It's Christmastime once again! And Superromance is bringing you a gift...**The Gift of Christmas.**

These are three great stories by three great authors.

"Stuck with Each Other" by Jan Freed
These are the Andersons, and they're about to get an unexpected present from Grandpa.

"Undercover Santa" by Janice Kay Johnson
Meet a reluctant department-store Santa who's about to learn the real meaning of Christmas.

"Epiphany" by Margot Early
When Carmen Dinesen marries Blackfeet Indian Chris Good Rider, she and her twelve-year-old sister move to his Montana ranch—just in time for Christmas.

The perfect gift to give yourself (and the romance readers you love!).

D0802622

ABOUT THE AUTHORS

Jan Freed is the recipient of a *Romantic Times* Reviewer's Choice award, as well as a multiple RITA® Award nominee. She lives near Houston, Texas, with her husband and teenage son, a cat who fetches balls and a golden retriever who doesn't. Her daughter attends college. Jan loves hearing from readers and can be contacted at www.superauthors.com.

Janice Kay Johnson has written books for adults, children and young adults. When not writing or researching for her books, Janice quilts, grows antique roses, chauffeurs her daughters around, takes care of her cats (too many to itemize!) and volunteers at a no-kill cat shelter. Janice has four times been a finalist for the prestigious RITA® Awards. This summer watch for a new trilogy by Janice to be published in Harlequin Superromance. You can reach her through www.superauthors.com.

Margot Early is a multiple-award-winning author and a two-time RITA® Award finalist who is known for her dramatic and emotionally compelling stories. Watch for her next Superromance novel, coming in late 2003.

The Gift of Christmas

Jan Freed
Janice Kay Johnson
Margot Early

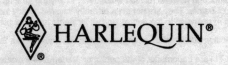

TORONTO • NEW YORK • LONDON
AMSTERDAM • PARIS • SYDNEY • HAMBURG
STOCKHOLM • ATHENS • TOKYO • MILAN • MADRID
PRAGUE • WARSAW • BUDAPEST • AUCKLAND

ISBN 0-373-71092-5

THE GIFT OF CHRISTMAS

Copyright © 2002 by Harlequin Books S.A.

The publisher acknowledges the copyright holders of the individual works as follows:

STUCK WITH EACH OTHER
Copyright © 2002 by Jan Freed.

UNDERCOVER SANTA
Copyright © 2002 by Janice Kay Johnson.

EPIPHANY
Copyright © 2002 by Margot Early.

This edition published by arrangement with Harlequin Books S.A.

® and TM are trademarks of the publisher. Trademarks indicated with ® are registered in the United States Patent and Trademark Office, the Canadian Trade Marks Office and in other countries.

Visit us at www.eHarlequin.com

Printed in U.S.A.

CONTENTS

Stuck with Each Other
Jan Freed

Dear Reader,

In our transient, fast-paced society we enjoy the freedom to change many things. Hate your boss? Get a new job. Unhappy in your marriage? Get a divorce. Think blondes have more fun? Get a package of Clairol. Family driving you crazy? Get used to it or get over it, because none of us can divorce our kids, parents, grandparents, uncles, aunts, siblings, etc. For better or worse we're stuck with each other, if only on special occasions and holidays.

I'm convinced that's a good thing. We can't run away from conflict easily when it erupts in our living room. We're forced to develop relationship skills. In the best-case scenario, we learn to accept flaws and differences in family members without diminishing our love for them. Which is, after all, the truest form of love.

I hope you'll slow down long enough during the busy holiday season to appreciate the family you're stuck with. They're not perfect, but then, neither are you. So be patient, hang on to your sense of humor and enjoy your exasperating lovable family to the fullest. The bonds you strengthen now will help support you through rough times ahead.

Warmly,

Jan Freed

CHAPTER ONE

JIM ANDERSON DRUMMED three fingertips on the steering wheel and glared at the clogged freeway exit ahead. Every surrogate Santa bound for the adjacent mall should be stripped of all credit cards and lashed with mistletoe!

A continual stream of ads warning "Only sixteen shopping days left!" had begun at dawn. Why some people insisted on waiting until dusk to panic was beyond him.

Couldn't they at least stay off the interstate?

They had no business using I-10 while Houston's downtown workforce headed for the suburbs. His normal commute home took long enough without deadwood compounding the logjam. He'd be lucky to be only an hour late. Darkness had snuffed out the last streak of gold on the horizon ten minutes ago.

He glanced at the cell phone mounted in front of the console. To call, or not to call: that was the question.

Whether 'twas nobler in the mind to suffer the slings and arrows of outrageous fortune now, or later? Either way, he was probably screwed. Sharon would tell him he should've left the office earlier, that the kids were starving, that just once it would be nice if he'd be on time to eat with the rest of the family.

Easy for her to say. She worked in a home office above their attached garage. Dinner was a mere trip down the staircase away.

Still, she *was* cooking the meal herself, not picking it up in a bucket. The least he could do was give her an estimated time of arrival.

Then again...miracles did happen. The traffic could feasibly clear. Or his car could sprout wings so he could actually get home before Sharon called him for a location report. Postponing her long-suffering sigh sounded like a pretty good plan to him.

A worm of guilt squirmed through his conscience. Excuses trailed close behind.

Anderson Architects was busier than ever. He needed to work noticeably harder than his hardworking employees. He needed to go that extra mile for his demanding clients. He needed to maintain company strength, attract new business and survive in a competitive environment. He needed to do all that, and more, or risk losing the momentum he'd struggled to build.

Then there was that little detail called money. He needed to earn it. A lot of it, preferably. The faster the better.

Sharon's fledgling interior design business hadn't taken off as quickly as they'd both hoped. Maybe it never would, and raising three kids today wasn't cheap—never *mind* the cost of giving them an educational edge in the cold cruel world of adulthood.

Incredible as it seemed, their son would start high school next year. College bills loomed right around the corner. So uh-uh. He wasn't going to beat himself up for working long hours in order to provide financial security for the future.

Besides, like he'd told his dad at Thanksgiving, it wasn't the quantity, but the quality of time spent with children that was important. All the experts said so.

He pat-patted his shirt pocket, reassured by the crackle of paper inside.

Pete Anderson's recent lecture might've been the catalyst for planning a surprise gift, but Jim took full credit for brilliant execution. Sharon couldn't stay mad at him for being late once he sprang his news. Hell, she hated the chaos and commercialism of the holiday season as much as he did. And the kids always complained there was nothing to do during school break.

As for him, the Westlake development project required constant supervision, yet in about a week, he would delegate full responsibility to his staff. If that didn't show his commitment to family bonding, he didn't know what would.

All that remained was to tell Sharon and the kids, phone "Grandpa Pete" in New Mexico and bask in their excitement and gratitude.

Assuming, of course, that he ever got home.

Jim lifted his right foot and stretched his cramped leg, letting the car roll forward without gas to the next bumper. Funny, how the silence he craved in daylight became an actual noise after darkness fell. The interior of his Lexus seemed more intimate, the surrounding vehicles more impersonal when driven by shadowy forms behind reflective glass.

He reached out and tuned in several radio stations, settling on Bing's rendition of ''White Christmas'' simply to fill the quiet. As far ahead on the freeway as he could see, a sluggish flow of red brake lights winked on and off…oh, *damn.*

He'd promised that morning to string twinkle lights on the friggin' tree tonight, no ifs, ands or buts.

Which meant dragging down dusty boxes from the attic and untangling strands he'd stored like spaghetti dumped from a colander. Probably a trip to Home Depot for replacement bulbs before all was said and done.

Then there was Sharon's compulsive need to relocate every ornament anyone else tried to hang, sure to be even worse this year than last, since she'd bought all new stuff for the tree. Mustn't forget Rick's almost guaranteed sullenness, which would set off Jim's temper, which would send the fourteen-year-old sulking off to play his god-awful electric guitar. Then twelve-year-old Caitlin would escape to talk on her precious phone. Which would leave Bethany more anxious to please than any seven-year-old should be, and Sharon deflated and hurt, and Jim wondering how in hell the situation had gotten so out of control when his intentions had been so good.

Bah, humbug didn't begin to express his feelings about the annual chore.

Just then a Ford Explorer rumbled up on his left

and tried to muscle in front of the Lexus. No waiting for a gap to open. No warning turn signal.

"No way," Jim muttered, honking his horn and forcing the Explorer to veer back into the left lane.

He grunted in satisfaction. That'd teach the jerk—

The blast of a horn yanked his attention to the left. An overhead light switched on inside the Explorer, revealing the driver. White male. Early thirties. Nice business suit. Middle finger raised. For long, creepy minutes he maintained his crude hand signal and exact parallel speed.

One look into malevolent dark eyes made Jim grateful the guy's finger wasn't attached to a trigger.

From then on Jim studiously ignored the insult, and was rewarded when his peripheral vision noted the Explorer's interior cab light switching off. After several more tense seconds, the SUV swerved into the far lane and out of sight.

Little by little, Jim released his pent-up breath.

Talk about out-of-control situations! He'd been stupid to pull that macho territorial maneuver. Especially during the holiday season, when people were extra stressed, depressed—or a combination of both. Modern urban life couldn't possibly measure up to the holly jolly propaganda, and road rage was rampant. Residential break-ins, too.

Last week the Miller family walked in on a theft in progress. The scumbags got away with some jewelry and a few presents from under the tree, but everyone agreed the cost could've been much higher. At least no one had gotten hurt.

They lived only two blocks away.

Jim's chest expanded with a surge of love and irrational fear. Sharon wasn't much better than the kids about keeping the doors locked at home. If anything ever happened to one of them...well, it didn't bear thinking about, that's all. Getting out of the city for Christmas was definitely one of his better ideas. And his family would be thrilled at the news.

He drummed three fingertips against the steering wheel, more impatient than ever to see their reaction. A nostalgic smile tugged at his mouth.

It would feel damn good to be their hero again.

THREE QUARTERS OF THE WAY up the ladder, Sharon twisted and looked over her shoulder. "You did *what?*"

"I booked a family vacation for the winter school break," her husband repeated from across the den. His sofa companions, ordered to "sit and don't move" moments earlier, exchanged startled looks of disbelief.

My sentiments, exactly. "You booked a vacation," Sharon said evenly. "For the whole family. Without talking to me first."

Jim's laser-blue gaze dimmed a fraction. "That's what I said. Now, would you please come down from there so I can explain without getting a crick in my neck?"

Sharon narrowed her eyes.

She'd burned her wrist frying chicken that was cold and soggy by the time she'd learned he would be at least an hour late. She'd strained her lower back lugging boxes down from the attic that *he'd* promised to lug down days ago. She'd cut her finger unscrewing broken bulbs on tangled light strands *he* should've untangled and strung, not her.

A crick in his neck? Puh-leez.

She opened her mouth to speak, remembered their audience and settled for an exasperated sigh.

Jim stiffened visibly. "Fine. Stay up there, if it's that important to you. God forbid the tree not look perfect. Martha Stewart's SWAT team might raid the house any minute."

Sharon blinked. That was the sharp scent of pine stinging her nose, *not* tears, she told herself fiercely.

"Please, Mom," Bethany chimed in, ever the family peacemaker. "You can sit by me. There's plenty of room." Scooting away from her father, she elbowed her older sister into the sofa corner, which forced their grumbling brother up onto the padded arm.

"Thanks, sweetie." Ignoring Jim, Sharon turned with wounded dignity and began to slowly descend the ladder.

What in the world was his problem, anyway? Of course she wanted the tree to look perfect! Clients would pass right by it on their way to her office. This tree might mean the difference between getting an interior design job, or not. So yes, it was "that" important to her. It was important to *them*.

So why wasn't it important to him?

She'd spent days finding the exact right ornaments

to replace their hodgepodge collection from years past. The frosted glass peach, ivory and mint green globes were elegant and simple. The iridescent ribbon garland added a touch of dazzle, more sophisticated than icicles. But did he appreciate her painstaking efforts? Only as joke material. She'd like to see *him* make wire ribbon and three kids bend to his will for two hours.

A bough brushed Sharon's shoulder and rebounded. Ornaments tinkled and clung for dear life. Scanning the ten-foot tree for casualties, she spotted a peach sphere dangling mere inches from an exact duplicate—as glaring and unsightly as two pimples on a flawless complexion.

Freeze! her mind warned, about three seconds too late.

Sharon stared stupidly at her outstretched hand. She was so close…so very close to restoring color symmetry. Only the knowledge that four pairs of eyes watched gave her the strength to pull back her itching fingers.

Okay, so maybe Jim had a teeny point.

Subdued, she resumed her descent and decided the least she could do was hear him out. A short getaway might do them all a world of good. It might even be a blessing. Lord knows when else she'd have the time to knock off her Christmas shopping. She stepped down to hardwood floor, turned to face the sofa and paused.

Wow. Sometimes she forgot the visual impact of

her family. She swelled with pride and admired the picture they made.

White shirtsleeves rolled up, power necktie loosened, glossy black hair a finger-combed mess above electric blue eyes, Jim was undeniably gorgeous, but no pretty boy. A hawkish nose and aggressively masculine chin saw to that. In college, he'd turned feminine heads wherever he and Sharon went. Now he also turned the heads of heterosexual males. A tribute to the air of competent authority he possessed at age thirty-eight.

Slouched on the opposite arm of the sofa, Rick was a mirror image of his dad—minus the muscle mass and six-foot-one height. Plus a ponytail and diamond-stud earring. His baggy cargo jeans, shapeless T-shirt, thick-soled biker boots and challenging scowl couldn't disguise the sensitivity Sharon had cherished when he was little.

But it was a darn good camouflage.

Wedged in the corner, Caitlin looked enough like Rick to be his twin. Tonight her low-rise jeans emphasized boyish hips, her tight red sweater the pads in her first bra. But all too soon her body would catch up to her exquisite face, and then there'd be trouble. She was a vivacious, sociable femme fatale in the making.

And Bethany…ah, sweet Bethany, who'd inherited her mother's brown eyes and hair, but a much gentler nature. Sharon had grown up scrappy and tough amid a litter of average-looking mutts like herself. She could only imagine what being described as "the plain one" did to a sibling's self-esteem. Especially when the label was not only unkind but vastly untrue.

"C'mon, Mama," Bethany urged. One small hand patted the space she'd created on the ivory leather cushion.

Sharon's heart squeezed. Smiling, she picked her way toward the sofa through cardboard boxes, rippling snakes of ribbon, and the makings of a new front-door wreath.

Rick shifted restlessly and caught her eye. "I have an algebra test tomorrow," he said, paving the way for a parent-sanctioned escape.

Sharon sat in her reserved seat and draped an arm around her cuddling daughter. "You told me you finished your homework before dinner."

"My homework, yeah. There wasn't time to study for a test."

She arched a brow at her savvy son. "That's odd. I could've sworn I heard you playing your guitar at least thirty minutes before I called you to the table."

His gaze faltered and dropped.

Sharon would've launched into her lecture on lying if she hadn't glanced at her husband first. She was too tired to referee another fight.

"So, Jim," she said brightly, attracting his glowering gaze. "Now that I'm ground level and all ears, tell me more about this trip of yours."

His expression cleared. "Not my trip. *Our* trip. Dad got me to thinking about how fast time flies, and how tied up I've been at work. Do you realize we haven't taken a family vacation since we rented that beach house on South Padre Island three years ago?''

Had it really been that long? Sharon was startled to realize that it had.

He drew in his legs and sat straighter, suppressed excitement humming in his eyes. ''Then I got to thinking how, every holiday season, we complain about the same things. How crowded the malls are. How exploitive the advertising is. How commercial Christmas has become. How cranky we all get. And how every year, we talk about taking the money normally spent on presents, and doing something more meaningful with it for the whole family. Am I right?''

Yes, but she didn't at all like where this was headed. She managed a wary nod.

''Well, for once I actually did something.'' With a grand flourish, he pulled a fat envelope from his shirt pocket and swept a satisfied gaze over them all. ''The Anderson family is having a bona fide white Christmas this year.''

Bethany was the first to respond. ''What's in there, Daddy?''

He lowered the envelope and beamed. ''Round-trip airline tickets to New Mexico, a week at Taos Ski Resort, and seven-day lift passes for each of us!''

Sharon could only gape.

He reached out and swiped a playful finger down Bethany's nose. ''So wha'd'ya think, pumpkin?''

''We're going *snow* skiing? For real, Daddy?''

He looked pleased at her awed tone. ''For real. You kids have never been away from Houston during the winter. And Mom's only seen snow in New York and Chicago. She's never had the chance to ski. It's high time you all expanded your horizons.''

To someplace close, Sharon amended frantically. Someplace suitable for a short trip, not for an entire week! She couldn't be gone from her business that long.

''But we don't know how to ski,'' Bethany pointed out.

''You'll take lessons. All of you. I promise it's no harder than waterskiing, and y'all learned that really fast. My guess is you'll pick up the basics and be off the bunny slopes in no time.''

Sharon suppressed a shudder. After three days and countless gulps of Lake Summerville, she'd finally risen to wobble on skis for longer than a boat length. She hadn't attempted a repeat performance, preferring instead to retire at the peak of her ability.

''Grandpa Pete lives in New Mexico,'' Bethany continued. ''Will he go skiing with us?''

''No. But we'll see him. In fact, we're going to take him up on his invitation to spend a few days at his cabin. Then we'll go on to the ski resort. How does that sound?''

Like he'd lost his mind, Sharon thought bleakly. Plus any respect he'd ever had for her wishes.

Bethany bounced once beneath Sharon's arm. ''I can't wait! Will I see some deers?''

''You betcha!''

''And ride on his snowmobile?''

''Sure, if you wear a helmet and hang on to me

tight. So can Caitlin. Your brother's old enough to ride by himself, if he wants.''

Jim's joviality sounded a bit strained. Apparently he'd finally noticed the rest of his family's conspicuous silence.

Bethany was oblivious. "Don't forget Mom. She gets a turn, too."

"I could never forget Mom, pumpkin. She always comes first." Flashing his gotta-love-me grin, he met Sharon's eyes.

His grin slipped, fell and flattened.

"Can we build a snowman, Daddy?" Bethany persisted.

"Um, sure thing."

"Can we have snow fights?"

"Yep."

"And make snow angels?"

"Yes, honey."

"Can I milk Grandpa Pete's cow?"

He hesitated. "Your allergies—"

"A cow's not anything like a cat or dog. I probably won't sneeze at all. Ple-e-ease?"

"Well…"

"Thanks, Daddy! Can we fish in the pond behind the cabin?"

"It's frozen."

"Can we—"

"*Jesus!*" Rick blurted. "Will you shut up?"

Caitlin giggled.

Her nerves raw, Sharon shot her son a lethally loaded look.

"What?" he asked belligerently, as if he didn't know.

"We had a deal."

His face crumpled in disgust. "Aw, Mom. She needs a chill pill. Admit it, she was bugging you, too."

"Don't change the subject."

"But Jesus isn't a bad word."

"No, it's not. It's one of the best. And I expect you to use it respectfully from now on." Holding his resentful gaze, Sharon willed herself not to crack. "Do you really want to fight about this now?"

He glanced at his father and back, then shrugged. It was as close to a victory as she'd get.

Lately she felt more like Professor Henry Higgins than Rick's mother. Only, her challenge wasn't cleaning up Cockney English, but MTVese: the crude language of America's young wannabe rock stars.

"What's this about a deal?" Jim asked with deceptive mildness.

Sharon hesitated.

Caitlin had no such qualms about ratting out her brother. "Rick has to pay Mom a dollar every time he uses 'foul language.' He already owes her six this week."

Seven, actually, but Sharon let it go.

Rick glared down at the helpful informant. "Thanks, bitch."

So much for leniency. "That's eight dollars you owe me," Sharon snapped. "At ten, I'll start washing your mouth out with Clearasil."

Caitlin snickered.

"Shut up, moron," Rick ordered.

"*You* shut up!"

"Brilliant comeback, moron."

She made a raised knuckle fist, reared back and punched his thigh with startling force.

He yelped and then twisted, grabbed her ponytail and yanked hard enough to jerk up her chin.

Leather scrunched and squeaked as they scuffled.

"Settle down," Sharon warned.

Rick obeyed by immobilizing his sister in a head-lock.

"Da-ad," Caitlin wailed.

"Let her go, Rick!" Jim ordered.

Rick thrust out his chin, looking uncannily like his father at that moment. "But she started it!"

"She's a girl."

Releasing his sister, Rick straightened. "You mean she can hit me as hard as she wants, and I have to sit there and take it, just because she's a girl?"

"I mean that a man never, ever, physically hurts a girl—no matter how angry she makes you."

On cue, Caitlin turned a misty sapphire gaze Jim's way. She even summoned enough moisture to squeeze out a big fat dramatic tear. "He called me a bitch and a moron, too," she reminded her father.

Jim's mouth thinned. "So he did." The gaze he wrenched back to Rick could've drilled holes in titanium. "A man never, ever, talks to a girl, or talks *about* a girl, in a disrespectful manner. Is that understood?"

Rick aimed a murderous glance at Caitlin before nodding sullenly.

Sharon, who wasn't bound by any chivalrous male code of conduct, reached for Caitlin's arm and pinched the smug look off her face.

Unmoved by blue eyes swimming with genuine tears, Sharon waited for her daughter's full attention before speaking. "A girl never, ever, tells someone else's personal business without that person's permission. If she does, she's not only a moron, but a card-carrying bitch. Is that understood?"

Rubbing her arm, Caitlin nodded mutinously.

"Tell your brother you're sorry."

"So-*ree.*"

Not very gracious, but acceptable.

"So...getting back to this ski trip," Sharon said, focusing on the larger problem at hand. "What's the flight schedule?"

Brightening, Jim thumbed through the envelope on his lap, removed a folded sheet of paper and snapped open what looked to be some kind of itinerary. "We depart from Bush Intercontinental on Wednesday, December 18, and return on Friday, December 27. That gives us three days to visit with Dad, and seven days at the ski resort."

Which gave Sharon only—she calculated quickly in her head—nine days from tomorrow to get everything done. *Nine days?* Impossible!

"Please tell me those aren't nonrefundable tickets," she begged on a rising note of hysteria.

Jim tugged his tie looser, the movement defensive.

"It was a smokin' deal on the Internet, Sharon. If I hadn't snapped up the tickets right then, they would've sold to someone else."

A cauldron of emotions churned in her chest. Anger bubbled to the surface. "Did it occur to you that I might be too busy to leave at the drop of a hat for ten days?"

He blinked.

"No, I can see that it didn't. To you, my work is just a hobby, isn't it?"

His brows slammed together. "That's not true. You know how much I believe in your talent. But you can't deny that clients aren't exactly beating down your door these days." He held up a forestalling palm. "Not that I think they won't ever. Which is why I booked a trip now, when you can get away easily, instead of after you start getting busy."

Rick wasn't the only savvy male in the family, Sharon thought coldly. He'd learned from a master.

"I have two jobs in progress now," she told her obviously startled husband. "Kelly Dobson expects her dining room and guest bedroom to be completed when her in-laws arrive on Christmas Eve. And the Harrisons expect a design proposal and estimate on January 4."

"So, hire extra help if you need to."

He didn't have a clue how her business operated, and the knowledge hurt. Deeply. "Even if Kelly would accept another designer stepping into my shoes at this late date, I can't afford to hire help. And I'll need every one of the fourteen days left until Christmas Eve to finish the job. You would've known that, if you'd showed enough interest in my work to ask. You wouldn't have wasted money on a nonrefundable ticket if you'd had the courtesy to talk to me first.''

Amazingly, he seemed hurt. As if *he* were the victim, not her.

''I wanted to surprise you,'' he said stiffly. ''And since we'd talked for years about doing something exactly like this trip for Christmas, I thought you'd be excited. Silly me.''

''I'm excited, Daddy,'' Bethany piped up in a small voice.

He looked at his daughter, his gaze softening. ''Thanks, pumpkin. It's nice to know I can count on *someone's* support in the family.'' He met Sharon's eyes, his implication clear.

She couldn't hide her flinch of pain. ''Your definition of loyalty must be different than mine. I thought that putting my own career on hold for fifteen years while you established Anderson Architects was a pretty good show of support. Silly me.''

A flush deepened his tan, heightening the contrast between crisp white collar and strong brown throat. ''Sharon—''

''It's my turn now, Jim. My chance to build a successful career. And I won't throw it away for the sake of a frivolous ski trip.''

''Frivolous?'' He made a huffing noise. ''I'm trying to give our family a chance to reconnect. Hell, any woman but you would think a three-thousand-dollar trip was dead serious. She'd put in the extra hours it took to make Kelly Dobson's in-laws happy, and then she'd plant her butt on a plane to New Mexico and be thankful she was there."

Ha! As if. "I'm staying home, Jim."

"Be reasonable, Sharon. If not for me, then for the kids."

"I'll stay home with you, Mom," Rick said loyally, then promptly ruined her gratified glow with his next words. "I told Kevin I could practice with the band every day during winter break. Auditions for the Valentine's Day dance are the week school starts back up. He thinks we can get the gig—if we nail down three more songs."

"I'll stay home too, Mom," Caitlin chimed in. "Linda Nicholson's Christmas party is December 21. You promised to take me shopping, remember? It's at the country club, and there's gonna be a DJ playing whatever we want. The girls get to dress up, and the boys even have to wear a tie. I *have* to stay home!"

"No one is staying home," Jim said in an ominous tone.

Rick let out an explosive breath. "But the band is counting on me, Dad! You always say I should keep my word and not let people down. You should've told me about the trip before I promised the guys I could practice every day."

Caitlin plunged into the opening. "And you should've told *me* before I promised Linda I'd go shopping with her for the party. We're gonna buy stuff for dance prizes and decorations, and she's *counting* on my advice. I can't let her down!"

"That's admirable," Jim said dryly. "But you'll both have to give your regrets. Blame it on your self-ish ogre of a father, who's forcing you to suffer a week of agony at a first-class luxury ski resort."

"But Da-ad," Caitlin whined. "Jimmy Taylor will ask out Stephanie Harris if I'm not at the party. I know he will!"

"And if I don't practice with the guys, Dirty Fin-gernail will land the Valentine's gig—and we're way better than them," Rick said in disgust. "Why can't I just stay here with Mom?"

"Let me stay, too, Dad," Caitlin pleaded. "You go on without us and have fun. Me and Rick have too much—"

"Rick and I," Sharon corrected absently, watching the pulse tick in Jim's temple, a sure countdown to detonation.

"Rick and I—" Caitlin rolled her eyes "—have too much to do at home. Besides, what about all our Christmas presents? We can't take them with us on the plane."

Five.

"Yeah, Dad, Caitlin and I will make sure they don't get stolen."

Four.

"So you can leave and not have to worry."

Three.

"You should take Bethany with you."

Two.

"Yeah, Dad, take Bethany."

One.

"She's the only member of the family who wants to go to that stupid ski resort, anyway."

Boom.

"Enough!" Jim thundered, making them jump nearly out of their skins.

Including Sharon, who'd been prepared.

He leveled an implacable stare all around. "Each and every one of you is boarding that airplane on December 18 if I have to carry you on my back kicking and screaming. We're going to fly to New Mexico and stay at Grandpa Pete's cabin like he's asked us to do for the past four years.

"And then we're going to go to that stupid ski resort and spend an obscene amount of money on meals, equipment rentals and ski lessons. And we're going to have snow fights and make snowmen and have lots of fun, damn it!"

He looked straight at Sharon. *"Is that understood?"*

CHAPTER TWO

BETHANY BUCKLED her seat belt and pulled the strap as tight as she could stand. Better. Her stomach didn't feel quite so much like it would flutter straight up to the ceiling now. It was still kind of queasy, but the good kind—not the bad. The kind she got on her birthday before everybody else woke up and the fun started.

Not the kind she got lately, before everybody fell asleep and the fighting stopped.

She leaned forward and glanced over Caitlin and Rick at her parents, who sat across the aisle on the right side of the plane. Her mother was bent over the big canvas tote bag Daddy said wouldn't fit under the seat. But it did. Once she took out some books and a can of hair spray, it slipped right under with only a little shove.

Mama was good at making things fit.

Bethany settled back and turned toward her window, happier than she could remember being in a long time. After waiting and waiting and waiting for December 18 to get here, she was finally on a real airplane headed for real snow, sitting where she'd really, really wanted to sit!

A minute ago she'd complained to her brother that she couldn't see out the plane from her aisle seat. Daddy had heard and given Rick a long look that got meaner the longer her brother didn't move. When he got ordered to switch places with his little sister, she'd felt sorry for him until he'd said "that sucks!"

Anybody that dumb deserved to lose the window seat. Sometimes it almost looked like he *tried* to make their parents mad. And that Caitlin did her very best to help him.

Like just now, she wouldn't get up from the middle seat when he'd asked, so he'd squeezed past her knees and nearly fallen in her lap. And she'd punched him hard in the ribs, even though she *knew* that wasn't fair because boys weren't supposed to hit girls back.

Then he'd gone and thumped her on the head anyway! Even though he *knew* she'd squeal like he'd stabbed her and their parents would hear, and he'd get in more trouble.

Bethany pressed her nose against the cold window and sighed. Maybe she didn't really want to have children when she grew up. Maybe she'd just get a puppy instead. A soft furry one that shed lots of dander all over the house—*her* house. So what if she had a stupid episode?

Her mother and Dr. Harris wouldn't even have to know.

Dazzled by her glimpse of future freedom, she stared blindly through the glass.

Behind her, Caitlin crowded close. "Quit hogging

the window. Do you see our suitcases down there anywhere?''

Bethany blinked, then focused below. The gray overcast morning was windy, flapping the orange vests of two men unloading luggage from a trailer bed. One of them grabbed a dark green bag that could be Rick's, but Caitlin's was red.

"Yours is probably on the plane already," Bethany said, answering her sister's real question.

Caitlin flounced back in her seat. "I sure hope so."

Bethany sure did, too.

Caitlin had borrowed a whole bunch of ski clothes that her friends said made her look at least sixteen. She couldn't wait to test them out on the fine high school guy she planned to kiss, once she met him. Which was why she'd finally stopped whining about going on this trip. Rick had stopped after Kevin said snowboarding was awesome, and any dude who carried one under his arm was a chick magnet—even if he never took it up on the slopes. Rick was supposed to take pictures of all the babes he met for the band to look at when he got home.

Bethany knew a lot of stuff about her brother and sister that they didn't know she knew. Being little and quiet made her invisible sometimes.

But it didn't make her deaf.

"Good afternoon, ladies and gentlemen," a woman's voice said through a loudspeaker. "Welcome aboard Continental Airlines flight 1476 nonstop from Houston to Albuquerque. I'm Kelly, and that's

Nancy and Greg standing next to me. We'll be your flight attendants today.''

Bethany located the three people at the front of the plane dressed in the same blue uniform, except the man wore pants instead of a skirt.

The blond woman, Kelly, held something that must be a microphone next to her mouth. "We look forward to making your experience on this flight a pleasant one. But first, please take a moment to make sure all seat backs are in the upright position, food trays are securely locked, and carry-on bags are stored safely beneath the seat in front of you or in an overhead compartment bin. And of course, fasten your seat belts.''

Smiling, she lowered the microphone and waited for passengers to do what she'd asked.

Loud engines rumbled to life, exciting and scary. The good kind of scary, not the bad. Buckles clicked and doors slammed. Nancy and Greg moved down the aisle handing out pillows and rearranging stuff overhead. One time Nancy yanked out a big fat leather bag and took it to the front entrance, then came back without it.

Whoever it belonged to could've really used Mama's help.

Outside Bethany's window, the two men she'd watched earlier hopped into a cart and drove off in a hurry, pulling the empty luggage trailer behind them. Somewhere near the back of the plane a phone rang loudly to the tune of ''Jingle Bells,'' then stopped.

Kelly laughed and raised her microphone. ''Thank

you for reminding me. All cell phones must be turned off for the duration of the flight. We should be taking off shortly, so let's review the safety features printed on the cards in your seat pockets ahead.''

While she talked about oxygen masks and flotation devices and emergency exits and blah, blah, blah, Bethany hoped her brother and sister were listening carefully. Because *she* sure didn't understand how to do anything Kelly explained.

''If you have any questions, ask me, Nancy or Greg once the captain extinguishes the fasten seat belt signs, and we'll be happy to assist you.'' Kelly hung her microphone on the wall and disappeared with the other two attendants behind the rest room.

Which Bethany never planned to use if she could help it. Not after Rick had told her that all the turds and pee going into the toilet got flushed out into the sky!

Shuddering, she glanced at her brother, who was trying to look cool, as usual. Like he'd flown a million times before instead of only once a long time ago.

She'd been too little then to remember much now about that plane ride to El Paso, but some things stuck in her mind. Like everybody's face when they got back from the funeral—especially Grandpa Pete's, whose puffy red eyes had made Bethany start to bawl without understanding why.

And she remembered the next day, riding all the way home to Houston in the back seat of Grandma

Kate's car that she wouldn't use anymore. Caitlin and Rick hadn't fought once. A family record, Mama said.

"It's about time," Caitlin muttered.

Startled, Bethany realized the plane was moving away from the terminal in a slow and jerky roll. She reached out and clutched her sister's arm.

"Hey!" Caitlin protested.

Bethany transferred her grip to the arm of her seat. The plane's speed picked up a little. The ride got bumpier. How would this big heavy plane ever get up in the air? How would it stay up? What if it crashed!

Horrible video images she'd seen as a six-year-old replayed now with a seven-year-old's greater understanding of terrorist attacks. All of a sudden, her stomach wasn't the good kind of queasy anymore.

She leaned forward and looked to her right—straight into waiting brown eyes the color of love.

Don't be afraid. Daddy and I are here. Nothing bad will happen. You'll be safe, Mama said without saying a word. And then she smiled.

Bethany had heard Grandpa Pete tell Daddy once that his wife's smile could start or stop wars. She still wasn't sure what that meant exactly. But from the way her father was staring at Mama now, Bethany knew it meant something really nice.

She started to relax.

But then Mama caught Daddy staring and her eyes stopped smiling. And his mouth got hard. And Bethany had to lean back and look away from a sight that was much scarier than any crash video replayed in her mind.

The plane rolled faster and faster. The engines whined louder and louder. Food trays rattled. Runway markers sped past in a blur. Her cheeks vibrated. She closed her eyes as the plane swooped up and invisible hands pressed her body deep into the seat.

"Wow, look at that," Caitlin said in an awed tone.

Bethany cracked open her eyes and gazed out the window. The ground below was getting farther away by the second and the rattling had stopped. She could see rooftops, crisscrossed roads and entire fields surrounding the airport. Back toward the city, several groups of tall buildings stood out against the gray sky, but one place had taller buildings sticking up than the others.

"That must be downtown," Caitlin said, pointing to where Daddy spent most of his time.

Bethany tried to pick out the building where he worked. She knew the lobby had a big fish aquarium and the elevators had shiny brass doors, but that didn't help. They all looked alike from the outside.

The next instant, her window turned completely gray.

The plane started shaking, then rattling, then jerking up, down, sideways, worse than a carnival ride. A few ladies shrieked. A man behind Bethany cussed all the bad words she knew.

Then he taught her a few she didn't.

"Don't worry, folks," Kelly said calmly over the loudspeaker from somewhere out of sight. "Once we get clear of these clouds, we should be free of this turbulence. Until then, sit tight and stay in your seats.''

''I'm scared,'' Bethany whispered to no one in particular.

Rick leaned forward, studied her face and winked. Then he snatched a narrow bag from the seat pocket in front of him, opened it next to his mouth and doubled over, pretending to barf. The noises he made were loud and really disgusting.

Bethany giggled. She couldn't help it. Caitlin's snorts turned into snickers.

''Oh, honestly,'' Mama said from across the aisle.

''Stop that, Rick,'' Daddy ordered in a strange voice, sounding more like he was trying not to laugh than like he was mad.

Sunlight burst through the glass and struck Rick in the face. He raised his head from the bag, stared out the window and gaped. Bethany followed his gaze.

The sky was crystal clear and bluer than Rick's eyes. Bluer than she'd known any sky could get. It stretched as far in every direction as she could see. And down below…oh, it was so beautiful it hurt her eyes! If she hadn't known better, she would've thought that was fresh white snow.

Smiling, she pictured falling back with her arms spread wide and making a snow angel in the clouds.

Kelly reappeared in front of the rest room, unhooked the microphone and spoke into it with a smile. ''Is everybody okay? Are we having fun yet?''

"Ask me again after my second Bloody Mary," a nearby voice called out.

Laughter filled the plane.

Mama had said that?

As Kelly reassured passengers that both complimentary and alcoholic beverages were on the way, Bethany shared a wide-eyed look with her brother and sister.

Mama didn't make jokes about drinking. She was always lecturing Rick on the dangers of alcohol. Her parents had been killed by a drunk driver when she was in high school.

Bethany unbuckled her seat belt and drew a deep breath.

The plane had finally settled and calmed. She wasn't scared anymore. Now, if only her safe, familiar world would stop turning upside down, she might not need Rick's barf bag after all.

THANK YOU, LORD, Jim thought fervently as the plane rolled to a complete stop.

The bucking descent through a thunderstorm had made the turbulent takeoff seem tame. Even seasoned travelers had cheered in relief when the wheels had finally touched down.

Jim leaned forward to look at the kids. Rick and Caitlin chattered post adrenaline rush about not being scared and wanting to do it all over again, as if they'd just ridden the Texas Cyclone at AstroWorld instead of a Boeing 727 lightning rod. Bethany, who'd been openly frightened, gave the adolescent gods their due worship.

Oh, to be young and immortal again. To be able to impress baby sisters with sheer bullshit and bravado. To be naive enough to be impressed.

Leaning back, Jim decided Bethany needed more safe thrills in her overprotected life. Like climbing aboard the kind of rides at AstroWorld she could brag about afterward. She'd been too little the last time he'd taken the family there—what, two summers ago? Three?

Yeah, three. Damn.

In kid years, that was more like nine. Rick probably wouldn't be caught dead now riding a roller coaster with his old man...

Clicks and rustles throughout the cabin penetrated Jim's disturbing thoughts. Overhead compartment bins unlatched. Passengers stretched cramped muscles and gathered their personal belongings. Time to collect his, Jim realized. He turned to Sharon.

Uh-oh.

Somewhere between the landing runway and the terminal, her last Bloody Mary had kicked butt. He should have stopped her after two, but warm and friendly had been a definite improvement over stone-cold sober.

"Honey?"

No response. Slumped boneless against the window, her cap of light brown curls tufted in odd places, she slept with one cheek against the glass, her pretty mouth parted slightly. She breathed heavily. Not snoring, exactly, but close. Drool bubbled every time she exhaled.

She'd be horrified if she knew.

She looked adorable.

Grinning, he nudged her pliant shoulder. "Wake up, Sharon."

She snuffled and broke into a genuine snore.

He laughed, wanting to scoop his tough, stubborn, lovable wife onto his lap and cuddle her close while her defenses were down. It wasn't the right time or place, of course. Lately, it never was.

"Dad!"

Jim swiveled toward the agonized voice.

Rick was watching his mother snore like she suffered from flatulence rather than too much vodka. The boy's mortified gaze wrenched to nearby rising passengers, obviously checking to see if they'd noticed her affliction.

Oh, to be young and painfully self-conscious again. No thank you! Once was torturous enough.

Jim turned back to Sharon and nudged her harder. "C'mon, honey. We're here."

Stirring, she mumbled something unintelligible, then sank back into oblivion.

Great.

The aisle was packed now with weary travelers anxious to get off the plane and go about their business in Albuquerque. Those near the front exit started shuffling forward in single file. Inner seat passengers stood hunchbacked, awaiting their turn to slip into the flow.

Rick rose to stand by Jim's seat and hold the Anderson family's place in line. Their window of opportunity would open up soon.

Jim leaned close to his wife's ear and yelled, "Sharon!"

She jerked upright from the window and blinked, her gaze unfocused. Baby-fine curls clung like pressed flowers to the rosier skin of one cheekbone.

He gentled his voice. "We're at the terminal, honey. It's time to get off the plane. Grab your purse and tote bag from under the seat."

Awareness entered her sleepy brown eyes, and with it, extreme distress. "Stop the world. I wanna get off."

Not good. "Take a deep breath—"

"Hurry up, Mom," Rick interrupted. "It's almost our turn."

She bent over swiftly, her head facing Jim's knees. "Oh, God," she whispered, swaying.

Before he could react she grabbed for his leg.

One arm wrapped his shin in a breast-hugging embrace; her forehead came down on his thigh. Her fingers clutched denim in spasms of misery, caressing the skin beneath.

Oh, God.

A long, muffled moan worthy of a porno queen steamed the jeans two feet south of his crotch.

Please help me not get turned on, Jim prayed as his wife battled nausea.

Unfortunately Pavlov's wasn't the only dog conditioned to respond automatically to certain stimulus.

His neck heating, Jim slanted a look up at the son who'd thought snoring was embarrassing.

Rick stared rigidly straight ahead, pretending not to see or hear or care. But that damn stud earring he insisted on wearing glittered conspicuously on a lobe that was fiery red.

Sharon moaned louder. Curious eyes turned their way. Rick's blush deepened.

Amusement rushed to Jim's rescue. This would teach the kid not to underestimate his parents' ability to humiliate him. He wouldn't make that mistake again.

Jim leaned forward and spoke for Sharon's ears alone. "I know you don't feel well, hon, but could you try and keep it down?"

"I *am* trying," she mumbled. "But keep the barf bag handy just in case."

"Mom, Dad, let's go. People are waiting."

Without lifting her head, Sharon flapped a weak hand. "B'bye. Y'all have fun. Come back for the funeral, that's all I ask."

Jim met his son's worried gaze. "Go back to your seat. We'll wait for everybody else to get off first."

Rolling his eyes, Rick obeyed. His vacated space instantly filled. The conga line of jostling passengers pressed forward.

Jim thought of his father waiting outside the baggage claim area, and squeezed Sharon's shoulder. "Think you can sit up now?"

"Do you like to live dangerously?"

He suppressed a smile. "I've lived with you for fifteen years. What do you think?"

Her chuckle turned into a groan. She lifted an ashen face. "Shoot me. Please."

"You'll feel better once you get some fresh air. Hang in there."

"Shooting's faster, but I'll take what I can get. Where's the rope?" She paused the requisite beat. "Har-har-har."

Always the jokester, especially during physical or emotional duress. A diversionary tactic he'd learned to ignore.

He helped her slowly straighten to a sitting position. "I'm pretty sure I packed a bottle of Pepto-Bismol. A few tablespoons should settle your stomach."

"On top of peanuts and Bloody Marys? Ugh. Wouldn't that be a pretty sight the second time around?" Shuddering, she massaged her temples. "Just find me some aspirin. I'm getting a killer headache."

Noting the tiny pearls of sweat beading her blanched complexion, Jim rubbed soothing circles between her shoulder blades. "I asked Dad to put the third seat in his Suburban. You can stretch out back there and relax. Sleep all the way to his cabin if you want. I plan on catching a nap, myself."

"No, I need to work on the Harrisons' kitchen remodel proposal. I've got a—"

"—presentation the day after we get back," he finished. "Yeah, I know. I heard it the first twenty times you told me.'' When she hadn't been giving him the silent treatment, that is.

She pulled stiffly away from his touch. ''Then you know I don't have the luxury of 'catching a nap.' Unlike you, I didn't have a chance to prepare for leaving my office with jobs unfinished.''

Bending over, she gathered her purse and tote bag with the slow, cautious movements of someone in pain. Jim watched and winced in silence.

He recognized that cold expression. She'd rather toss her cookies than accept his help now. They were back to square one.

Me and my big fat mouth.

Sighing, Jim rose from his seat and slung the strap of his bulky camera case over one shoulder. Rick and Caitlin stood in the aisle squabbling over who had to carry the backpack stuffed with video games, CD players and similar essential gear. Behind them, Bethany hoisted the pack at their feet into her frail arms, then gamely staggered toward the front of the plane.

Jim brushed past his older children in disgust. He caught Bethany in two strides, relieved her of the heavy burden, and added it to his own.

What was one more in the scheme of life?

PETE ANDERSON LOWERED creakily to one knee, his heart turning youthful handsprings. ''Peanut!''

''Grandpa!'' Bethany darted past the baggage claim attendant who was matching stubs to exiting luggage. She pounded across the tile floor and into his open arms.

Wrapping her in a hug, he closed his eyes and pressed his cheek against mink-soft curls that tickled his nose. Since Kate's death four years ago, moments of pure joy had been few and far between. He stored the memory of this one to savor during the hardest part of the next ten days.

After a last, fierce squeeze, he held Bethany at arm's length and studied her animated face. "You cut your hair. It suits you. I swear, you look more like your mama every day." He cocked his head. "Something else about you is different, too. What am I missing?"

She lifted her chin, bared her teeth and pointed proudly to the gap where her left bicuspid should've been.

"Oh-ho!" he chortled. "Looks like the tooth fairy paid a visit to your house after I left."

Her happy expression faded, leaving big, sad Bambi eyes. "There's no such thing as the tooth fairy. She's make-believe, like Santa Claus."

Huh? Only last month, he'd helped her write a letter to Santa. She'd been jumpier than spit on a hot skillet about asking for more than the puppy she wouldn't get, but he'd finally convinced her she wouldn't seem greedy.

He collected his composure. "Why do you say that?"

She shrugged, not quite meeting his eyes.

"Some people don't believe in anything, Peanut. Doesn't mean you should believe them instead of your own heart." That got her attention.

"Caitlin told me they weren't real. *Saturday Night Live* was making fun of them, and I made her tell me the truth." She searched his face and added hastily, "It wasn't her fault."

It damn sure wasn't. "You're allowed to watch *Saturday Night Live?*"

"Don't you like that show?"

He chose his least serious objection. "It comes on pretty late past your bedtime."

Relief flooded her face. "Comedy Central plays re-runs early. Me and Caitlin watch all the time. It's funny."

"What about your mama and daddy?"

She paused. "Well, Mama jokes a lot, and Daddy makes these funny faces—what?" she asked at his bark of laughter.

Shaking his head, he tweaked her nose. "I love you, Peanut. I wish…" *That you still believed in magic, that you never had to learn things the hard way, that you were safe from real world dangers that might cause you harm or pain.*

Her seven-year-old gaze was far wiser than it should have been. "It's okay, Grandpa. I'm not a little kid anymore."

He could see that, and it broke his heart.

Snatching her close for another long hug, he cursed today's screwed-up culture. Advertising, music, TV shows, movies—hell, *everything* forced kids to grow up way too soon. Parents were a child's best protection. But even loving ones like Jim and Sharon sometimes got off track. Pete had been right to take matters into his own hands.

"I can't breathe," a squashed voice protested against his chest.

Instantly he relaxed his arms. "What's the matter? Don't you want me to call you Peanut Butter from now on?"

Bethany's giggle became a happy shriek when he tickled her ribs.

Smiling, he set her aside and clambered to his feet, feeling every one of his sixty-two years. As he massaged his knee, his gaze snagged on the two older grandchildren walking his way.

Rick carried a large black duffel bag that banged his shin every other step. His hair was still long, tied back in a girly ponytail, exposing that damn earring he'd borrowed from Caitlin and never given back, despite threats of bodily harm. His britches were big and swishy, but his stride was masculine and strong.

Beside him, Caitlin towed a red overstuffed bratwurst of a suitcase on uneven squeaky wheels. Her ponytail was thicker than Rick's, her britches were tighter, and she wore two earrings to his one. She had no hips to speak of but she walked like she did, and Pete experienced a twinge of sympathy for his son's future sleepless nights.

They flashed identical tired smiles, and Pete was unable to suppress a thrill of pride. The Anderson genes done good with these two.

Still, time would tell if they developed strength of character to match the looks they were born with.

They'd seemed mighty self-centered during his last visit.

The next few minutes passed in a flurry of hugs and greetings, plus stories of their death-defying flight. Sharon and Jim dragged up to join the group, pretending they weren't avoiding each other's eyes. Pete noted their tense smiles and frazzled appearance, their strained effort to seem happy for his benefit. But he made no comment. He had his own pretense to pull off.

After hustling everyone into jackets, he herded the family and a staggering amount of luggage outside into the rain-washed knife-cold evening. He got a kick out of the kids' exaggerated shivers, and a bigger one at their awe over the Sandia Mountains on the horizon. Wait'll their semitropical Houston blood hit 10,000 feet above sea level. They'd think Albuquerque was Cancun.

It took some muscle and engineering, but they finally crammed everything but the bratwurst into the back of Pete's Suburban. They shoved that onto the third seat, where it occupied the space of two large German fräuleins.

Caitlin was ordered to sit beside her suitcase and quit complaining, else she'd be dumped at the curb and her clothes distributed among needy orphan children. Rick was ordered to stop cackling this instant, else he'd have to switch places with his sister.

Jim wanted to ride shotgun up front, but Pete recognized signs of a nasty hangover when he saw one. He settled Sharon there instead, reclined the bucket seat, and ordered his son to quit whining about cramped legs or he'd personally chop them off.

When he gave Sharon a bottle of water and two aspirin from the glove compartment, she thanked him profusely and smiled. *You are the most chivalrous, virile, exceptional man on the face of the planet.*

Pete blinked, then slammed her door.

Rounding the truck's hood to climb into the driver's seat, he chuckled at himself. The first time he'd met his daughter-in-law she'd reminded him of a common little brown wren—cute, but nothing special in the looks department. Within minutes, her humor, spirit and intelligence had him reconsidering his opinion. It had taken that smile of hers, however, to make him fully see the light.

Warm and caring, excluding all others but the lucky recipient, Sharon's smile was a thing of rare beauty. It was also sexy as hell.

Any man who wouldn't bust balls to earn that smile as often as possible was a damn fool. He hadn't raised a dummy, so what was his son's problem?

The four-hour drive to his cabin provided a clue.

He'd hoped to show off his adopted new state during the remaining hour of daylight. The progressing sunset was spectacular, the terrain dramatic, especially compared to the flat Texas Gulf Coast. The route north from Albuquerque via I-25 was smooth. But inside the Suburban, it was one helluva bumpy ride.

Instead of relaxing and enjoying the scenery, Sharon hauled out paperwork with a martyred sigh.

The third time she refused to look up from her note-pad at a sight Pete pointed out, Jim told her to take off the hair shirt, for God's sake. Of course, she really got prickly then. And Caitlin and Rick didn't help.

Even sitting in separate seats, they spat and hissed like two wet cats in a sack. The more their parents ignored them to fight their own private battle, the louder the hissing got.

Darkness fell, letting Pete off the hook as tour guide, but testing his skills as mediator. He got a break passing through Santa Fe, though. The city's trademark adobe structures and Native American influence captured his passengers' interest. They ate a fast-food hamburger there in relative peace. Back on the road, the truce ended.

The last forty miles on NM 518 reminded Pete why he liked living the life of a hermit. Silence was golden.

By the time he unlocked the gate to his property, switched to four-wheel drive, added snow chains and headed up the long, winding mountain road, he was as exhausted and cranky as everyone else.

He loved Jim's family dearly. But what they all needed was a wake-up call, not a luxury vacation. They were pampered and spoiled enough. Pete knew they might hate him the next ten days, but he was willing to take that risk.

If they survived the experience without killing each other, they just might be fit to live.

CHAPTER THREE

SOMETHING TANTALIZED...teased...dragged Sharon up from the murky depths of slumber. She bobbed on the surface of consciousness, resisting sleep-hungry tugs from below. Her lids cracked open. She winced at the dim light penetrating the closed miniblinds.

Where was she? Who was she?

Memory returned in a rush, and she squirmed beneath the covers.

The warm, snuggly covers of the king-size bed in Pete's bedroom, which he'd graciously given up, along with the private bathroom, for her comfort. A small TV on the dresser seemed possessed with demonic eyes, a reflection of embers glowing in the corner fireplace.

That answered the where. As for the who...she grimaced.

Only an idiot would knock back four stiff drinks, knowing her tolerance limit was one. Only a spiteful child would do such a thing to deliver the message *I'm here against my will, so don't expect me to behave.*

She'd really showed Jim, all right.

That she was stupid, immature and a mean drunk

to boot! She hadn't driven while intoxicated, but she'd hit and run just the same. Falling asleep without apologizing.

She peeked at her sleeping husband, who—for the first time since saying I do—had failed to at least grope for her hand in the dark and whisper good-night. Usually he tested her mood more thoroughly.

Then again, usually there was a chance in hell he'd get lucky. All her signals last night had told him to back off.

After snapping at him on the plane, she'd continued her peevish grudge match on the long drive here. Bad enough that the kids had watched from the back seats. Even worse, Pete had sat ringside. Of all people to see her shameful performance!

Unlike her children, he'd still thought she was a nice sane woman. A delusion she'd cherished and tried to maintain, which hadn't been difficult, since his visits were short and infrequent.

And? her conscience prodded.

Okay, and unreciprocated.

And why is that, missy?

Well, at first the kids had been so little, the drive to El Paso so long, the money so tight and flying so expensive, she and Jim had balked at the hassle. Then Kate had died, and Pete had gone off the deep end, refusing to move to Houston, refusing to live in any city without his soul mate. The avid outdoorsman had sold his house and hardware store and everything else he could convert to cash, bought himself mountain property twenty miles from the nearest neighbor, and retired from civilization.

And you think the mountain should come to Muhammad, is that it?

Well, no, but visiting Houston had forced Pete out of unhealthy reclusion. And frankly, the kids had lessons, recitals, ball games and camps. She and Jim had dual careers and parental duties to juggle. Their schedules simply hadn't permitted a trip to the boonies in New Mexico, when traveling was much easier for Pete.

Oh, really? What kind of condition was your family in after making that "easy" trip?

Well...they'd been stumbling tired.

Sharon grabbed an extra pillow, pressed it over her face and stifled a shamed groan.

If Jim hadn't virtually forced her onto that plane, no telling how many more years she would have made excuses for her selfishness. She was a terrible daughter-in-law! A horrible person! Undeserving of even minimal hospitality!

Flinging her pillow to the floor, she blinked rapidly and sniffed.

Then sniffed again.

Then sat up slowly and lifted her twitching nose. The scent that had teased her awake earlier was much stronger now.

Coffee.

She swung her feet to the floor, grabbed her terry robe from the foot of the bed and hesitated. She was not worthy, remember?

A Columbian curl of fragrance beckoned a seductive come-hither finger.

On the other hand, Sharon rationalized, she wasn't worth spitting on until after that first jolt of caffeine hit.

She stood and tiptoed to the bathroom, took care of business—which included vanquishing hangover mouth—and crept back out toward the closed bedroom door. Pete was a saint to remember she had the internal alarm clock of a rooster. And he'd been so sweet the night before, insisting that she and Jim take the master bedroom, getting the kids settled in the sleeping loft.

She'd been unable to muster the strength to object, then. But the dear man would sleep in his own bed tonight, Sharon vowed.

The hinges squeaked loudly as she opened the heavy oak door. She glanced over her shoulder, but Jim didn't stir. Good. She'd have time alone with Pete to make her apologies. There was a lot of ground to cover, including a proper tour of his cabin.

She eased the door shut, turned and corrected her initial muzzy-headed impression. "Wow."

Cabin was too humble a word to describe the two-story vaulted room she faced. Roughly twenty by thirty feet, it encompassed a kitchen separated by a unique bar counter made of stacked stone topped with…a split log? Cool.

Her gaze moved to the matching stone fireplace and soaring chimney on her right, its split-log mantel another spectacular focal point. No Christmas stocking.

No festive tree or decorations of any kind. The whole room was masculine and sparse. She itched to examine everything thoroughly. And she would.

Right after she looked her fill through the undraped windows flanking a door on her left.

Drawn irresistibly closer, she saw that the door opened onto a large wooden deck enclosed with a waist high rail. Four cushioned patio chairs and a table looked fresh off the showroom floor. Smiling at more evidence of Pete's hospitality, she stepped outside on impulse.

Her gasp was as much a reaction to the glorious view as it was to frigid wood and frosty air.

Pete's house sat on top of the world!

Higher than the surrounding craggy peaks, but not above the timber line. Majestic pine trees hid the rising sun and crowded the two-acre compound containing house, a weathered gray barn and…some kind of shed? Pete had parked the Suburban in an attached garage off the kitchen. So possibly the shed stored his snowmobile. Whatever, it was a charming replica of the barn.

And the snow! Holiday greeting card perfect. A veritable winter wonderland of the stuff, undisturbed but for a trampled path to the barn. The kids would go nuts playing in this thick, pristine blanket of…frosted pink, actually. Growing whiter and more dazzling as she watched.

Sharon drew in a lungful of alpine air smelling almost as wonderful as coffee. Fortunately no wind added a chill factor to drive her back inside. She hugged herself happily.

Coming here was not only the right thing to do for Pete, it was also good preparation for Taos.

No ski resort snobs would be around to snicker at the Texas bumpkins who'd never seen more than sleet in their part of the state. Rick and Caitlin wouldn't have to act blasé. For once they could simply be children.

Her gaze lifted to the cloudless sky. Such a beautiful shade of blue. Not a trace of pollution. And the hue intensified each second the sun climbed higher. If she could locate that vivid color in silk, she'd get the Harrison job for sure.

What would it be like to wake up to this sky, this view, every morning? Had Pete grown immune to it by now?

As she absorbed the breathtaking scene with a growing sense of awe, trivialities like fabric and budget proposals faded. The most magnificent interior ever created by human hands could never match the grandeur of these mountains.

Humbled by her insignificance, she was inspired by the same. She'd never been more certain of a natural order to seeming chaos. Of a higher purpose and existence beyond this life. Thoughts of her parents were gentle and warm, devoid of the usual pain…oh, my.

Understanding burst within Sharon like sunrise clearing the treetops.

She blinked to clear her vision, lowered the hand she'd unconsciously pressed to her heart. Oh, my. She and Jim had totally misjudged Pete's reasons for living like a recluse.

He hadn't withdrawn from civilization in order to brood over his devastating loss. He'd moved as close to heaven as a mere mortal could get in order to remember Kate's gain.

And to heal in the presence of boundless love.

"Are you crazy?"

Sharon whirled around and nearly stumbled. Her bare feet were like blocks of ice. But her heart warmed at the sight of Jim scowling ten feet away in the doorjamb. He wore a rumpled white T-shirt and gray flannel boxers. His hair was tousled and his jaw shadowed with beard. He looked the same as he had every morning for the past chaotic year. Only her response to the sight was vastly different.

If she ever lost him... Her throat closed.

"What's wrong?" he asked sharply.

"Nothing." For the first time in recent memory, she appreciated how right so many things were. "It's beautiful out here, isn't it?"

"Through the window, maybe. Out here it's freezing. Aren't you miserable?"

"Nope." *Just ashamed.* "Today I'm a happy camper."

He eyed her as if waiting for a punch line, then folded his arms. "Have you been into that little bottle of airline vodka you slipped into your purse?"

She might've been offended, if his biceps hadn't bulged and drawn attention to his impressive pecs. His shoulders spanned the entire doorway.

He misunderstood her silence. "Didn't think I would notice, huh?"

Lord, his eyes were incredible. Caribbean Sea blue in the mountain dawn. The color intensified as she watched, just as the sky had earlier.

"Sharon?"

His mouth was incredible, too. A sensual master-piece framed in dark beard stubble. She'd stared at those lips for three semesters at Texas Tech before learning how skilled they were—

"*Sharon.*"

Oops! "Yes?"

Keenly alert, he tilted his head. "What are you doing?"

She widened her eyes. "Nothing."

He narrowed his.

"I'm just looking at you," she said defensively.

"I'm aware of that. Believe me."

Her dormant libido was finally stirring to life, but the timing was lousy. "Guess I was kind of day-dreaming. I haven't had my coffee yet, and you know how I am before that first cup. Totally out of it." The more she babbled, the brighter his eyes gleamed. "Pete must've set the automatic timer last night to brew at dawn, bless his heart. Is he downstairs?"

"Didn't see him."

"I'm assuming he bunked with the kids. He's probably still asleep in the loft."

"Probably."

"I suppose he could be in the barn, but I didn't hear him leave. Did you?"

Jim didn't bother to respond, just stood there with

his cut muscles and hooded eyes and libertine mouth radiating watchful tension.

Ridiculous, to be so flustered. She washed the man's dirty underwear, for heaven's sake!

"He's probably still asleep," she repeated, untying the sagging belt at her waist for something to do. As the knot came free, her terry-cloth robe parted for an instant.

His gaze latched instantly on to her chaste cotton nightgown.

She caught her breath. A delicious shiver rippled over her skin.

Frowning, Jim studied her face. "Would you please get in the house before you make yourself sick?"

She closed the flaps of her robe. "Worried I'll ruin the rest of your vacation like I did the beginning?" Knotting her belt tight, she offered a rueful smile. "Let's be honest. I've been acting like a spoiled, ungrateful brat about this trip."

He pretended to stagger before muttering, "So have Caitlin and Rick."

"True, but at least they had a good excuse." She thrust chilled fingers into the pockets of her robe. "They *are* spoiled, ungrateful brats. They weren't acting."

His snort of amusement eased some of the tension from his crossed-arm posture.

"Seriously, Jim, you gave the family a wonderful Christmas gift. I'm not saying you were justified in hurting me—no, in hurting my professional ego, by assuming that my clients and schedule weren't as important as yours."

"Sharon—"

"I *do* admit that my professional ego is way too fragile. I overreacted, and I apologize." She withdrew a hand and gestured broadly to the panoramic view. "I would've missed experiencing something special if I'd stayed behind. So thank you for making me come. It couldn't have been much fun for you."

Just that fast, Jim's palpable tension was back. "That's where you're wrong."

Unaccountably her heartbeat accelerated.

"Making you come is one of my greatest pleasures."

Sharon blinked, startled more by her body's thrilled response than by his crudeness.

"That obviously shocks you. But just because you've lost interest in sex doesn't mean I share your lack of enthusiasm."

Whoa! "What?"

A tropical storm of emotion gathered strength in his sea blue eyes. "Well, hell, Sharon, what else am I supposed to think when you're always exhausted and want to go straight to sleep?"

She crossed her arms and mimicked his pose. "Gee, I don't know, Jim. That I'm exhausted and need some sleep, maybe? When I leave my office after a full day, I walk straight into my second job. I don't get to relax, like you do."

"That's funny. Because whenever I start to touch you, it seems like there's always a chapter you want to finish reading, or the end of a movie you want to watch, or some fascinating documentary on the life cycle of crustaceans in the Strait of Gibraltar that you're dying to see."

His bitterness stunned her anew. "Why are you being such a jerk?"

"You said let's be honest, didn't you? I can't help it if you don't like hearing the truth."

"You know, Jim," she said through her teeth. "Just because my legs don't automatically spring open on impact with a mattress doesn't mean I've lost interest in sex."

"Sorry. I stand corrected. Watching the mating habits of crustaceans gets you hot and bothered. It's only our sex life that puts you to sleep. Either that or you make up excuses."

"I do not!"

"Please. It's one excuse after another. The kids aren't asleep yet. Or they're asleep, but one of them might wake up. Or you're about to get your period and don't feel well. Or you've *got* your period and are out of commission. Or you finished your period, but now you have a headache—"

"Hey!" she exploded, quivering with outrage at his gross exaggeration. "Pardon the hell out of me for being an overworked mom with inconvenient plumbing! If you wanted 24/7 playtime with a sex toy who doesn't ever complain, you should've married a blow-up doll and adopted children who aren't spoiled brats!"

The muscles in his folded arms bulged alarmingly. "I don't want a sex toy. I want you."

"I can't tell you how flattered that makes me."

"And I don't expect you not to complain when you're not satisfied. There's a difference between complaining about your love life and making a million excuses to avoid having one."

She blinked back angry wounded tears. "For one thing, I don't make a million excuses. For another, you've made it quite—" She stopped to firm the wobble in her voice. "You've made it quite clear that you haven't been happy for a long time, but this is the first time you've complained to me. It's not—" *damn* "—it's not fair to blame me for something I haven't had the chance to try and fix."

"Sharon...honey..." He uncrossed his arms and took a step forward.

She retreated a step and he stopped.

A turbulent mixture of love, pain and self-disgust roiled in his eyes. "Please don't cry."

Of course that squeezed a tear free. She dashed it away and willed the weakening dam not to break.

"You were right. I was being a jerk." He lifted a hand entreatingly and started to move.

"Don't," she ordered, shrinking back.

His mouth twisted. He slowly refolded his arms. "I never should've said anything."

She thought of the nights she'd been less than receptive and he'd gone through the dutiful motions of foreplay. She loved him, and she loved his touch, so she'd always responded. But she'd also secretly wondered if any convenient warm body would've sufficed.

Apparently a blow-up doll would have worked just as well. Maybe better.

She raised her chin in a show of strength and cursed her trembling mouth. "Actually, you should've said something sooner. This is important. I've been working so hard to get the business going I didn't realize you were dissatisfied with our sex life. With *me,*" she added, her throat constricting.

"With you?"

"Isn't that what you've been trying to tell me? The honest truth?"

"No— I mean, yes!" His brows formed a bank of dark thunderclouds. "Damn it, Sharon, I'm not blaming you."

"Could've fooled me," she said thickly.

"I tried to fool myself, is the problem. I didn't want to admit the honest truth."

"You're talking in circles, Jim. Do me a favor and just spit it out."

His complexion grew ruddy, his breathing agitated. "The truth is that it's *my* fault. You can't help it if I don't turn you on anymore."

For a second, she wondered if she'd heard right.

But his turmoil was too genuine, his struggle to regain composure too obvious. He actually believed himself!

Oh, my.

Oh, *no.*

His carefully blank gaze moved to a spot somewhere over her shoulder.

Reeling from his confession, Sharon stared at her tall, strikingly handsome husband with fresh eyes. And lo and behold, he changed. To an overworked dad with inconvenient plumbing, who felt as inadequate sometimes as she did. Which was such a joke. He was the most competent man she knew. Also the kindest. Not to mention the most honorable. She'd lusted after him from afar as a coed; she'd loved him heart and soul as his girlfriend, fiancée and wife. He was everything she most wanted in a husband, a father, a best friend, a soul mate. He knew that.

But when had she last made him feel wanted as a lover?

"Jim Anderson, you are so clueless. You stood at that door not ten minutes ago and caught me staring at you. Did you really think I was daydreaming?"

Though he didn't look at her, such guarded hope crept into his expression she didn't know whether to laugh or cry.

Given a choice, she always preferred humor. "Get real, stud muffin."

His gaze snapped to her face.

"I was swooning over your manly muscles, idiot. Mmm-mmm-mmm," she murmured while admiring said muscles all over again. "Linda Nicholson thinks you're a hottie, you know. I overheard her tell Caitlin." Sharon finished her examination and met his riveted gaze.

"She's twelve years old," he pointed out.

"She's a female between the age of ten and dead. She wants you bad. Fortunately, she's kinda scrawny." Shoving her sleeves to the elbow, Sharon sniffed. "I think I can take her."

His mouth twitched. "Nice to know my virtue's safe."

"Oh, I'll protect you from Linda. Who's gonna protect you from me?"

Jim didn't look vulnerable now. He looked intrigued, and a little dangerous. Like she'd better not flirt with the new storm brewing inside him unless she was prepared to weather the consequences.

"You have, without a doubt, the sexiest, most

beautiful eyes of any man I've ever known. Remember that private cove we found on our honeymoon in St. Martin?" *The one we skinny-dipped in?*

Whitecaps of warning said that he did.

"Your eyes are the same shade of blue. And then there's your mouth," she said recklessly, breathlessly. "I guess I *was* daydreaming about that. It used to drive me crazy in college. Did you know that I filled a whole sketchbook with drawings of your mouth? I'd flip through them at night and wonder how your lips would feel—"

"Sharon?"

She swallowed hard. "Yes?"

His spiky lashes closed over eyes that were anything but sleepy. "What are you doing?"

"Trying to tell you what a hottie I think you are." She smiled nervously. "How am I doing?"

He unfolded his arm in a slow, deliberate movement. "I think you need to stop talking and start demonstrating."

CHAPTER FOUR

HER PULSE LEAPED as he walked forward, stealing her air, weakening her limbs, sluicing heat to the parts of her primed for his touch by her own seductive words.

"God, I've missed that look in your eyes," he said hoarsely. "Yeah, that's the one. Like you want me to kiss you. Like you want my hands all over you. Like you want your hands all over me." He loomed close.

She tilted her head back as he swept an arm behind her waist.

"Like you want me right here—" he yanked her against his thighs "—right *now.*" Desire glittered and crested in his gaze.

Gasping, Sharon caught a glimpse of Caribbean blue before his mouth came crashing down.

The wave of passion knocked her into a rolling tumble of wet thrusts and sandpaper beard scrapes. Filled with the taste of him, surrounded by the heat of him, she grabbed for his shoulders and clung. She'd grown accustomed to a lazy float on a lovely lagoon.

This was like riding a muscular surfboard in a squall of lust.

An exhilarating, disorienting, wet and wild rush

that left no doubt she wasn't a convenient body; she was as necessary to him as air.

The knowledge was a huge turn-on.

She met the thrust of his tongue and suckled it strongly, swam over and under it sleekly. Her hands stroked the sculptured contours of broad shoulders, muscular arms and powerful chest. Her eager fingers dove through his hair and raked bottom from forehead to nape.

Rumbling his approval, Jim pulled her hips closer and showed her the granite result of her fierce ardor.

Her pleasure spiraled. She wanted him right here. Right now. But he was a little off target. Sweet, sweet torture. Standing on tiptoe helped, but not enough. No problem. Easily fixed.

She paddled a hand between their bodies, found the gap in gray flannel she sought, and closed her fingers around hot rigid velvet.

Jim broke off the kiss with a choked "Stop!"

Chest heaving, he disengaged her fingers and leaned his forehead against hers. Panting shallowly, she wondered if her eyes looked as dazed and crossed as his.

"Don't touch me," he begged in a ragged voice. "We can't do this."

"Why not?" She struggled to focus and gave up. "Are you getting your period?"

His chuckle sounded desperate. "I'm getting my payback for kissing you out here. Give me a minute to cool off."

The incongruity of his statement, given the temperature, struck them at the same time. They broke into big dopey grins that slowly faded.

Her hands found their way to his stomach and she thrilled to his low growl of warning.

"Okay, hussy. You've pushed me too far. Let's take this inside."

"To do what?" she asked archly.

"There's a fascinating documentary on the life— Ooph!"

"Ow!"

Straightening simultaneously, he massaged his abdomen and she cradled her knuckles.

Frowning, she examined her reddening joints. "I think your stomach just broke my hand."

He looked more flattered than concerned. "What can I say? My muscles are manly. If you're a good little hussy—" he lifted her hand to his mouth "—I'll show you all of my manly muscles—" he kissed her knuckles and waggled his brows "—in the bedroom."

Grabbing her wrist, he pulled her behind him toward the open door.

Her feet truly were frozen numb, she realized. Everything else had warmed up quite nicely thanks to that steamy X-rated kiss. Out on an open deck. In full view of anyone coming downstairs.

She had a sudden horrifying vision of her children staring through the window while she fondled their father through his boxers.

Nothing could have chilled her faster or more effectively.

Jim entered the cabin, closed the door and headed for the bedroom, still gripping her wrist. She scanned the kitchen and main room for bodies. Empty, thank God!

Except for a rich and glorious scent. She dragged her feet on the pinewood floor.

Jim pulled harder. "Come. I have many muscles to show."

Resisting harder, she tottered behind. "Doesn't that coffee smell wonderful?"

"No."

"I'd love a hot cup, wouldn't you?"

"No." He'd almost reached the open bedroom door.

"Just a few sips. I'll be fast," she promised.

"Me, too."

"But I *really* want some."

"So do I."

"Mama?" a sleepy voice called from above.

Sharon dug in her heels and stopped, her head tilted toward the loft. Anyone standing by the balcony rail would have to lean far over to see them, or be seen.

Bethany must have called from her bed. "Yes, sweetie, what is it?"

"I had a bad dream."

Jim bumped his head woodpecker style against the door frame.

Sharon weighed needs. "Everything's fine. Go back to sleep."

"I'm thirsty. Can I have some water?"

She mouthed *I'm sorry* to Jim. "I'll be up in a minute, honey."

With a heartfelt groan, he released her wrist.

Poor man. She would make it up to him later. She looked forward to it more than she had in a very long time. But since she had to make a stop in the kitchen anyway...

Following her nose, she located a small glass and filled it with water, then found a large assortment of mismatched dishes and pulled down two ceramic mugs. Exchanging the cracked brown one for a chipped green one that at least wouldn't leak when she sipped, she decided Pete could use a complete new set of dishes.

Too late now for Christmas. She'd already bought him a new wristwatch from the family. But his birthday was in March. She would look for a good sale on stoneware when she returned home.

Fortunately his automatic coffee brewer was in good working order.

She glanced at the bedroom doorway. Jim had disappeared. No lamps were on. Was he stretched out in bed, all of his manly muscles bared, hard and waiting for her to explore?

Anticipation made her tingle. She poured herself a full mug, added sugar and lifted the rim slowly to her mouth.

At the first hot taste, her eyelids fluttered in ecstasy. Oh, God...oh, baby...oh, yes, yes, *yes!*

Only after her mug was half-empty did she pause long enough to remember her mission. She filled a glass with water and carried it toward the stairway leading to the loft, noting details along the way. Lovely grain on the pinewood floor. The black leather sofa was get-what-you-pay-for lumpy. Two cinnamon-red club chairs were worn to the chenille nub in spots. Nice contrast, though, with the large Navajo area rug.

Unable to resist squatting for a closer look, she set down Bethany's water and lifted a corner of the rug.

Well, Pete's housekeeping left something to be desired. But his taste in rugs was superb. An authentic Two Grey Hills weave if Sharon wasn't mistaken— and she usually wasn't, when it came to textiles. She lowered the corner thoughtfully.

The diamond pattern looked right, and no dyes had been used. Amazing how many shades of black, brown and cream could be achieved from raw wool. Something similar would be perfect in the Harrisons' breakfast room.

Collecting the water glass, she rose and glanced up at the balcony rail, curious about who had slept where. It was awfully quiet. Were they all dead to the world? Dead enough for her to return to the bedroom? She decided to take a quick peek.

She walked to the staircase, climbed to the top step, and froze.

She'd kill them when they woke up!

Every suitcase lay gutted on the floor, their entrails yanked out and left in obscene tangles to rot. Boots of all sizes tilted here and flopped there, exactly as they'd landed after being thrown at the nearest sibling's head.

The bathroom door was closed, but she didn't have the stomach to see what carnage awaited her there.

Rick and Caitlin were recognizable lumps in the heavily blanketed bunk beds. Bethany lay curled in on herself like a cold little snail in the double bed, her covers kicked down. No sign of Pete. He must be in the barn after all.

Sharon moved forward, her annoyance softening as she tucked in her youngest daughter and kissed a rose-petal cheek. Bethany stirred and opened her eyes.

"Shh, go back to sleep," Sharon whispered.

Bethany scrambled into a sitting position, instead.

It took four sips of water, repeated reassurances and a soothing back tickle using the lightest touch of Sharon's fingernails to get her daughter back asleep.

Straightening, she noticed the white, bony, extremely large foot hanging off the end of the top bunk, and sighed.

She wove around Samsonite carcasses to do the mom thing. Memories of playing This Little Piggy tugged at her heart as she covered her son's sasquatch toes. Leaning down, she removed the pillow covering Caitlin's head and admired her beauty. Snow White in the flesh. Truly the fairest child in the land.

At the top of the stairs, Sharon cast a sweeping glance back at her children. They were pains in the butt. A source of constant worry and unending responsibility—but also tremendous pride and immeasurable joy. That last point was a biggie in a world too full of ugliness and pain.

Okay, she wouldn't kill them.

Today.

When she walked down the stairs and spotted Jim across the room, her heart actually *ker-thumped* like an infatuated coed's. Silly, but wonderful.

He was fully dressed, stooped over and rummaging deep inside the refrigerator, his backside to Sharon, so he hadn't seen her yet. She'd been gone much longer than she'd intended. Apparently he'd settled for appeasing a hunger he could satisfy immediately.

Glad she was barefoot, she crept toward the denim buns of steel begging to be goosed.

The key to sneaking up on somebody successfully was not so much one's own stealth as the somebody's complete preoccupation. Her husband was in full hunter mode, intent on tracking down food for his belly. True to habit, he was inspecting all his options first. So far, so good.

She reached the island no problem, rounded the corner and approached her target one slow tiptoe at a time.

This was the critical stage. Al-most there. She stretched out both hands, her fingers in pinching position—

Jim whirled around and she screeched.

Straightening to his full height, he laughingly grabbed her hands and pulled her into a tight hug. Real funny. She'd nearly had a coronary.

But with her cheek pressed against his chest and

her heart no longer slamming, she found herself smiling at his cavernous chuckles. He sounded happy.

Which made her happy.

Nuzzling his wool-blend sweater, she savored the smell of Showered and Shaved Jim. A heady mixture of soap, woodsy cologne and the incense unique to his skin.

His chest and arms felt wonderful, too. Maybe not as good as Naked Jim felt, but a close second. She kneaded the muscles from his neck to his lower back before noticing that he'd grown quiet and very still. Hmm. She snuggled experimentally.

Oh, my. Yes, indeedy. His shower hadn't been cold.

She twisted and peered up at the balcony. No eyes peered down. They must've slept through her blood-curdling shriek.

"Sharon? What are you doing?"

Sometime in the past hour, an electrifying awareness had reawakened between them, an extraordinary gift she was ready to unwrap.

She turned around with a sultry smile, kicked the refrigerator door closed, clamped her fingers around one of Jim's wrists and began pulling him out of the kitchen.

For a fraction of a second, he resisted in confusion. Then he eagerly dogged her heels. Halfway across the main room he passed her by to take the lead, and began towing her instead.

She could get used to this caveman stuff. It made

her feel weak and feminine, desired and prized, innocent and chaste—

"*Mom?*"

Well, shit.

She stiffened and stopped, forcing Jim to halt just outside the bedroom doorway.

"*Dad?*"

Jim shot her a fulminating look and tugged at her wrist. She mouthed *I'm sorry* and didn't budge.

Sharon tilted her head toward the loft. "Yes, Rick? What is it?"

Releasing her wrist, Jim banged his forehead once on the door frame.

"Is Grandpa Pete down there?"

She exchanged a puzzled glance with Jim. "No. Why?"

"There's an envelope up here in the bathroom with y'all's name on it in big letters. I think it's from Grandpa Pete. It wasn't here last night when I brushed my teeth." Rick was trying to sound nonchalant, but there was an odd note in his voice that alarmed Sharon.

Frowning, Jim moved back from the bedroom door and looked up at the loft. "Bring the envelope down here, son. I'm sure it's nothing to worry about."

"THIS REALLY SUCKS," Rick said for the tenth time in as many minutes. Elbow propped on the sofa arm, head in hand, he stared gloomily at the envelope on the coffee table.

Jim roused himself from his slouch on the club chair enough to mutter "Don't say that again, son."

Rick raised his free hand to scratch the electric guitar emblazoned on his T-shirt. "This really blows."

When you're right, you're right, Jim thought.

Even Sharon let the comment lie.

After spending a frenzied hour confirming the truth of the envelope's contents, they all sat staring now at the cursed thing like it was some damn voodoo doll bristling with stickpins. Not a bad analogy.

Good ol' Dad had stuck it to them but good.

Jim wouldn't have believed the Pete Anderson he knew capable of such deviousness, much less such high-handed meddling. What gave him the right to decide what was best for the family he only saw twice a year?

Jim still hadn't assimilated his sense of betrayal and helplessness.

In the opposite club chair, Sharon was equally upset. He could tell because she'd changed into pink sweats and high-top sneakers earlier, and sat curled with her legs beside her, rubber soles on the fabric. A startling transgression of her usual house rules.

She stirred and met his eyes. "What about tapping into the phone line? Is that possible?"

"Sure, for a phone company lineman. Even if I climbed the pole without breaking my neck, I don't have the equipment or knowledge to do anything but electrocute myself." Frustrated, he looked at Caitlin and Bethany on the sofa. "You girls sure that remote phone receiver isn't hidden somewhere in this cabin?''

"We looked everywhere, Daddy," Caitlin promised. "I found some rolled quarters stuck in one of the pots in the kitchen. And Bethany found a dead mouse in one of Grandpa Pete's boots—"

"What!" Sharon yelped.

"It only had a little fur left, Mama," Bethany assured her. "I didn't sneeze. It was mostly bones."

"Yeah," Rick confirmed, straightening with a show of interest. "It was pretty cool. All shriveled like a little mummy. Want me to get it out of the trash so you can see?" There was a twinkle buried in his innocent gaze.

Predictably, Sharon shuddered. "I'll stick to watching the History Channel, thank you."

"Not for the next eight days, you won't," Jim said.

All eyes turned his way, and his stomach knotted. He'd hoped to disarm this final bomb with a viable solution before releasing it on his family.

"None of us will be watching any TV while we're here. The activation card to Dad's satellite dish is missing. He must've taken that with him along with everything else."

The pall of horror that greeted this announcement surpassed their earlier shock. Then, they'd thought this might be a cruel practical joke. Now, they knew it was simply cruel.

The facts were grim.

They had no truck, no snowmobile, no telephone, no stereo unit, no functional TV. No backpack containing the kids' CD players and headphones, Game Boy color, and assorted fashion and music magazines. No way off the mountain except by hiking twenty twisting miles of private road to a sparsely traveled rural highway, where the chance of flagging down help was slim to none. From there, it was another thirty-mile walk to the town of Moran.

Which Jim would've gamely attempted, if his father hadn't canceled the family's reservations at Taos Ski Resort and paid the penalty fee.

Before they'd even arrived in New Mexico, damn it! Unbelievable. The reservation confirmation letter tucked in Jim's camera case was useless. Their rooms had undoubtedly been rebooked the minute they became available.

No hotel of any kind that was accessible to ski areas would have vacancies open during the next week. Especially not with recent record snowfalls. The past two dismal seasons had created a feverish demand this year.

Even if he did manage to fetch transportation for his family, where would he take them? To the airport and back home? What a perfect ending to the trip from hell!

Rick broke the silence first. "What about that guy on the CB radio? Sam, right? Why don't we let Mom talk to him, this time? She won't yell and piss him off like you did."

Jim grimaced. His father had left them a CB radio and instructions to use channel 12 for emergencies, only. He'd assured them that his nearest neighbor and good friend Sam would respond. And sure enough, Sam had answered right away.

Unfortunately he'd taken exception to an angry demand for immediate help but no life-threatening emergency to report. He'd also refused to divulge his location, which was somewhere within a ten-mile radius of the CB radio.

Rick looked at his mother. "C'mon, Mom, you know you can sweet-talk anyone into doing anything. I'll bet you can at least get him to drop some clues about where he lives. Then Dad and I can go steal Sam's—" he stopped at Sharon's frown "—*borrow* his car," Rick corrected.

Jim sighed. A father shouldn't have to deliberately tarnish his own image. "It's not that easy, son. Without specific directions, and probably a compass, too, we could wander in these mountains for days. Your grandfather's letter said that Sam's cabin is even more isolated than this one."

Sharon looked alarmed. "Your father's right, Rick. Besides, I don't think I could get anything new out of Sam. He sounded pretty determined not to break his word to your grandfather."

They'd all heard Pete in the background barking at Sam to stand tough.

Fingers threaded together, Rick bulldozed his palms from hairline to the top of his skull and stopped, trapping the strands that normally escaped his ponytail to obscure some part of his face. "So you won't even try?"

Sharon seemed as bemused as Jim at the instant maturation of Rick's features. Recovering, she shook her head. "I don't want you or your father traipsing through the forest."

"Okay, then, how 'bout this?" His locked hands slid down to his nape, releasing a slither of hair to dangle over one eye. "You radio back and make up some emergency. You know, like Caitlin cut off her finger chopping eggs for tuna salad or something."

"Gross! Cut off your own finger," Caitlin suggested.

He flapped his spread elbows. "Whatever. The point is to get all hysterical so we can get out of here."

Jim sought his wife's gaze.

We can't, Jim. What kind of example would that set?

Yeah, you're right. Good idea, though.

Amusement glinted and was quickly doused in her eyes. She turned to their son. "I won't lie and distress your grandfather, no matter how much we want to leave."

"Jesus, Mom, why not? Grandpa Pete sure didn't have any problem dicking *us* around!"

Her backbone steeled. "Two wrongs don't make a right. And I won't tolerate that language. You owe me two dollars."

"Fine!" He unclasped his hands and flung them wide. "Take all the money I brought! What do I care?" His flushed face and mulish expression belied his words. He crossed his arms. "It's not like there are any stores around here to spend it in. Merry freaking Christmas.''

Jim felt slightly sick.

''We're really staying here?'' Caitlin asked, her eyes rounding. ''For the whole vacation?''

Rick angled to face both of his sisters. ''Don't be spoiled, now. Just because we were supposed to chow down on fancy resort food, and go snowboarding, and sit in hot tubs, and sing Christmas carols on sleigh rides—'' he rolled his eyes ''—and pick out one thing we each wanted from the gift shops as part of our wonderful Christmas trip. Just because none of that's gonna happen now, doesn't mean we shouldn't be grateful we have each other.''

''That's right,'' Sharon snapped. ''I'm beginning to see the method in your grandfather's madness.''

''But, Mom.'' Caitlin's mouth trembled. ''There's nothing to do here. We'll be so bored. *Daddy*—'' she trained tear-spangled eyes on Jim ''—you've got to *do* something.''

Strangling the man responsible for ruining his family's Christmas vacation sounded good. But that probably wouldn't set a very good example.

Jim leaned forward, elbows on thighs, clasped hands forming a fist between his knees. ''We're all disappointed and resentful, and those are natural feelings, given the situation. I'll start looking for a safe way to leave, and somewhere to go that has vacancies and a lot of fun things to do. But for right now, we've all got to be flexible and go with the flow.''

Caitlin voiced the question lurking in all of their eyes. "But...what if we don't find a way to leave?"

He'd wanted to give his family a great trip and be their hero. Well, getting them off this mountain would make him Superdad. He started to assure them he wouldn't fail, then stopped himself.

All the dinners, Little League games, Open House nights and dance recitals he'd missed came back to haunt him. Promises were easy. Over the years he'd made and broken a lot of them.

It was high time he admitted that fact to himself.

"If we don't, then I guess we'll have to stick it out and make our own fun. It's all a matter of attitude. We have to decide to make the best of our change in plans and have fun with each other.

"That may sound corny, but I guarantee it's much harder to be corny than to be cynical," Jim said, noting his son's slight sneer before sweeping a solemn look over the others. "I need everyone's help and cooperation. Are we up to the challenge? Can we concentrate on something besides what we want individually and focus on what's fair and best for the family?"

Rick was the key, Jim knew. He sought and held his son's gaze. Not as a father demanding obedience, but as an equal requesting help.

The boy straightened from his slouch, his face registering a succession of emotions. Surprise. Wariness. Pleasure. And finally, a mature resolve that revealed a glimpse of the man he would soon become.

"We'll try, Dad, won't we?" Rick eyed his siblings until they nodded agreement. He turned back to his father and grinned. "Who knows? Maybe it won't suck as much we thought."

As far as Jim was concerned, it already didn't.

CHAPTER FIVE

No DOUBT ABOUT IT, Sharon decided. The cedar chest had saved their lives.

Sitting on a patio chair with her boots propped on the deck rail, she sipped a midmorning cup of coffee and contemplated the view. Since learning three days ago that they were virtually trapped on this mountain, she'd spent as much time out here as possible. Warm clothes provided physical comfort, and the awesome scenery never failed to soothe her soul.

Still, if Rick and Jim hadn't discovered the cedar chest that first awful morning, cabin fever would've run rampant by now. Pete would've returned to find the place littered with casualties.

Modern families were simply not prepared to spend fourteen waking hours together without the buffer of modern distractions.

A girlish shriek pierced the still mountain air just ahead. There was the sound of a dull thwack, a childish squeal. Two more thwacks, and husky laughter.

Sharon peered between the slats of the deck rail and confirmed the start of a snowball fight in front of the toolshed. Caitlin and Bethany against Rick, again. He'd creamed them consistently, so she had to give them credit. What they lacked in muscle they made up for in spunk.

Sharon's attention sharpened. You go, girls! *Use* those superior brains!

Bethany was on her knees assembling and supplying a steady stream of ammunition to Caitlin, who fired them rapidly at her brother's head. Hands screening his face, snow bursting against his gloves, laughing and taunting simultaneously, he backed away, stumbled and fell. His sisters surged forward like wolves going in for the kill.

Watching sweet little Bethany cram a fistful of snow up her brother's nose, Sharon grinned proudly before relaxing against the cushion.

She studied the horizon through aromatic steam and returned to her musing. To that first devastating morning.

United in panic, the family had combed the entire compound for anything that might help them survive. They'd split into traditional teams. Girls inside, boys outside.

Sharon had discovered a deep freezer in the garage packed with enough hamburger, chicken and steaks to last four burly men on the Atkins Diet a full month. The pantry was equally well stocked. No convenience foods or snacks, but plenty of staples and canned goods. The refrigerator bore the fruits of a huge grocery-store run.

Pete had seen to it quite generously that they wouldn't go hungry. He must have spent a small fortune, she'd later told Jim.

Glaring, he'd said they should eat steak every night until it ran out, then go to chicken, and leave the hamburger for last.

She and the girls had made a pile of interesting items they found. Cuban cigars. Ivory dominoes in a wooden box. A towering stack of *Reader's Digest*. Four bottles of merlot wine.

They'd been proud until Jim and Rick had returned from their hunt carrying a huge cedar chest between them like a slain bear. The two had deposited it in front of the fireplace and described finding it in a stall where the cow should've been.

Thank God. For many reasons, not the least of which was the fact that any poor cow who relied on them to milk her was in for a rough time or mastitis or both. Pete had humanely taken her from harm's way.

In her place, he'd left the chest with a big red bow on top, so there was no mistaking it was a gift. And what a gift!

Sharon took a smiling sip of coffee, remembering their amazement over the contents.

There were board games. The old-fashioned kind. Candy Land. Monopoly. Scrabble. Clue. Oh, and checkers. She'd barely recalled how to play that one, but Jim had given her a refresher course, and pretty soon she was whipping his butt.

Of course, Rick now whipped hers on a regular basis. She pretended to be upset, but she loved seeing his eyes sparkle, hearing him whoop and turn to his dad for an elaborate hand ritual involving slaps, bumped fists and curled fingers in some order she could never duplicate.

There had been craft supplies in the chest, too. Basic stuff like crayons, construction paper, scissors and glue. Fancy stuff like pretty ribbons and gold glitter. Interesting stuff like old buttons, pressed flowers and tiny shells.

The boys had snorted with macho disdain. The girls had exclaimed with delight. The order was reversed when an assortment of woodworking tools came out next.

But the coup de grâce, the item that had produced gasps as Jim unwrapped it from a blanket, was an acoustic guitar. Obviously old and well used. Not much to look at. But a guitar! Tears had sprung to Sharon's eyes as all trace of cynicism and discontent had vanished from Rick's expression and he'd reached for the instrument reverently.

He'd be inside right now practicing his songs if the girls hadn't pried him loose. Sometime during the past three days they'd accepted their fate and decided to make their own fun. The family was heading for the woods soon to cut a fresh Christmas tree. Jim had already built the stand, and the kids had begun making paper chain garlands. Imagine that?

At home she'd selected, purchased, hauled, set up and mostly decorated the tree by herself.

Oh, yes. No doubt about it. The cedar chest had saved their lives. And the man who had lovingly compiled the contents deserved their gratitude, not their anger.

"HOW 'BOUT THIS ONE, Mama?" Bethany patted the rough bark and anxiously watched her mother.

Arms crossed, head tilted to study the branches, Mama looked bright and cheerful in her yellow parka and red cap. But no gleam warmed her brown eyes to gold.

She wouldn't pick this tree, either.

"That's nice, honey, but the branches are too thin on the left. Let's keep looking."

"God almighty, Sharon!" Daddy bellowed, standing with Rick and Caitlin to Bethany's left. "If you don't hurry up and decide, I'm cutting the next tree I come across that's the right height."

"Yes, dear," Mama said in her I'm-not-listening voice. She whirled around and crunched forward through the snow, looking at each smaller tree that she passed.

Bethany shared a knowing glance with her father, brother and sister. Mama didn't see the same things they saw. Until she spotted whatever it was she was looking for, there was no use trying to make her think something else was fine.

Daddy picked up his ax, Rick slipped his arm and shoulder through loops of rope, Caitlin held out her gloved hand to Bethany, who rushed forward to grasp it gladly, and they all trudged after Mama.

The forest was spooky, with patches of sunlight here and there on the ground, but mostly shadows. Bethany craned her head back to stare at the sparkly treetops, feeling very small, but happy and safe. Her sister's hand was firm and warm. The rest of her family was within sight. Nobody was mad, or sad, or acting like they wanted to be anywhere else than right here.

Bethany was glad they weren't at some stupid ski resort. She was having more fun than she'd ever had!

If they were at a resort, her brother and sister wouldn't have helped her make three snowmen, each one better than the last. They wouldn't have played Candy Land with her, or taught her how to play Monopoly—well, she still wasn't sure about the rules, so she and Mama were partners in that game.

Caitlin never would have drawn pictures, leaving the insides white for Bethany to color with crayons. Rick would've *never* let her sit and listen to him sing and play the guitar in the bedroom with the door closed. Even if he'd been terrible, she would've told him he was good.

But he *wasn't* terrible. He was better than that singer in Staind, and she'd told him so. He'd looked surprised that she knew the band, and pleased at her compliment. And since then, he hadn't looked at her like she was a baby or ignored her once.

Straight ahead, Mama suddenly stopped. She was staring at a tree to her right. One with furry bluish branches.

''Oh, my,'' she said, moving to circle the tree slowly.

It didn't look much different from the last five trees to Bethany, but Mama's eyes were glowing as she walked toward Daddy and stopped.

"That's the one, Jim. Isn't it gorgeous?" She looked up at him with her biggest smile.

"Beautiful," he said in a funny voice, looking at her and not the tree.

Her face got all pink, and he kissed her quick on the mouth like he couldn't help it, like he did to Bethany sometimes when she'd said something cute. Only this wasn't like that at all.

Caitlin rolled her eyes at Rick, but they didn't seem disgusted. People who loved each other were supposed to get mushy.

Then Daddy yanked Mama's cap down over her eyes, and everybody laughed, and they weren't kids watching their parents, they were a family again.

Daddy made everyone move back as he started chopping the trunk with his ax. After a while, he complained that the edge was dull, and took off his coat. Then he asked everyone to stop giving advice. Then he stopped talking and only grunted. At last the trunk cracked and the tree fell, and Mama fussed over his red face dripping with sweat.

If she'd made the same deal with him about cuss words that she'd made with Rick, her money jar would've been stuffed by the time they dragged the tree to the cabin and finally got it to stand exactly, perfectly straight next to the fireplace.

Then Mama made them move it farther away so it wouldn't catch a spark and burn the house and everyone inside to crispy critters.

Finally they all stood back and admired how pretty it looked.

Daddy slipped an arm around Mama's waist and bumped her with his hip. "You know what I like best about this tree, don't you?"

"That wonderful pine smell?"

"Hell, no. I like that I don't have to string any damn twinkle lights."

"Hey, you got off easy this year at home. I did all the work. But there's a lot that still needs to be done here to spiff up the place. I could use everybody's help. I'm not close to having my presents ready."

Bethany's stomach jumped in excitement. They were making homemade gifts for each other, and all the whispers and shoving things out of sight and disappearance of craft supplies was almost as magical as the thought of Santa's workshop used to be. Grandpa Pete would be glad...

"Mama?"

Her mother looked down. "Hmm?"

"I think we should ask Grandpa Pete to come back early and spend Christmas with us." Bethany had everyone's attention now. "He shouldn't be alone on Christmas, and this is his house, and he gave us all that neat stuff in the chest, and he didn't leave us trapped here because me and Caitlin and Rick—"

"Caitlin and Rick and I," Mama corrected.

"Caitlin and Rick and I are spoiled, like I thought at first. I think he just wanted us all to stop being invisible."

Her parents exchanged one of those looks only they could understand before her father spoke. "What do you mean, invisible, honey?"

"You know, *invisible*. Like the invisible man." She struggled for the right words. "People know he's there in the room. He talks and moves around and has feelings, but nobody ever really *sees* him."

Frustrated, she turned to her brother and sister for help.

"Yeah, I know what you're saying," Rick told her, then looked at their father with that expression her parents hated. "Like playing my music. At home it's just noise to you. Something I do to interrupt the peace and quiet, or to keep from doing my homework. Here, you act like I might really be serious about something important to me."

Daddy opened and closed his mouth.

"Same with my drawing," Caitlin said, attracting all eyes, but staring only at Mama. "They were just silly paper doll fashions and doodling at home. It wasn't until I made coloring books for Bethany that you really *saw* what I can do, or acted like I might have talent."

Mama looked like Caitlin had hit her.

Bethany met the full force of her parents' searching gazes and wished she could make them feel better. But they'd taught her never to lie.

"At home we're invisible. Here—" she shrugged helplessly "—we're not."

WHEN SHARON SLIPPED INTO bed hours later, Jim was lying on his back, covers pulled to the waist, staring at the ceiling as if in deep thought. She switched off the lamp, converting the room into an intimate haven of flickering shadows.

Flames popped and hissed in the corner fireplace, limning his muscles in gold, dyeing the hair on his chest blond, providing a romantic ambiance she'd enjoyed to the fullest the past three nights.

She scooted to his side and used his biceps as a pillow. The discomfort was worth the comfort. Resting a hand on his chest, she absorbed the solid beat of his heart.

"We're terrible parents," she said miserably.

He covered her hand with his own. "No, we're not. Not all the time," he amended.

"Bethany's completely right. Out of the mouths of babes, yet. We've been so blinded by the trees we haven't seen the beautiful forest."

"Don't mix metaphors. The invisible man is cooler."

"Wasn't that amazing insight for a seven-year-old? She's so smart."

"Takes after her mother."

Sharon sighed. "No, I'm dumb. And selfish. And insensitive. How could I pay more attention to their dirty laundry and report card grades than to *them?*"

"Now that *is* dumb. You stand on your head for those kids. You have from the very beginning. They have no idea what you gave up to stay home and be there for them!"

His staunch loyalty thrilled the secret part of her that hadn't been sure *he* had appreciated her sacrifice.

She stirred a whorl of chest hair. "But did you see

Caitlin's face? She's right, Jim. I never paid much attention to her drawings because they're always of clothes and shoes and things I think are superficial. Everybody says she should be a model and I didn't want to encourage her interest in fashion. When her beauty fades, I want her to be on solid ground, courtesy of her brain.'' She snorted. ''Like making over the Harrisons' study and kitchen will cure cancer. I'm the worst kind of hypocrite!''

He squeezed the top of her hand. ''Did you see Rick's face? Did he have my number, or what? When I walk into the house and he's jammin' on that electric guitar after a day of phones ringing and clients bitching and horns honking in traffic for hours, I *do* only hear noise. Plus, what kind of life do rock musicians have? If I encourage him, what's his incentive to go to college?''

She turned her palm up and threaded her fingers through his. ''I know, but can you believe how he sounds on your dad's old guitar? Pete will get such a kick out of hearing Rick play.'' Pete had seemed so relieved and grateful at the invitation she'd felt doubly shamed for not thinking to ask him without prodding from a child.

''I listened to Rick through the door yesterday,'' Jim confessed. ''The kid's really good, and not only on the guitar. He's got a damn good singing voice. Where did that come from?''

''I have no idea.''

They shared a moment of proud wonder. Her tone-deaf parents had passed the handicap to all their kids.

Jim could carry a tune—but only if someone helped him hold it steady.

She shifted her neck, seeking a softer spot that wasn't there. "When it comes down to it, Rick is so enthralled with the music industry, our approval or disapproval may not matter. It's not the lifestyle I'd wish for him. Drugs are such an integral part of the culture…"

"Yeah." The silence pulsed with images of the worst case scenario. "It scares the hell out of me," Jim admitted.

"God, me, too." She lifted their joined hands and bumped his chest. "I thought parenting would get easier when they grew older."

"It's a myth spread by obstetricians so they can pay for their beachfront condos."

She laughed, loving that he understood, that she wasn't alone, that they were united in bafflement and good intentions.

Jim rubbed his thumb over her knuckles. "Fortunately the kids have you. Because I don't know what the hell I'm doing."

"Then our children are doomed, because I'm clueless most of the time. Remember what life was like in the old days—BC?" Before Children, they referred to it jokingly.

His low chuckle vibrated every part of her that touched him, which suddenly wasn't nearly enough parts. She turned on her side and snuggled closer. The forearm of her muscular pillow rose and warm fingers cupped her shoulder.

"Just think," he said in a musing tone. "Only eleven years and three months to go, and we'll be empty nesters. Free at last."

"The mind boggles."

He kneaded her shoulder with gentle strength. "We can walk buck naked through the house, make love on the living room floor—"

"Travel whenever we want, use our phone without kicking someone off first—"

"Make love on the kitchen counter—"

"Take a class at the community college—"

"Make love on the dining room table—"

"Ignore Open House Night at school—"

"Make love—"

"Jim?"

"Hmm?" One hand slid from her shoulder to elbow and back, the other pressed her fingers against his chest.

"I'm sensing a definite theme to your conversation."

"Really. What might that be?" His caressing palm spread delicious warmth through her limbs.

"Well, you either think that bedrooms make for boring sex, or you have sex on the brain, period."

"Boring sex is an oxymoron," he assured her. "It's that second thing."

"So you're okay with a traditional bed? Because we have a lot of years left before we can go wild outside a locked bedroom door." She pulled her trapped fingers free and scraped her nails lightly up his abdomen.

His stomach rippled in her wake. "Is this door locked now?"

"I believe that it is." She reversed the direction of her nails.

"You believe, or you know?" Tension hardened his muscles into ridged slabs.

Her body softened along with her voice. "I locked it myself." She circled his navel.

"Does that mean you wanna go wild?"

Everything in her screamed yes. "I dunno, stud muffin. Think you're up to the job?" Her nails leaped off the merry-go-round and hit elastic waistband.

He hissed.

One second she was on her side, the next she was flat on her back, her wrists manacled to the mattress on each side of her head.

Her heart pounding, she thrilled at the powerful torso looming above her, the intense stare glittering down from a shadowed face, the parting of her legs with a hair-roughened knee. He surged forward and stopped, his most manly muscle of all pressing the juncture of her thighs.

"What do you think?" he asked in a growl.

Even if she'd tried answering in words, she couldn't have been coherent. So she reached for him through his boxers and made a feminine sound of approval he couldn't misunderstand.

One stroke of the fist she'd made was galvanizing.

He grabbed the nightgown bunched at her thighs, yanked it over her head, scrambled out of his boxers and returned to her as Naked Jim. Her favorite. Desperate for skin-to-skin contact, she tugged at his shoulders to no avail.

"Not yet," he said in a guttural voice. Holding her gaze, he removed her hands. "Go wild for me."

He lowered his head and feasted.

On her mouth, with a deep, hot kiss that left her breathless and stunned when he moved to a breast, where he tasted and teased her nipple with soft, moist, suctioning bites. A beard-rasping trip to the other breast prickled nerve endings from her neck to her curling toes. Alternating flicks of his tongue and pulls of his mouth wrung a choked sob from her throat.

Dazed and flushed, unbearably aroused, she watched him sample this and that as if she were a buffet table. He nibbled the flare of her hip, swirled his tongue in her navel, murmured soft words of love and sex on her sensitive inner thighs.

When he centered his attention on the focus of hers, she arched her back at the exquisite sensation.

He took his time and made his enjoyment lustily clear. Knowing she gave as well as received pleasure made her wild. Her head tossing from side to side, her fingers digging into the mattress, she let the sweet tension build and build, then pulled him frantically higher and met his eyes.

"I want you inside me *now*."

He reached down, positioned himself where she ached, and buried himself in a single powerful thrust.

She gasped and trembled, joined to this man in so many ways that he filled her completely, as no other lover could. She lifted a hand to stroke his cheek.

"We're so lucky," she whispered.

"And about to get luckier."

Smiling, she lifted her head and met him halfway for a tender kiss.

As always, the tenderness vanished, replaced by a fierce passion that was no less loving. She went wild for him and surrendered to a shattering climax that triggered his hoarse cry of release.

Drowsing for long, contented moments beneath her husband's full weight, she thought again of how blessed they were to have found each other. But she really was beginning to suffocate.

She pushed at his chest.

He raised to his elbows. "So that's how it is, huh? My purpose has been served, and now you want to get rid of me."

"Not a chance, stud muffin." She wrapped her arms around his waist. "You're stuck with me for life."

This time her pinch on his butt caught him by surprise.

EPILOGUE

PETE HAULED the stock trailer carefully up the winding road to his cabin. Jezebel mooed her displeasure after a particularly nasty jounce. The trip down had been bad enough, she seemed to say. Sharing the ride twice with a snowmobile was asking too damn much.

He checked the rearview mirror of his Suburban. Nothing was damaged except her dignity.

Excitement mixed with dread as he thought of seeing Jim and his family again. Sharon had said to come anytime before noon. That they were in no rush to open their few presents. That Christmas wasn't about presents this year and that Pete should take his time.

So he'd tried not to leave before at least ten o'clock. He'd milked both the cow and as much time out of packing as he could.

But after days of wondering if Sam would *ever* shut up, once he'd left to spend Christmas in Santa Fe, Pete had missed his kind friend's jabbering. The peace and quiet this morning had been downright lonely.

Funny. Because he never minded the lack of voices or company in his own cabin. He couldn't wait to get home where he belonged!

The past week had been the hardest test of will he'd ever endured. First there had been the torture of listening to transmitted pleas for rescue, and having to convince Sam—and himself—not to respond. Then there had been the worse torture of not hearing anything crackle over the CB radio for days.

His imagination had filled in the dead silence.

The family had headed out on foot and was wandering lost in the forest, or lying frozen in the snow, or they'd turned on each other in the cabin like a pack of entertainment-starved wolves.

That last possibility had robbed him of sleep. If his extreme measures had caused irreparable harm to Jim's family, instead of forging stronger bonds, Pete wouldn't have been able to live with himself.

His relief at Sharon's radio contact and invitation had been overwhelming. She'd actually sounded cordial. He'd taken that to mean the situation had improved since those early desperate calls.

Whether or not he'd been forgiven…well, that was a whole other ball of wax.

Five minutes later, Pete crested the final turn and broke free of the towering ponderosa pines. The compound was visible straight ahead, and his heart lifted. Home sweet home at last.

No sign of life outside. Smoke billowed from both chimneys of the cabin. Three of the sorriest looking snowmen he'd ever slapped eyes on leaned drunkenly near one corner of the toolshed. Everything else looked the same as when he'd left.

Praying that some things had changed, he drove to the barn and parked close to the wide double doors.

He'd tucked Jezebel safely in her stall and was throwing her a bundle of hay when Rick burst through the door at a run, Caitlin close behind. Both stopped and leaned over, propped their hands on their knees and panted.

"Beat you!" he crowed breathlessly.

"You cheated. You were supposed to count to five before starting."

"So I count fast." He looked up at Pete and grinned. "Hi, Grandpa."

"Hi, Grandpa," Caitlin echoed. "Merry Christmas!"

"Merry Christmas to you, young lady."

They straightened and rushed forward as he opened his arms.

He took in their rosy cheeks, sparkling eyes and animated expressions with a surge of gladness, and locked an arm around each for a quick squeeze. "Looks like you two survived the week without killing each other. That's a relief. I was a little worried."

"Yeah, well, you should've been," Rick said. "I came close a couple of times with a snowball between her eyes."

"Oh, big talker," she countered. "Me and Bethany—"

"Bethany and *I,* moron."

"What-*ever.* We slaughtered him, Grandpa. He almost choked on a snowball Bethany shoved up his nose."

Pete raised both brows. *"Peanut?"*

They both laughed. Rick shook his head ruefully, "She got me good that time, I have to admit."

"Hey, look at the cow, Rick! Ooh, she's so cute."

By the time Pete had answered all their questions about Jezebel and walked with them to the cabin, he was tickled at the subtle changes he'd noticed. The bickering hadn't let up. But the tone was good-natured, not whiny or hostile. Once or twice they'd even smiled at one another like they might be friends one day.

He entered the mudroom more hopeful than he'd expected. The three of them stomped snow from their boots, took off coats, hats and gloves, and walked inside via the kitchen. He took two steps and stopped, bombarded with sights and smells.

Sharon turned, clasping a pan of fragrant biscuits she'd just removed from the oven, and smiled. "Merry Christmas! Your timing is perfect. I hope you're hungry, because Jim made way too many pancakes." She gestured with her elbow at a heaping platter on the counter.

Jim set down syrup and butter. "Speak for yourself, puny woman. We have manly muscles to feed." He winked at Rick, then glanced at Pete. "Hi, Dad. Merry Christmas."

Rick and Caitlin pulled out bar stools and claimed two of the six place settings.

"Grandpa Pete!"

Pete turned to see Bethany waving at him from behind the loft balcony rail.

She whirled around and pounded down the stairs, then hurtled across the room.

"Slow down!" Sharon called out too late.

Bethany barreled into Pete's thigh.

He stumbled and laughingly regained his balance. "Whoa, there, Peanut. Where's the fire?"

"Rick put it out already. He's a *hero*."

Startled, Pete searched out his grandson.

"No big deal," Rick muttered.

"It was too, Grandpa Pete," Caitlin insisted. "Yesterday Mom and Dad were in the barn, and it was my turn to make breakfast, and I took the bacon out, but forgot to turn off the burner. And there was this big *poof!* And I turned around and screamed like a moron, 'cause flames were shooting up and I didn't know what to do. So I grabbed a glass of water and was about to throw it on and Rick stopped me. He got the lid of that big soup pot you have? And he kinda tossed it onto the pan and smothered the fire."

Bethany tugged Pete's corduroy pants. "Yeah, and Mama said Caitlin would've burned herself *bad* if she'd thrown water."

Pete looked at his grandson. "Sounds to me like it was a pretty big deal. Good thinking, Rick."

The boy's flush of pleasure deepened when his father laid a hand on his shoulder and squeezed.

Sharon finished filling a row of glasses with orange juice and called over her shoulder. "Jim, help me get these on the table. Everybody else, sit."

Pete hopped as fast as Bethany to obey the direct order.

"Eat," Sharon commanded. "Before it gets cold."

And just that easily, Pete slipped back into the family's good graces. Not a word was said about their aborted ski vacation, or his sneaking away and leaving them stranded, or the backpack and satellite dish card in the Suburban. They'd obviously made some kind of pact to be nice, and were sticking to it. That was fine and dandy with him.

During breakfast, he marveled at the Christmas decorations in the cabin. They'd set up a pretty blue spruce tree by the fireplace, and wrapped it in red and green paper chains, then hung homemade ornaments. He'd have to look closer, later, but a lot of them used the glitter and ribbons that he'd left in the chest.

Pine boughs lined the mantelpiece. Paper Christmas stockings with names written in crayon hung down, taped to the edge. When he saw his name on one, he had a hard time swallowing his bite of pancake past the lump swelling in his throat.

After eating, the children begged to digest their meal before tackling the dishes. A phrase Pete remembered hearing Jim use at Thanksgiving. Relenting, Jim and Sharon led the way into the main room, and everyone claimed a piece of furniture.

"I feel bad that I didn't bring anything," Pete admitted.

"Are you kidding?" Sharon made a scoffing sound. "You filled a whole chest with wonderful presents. We want you to know how much your thoughtfulness meant to us. Even though you did force us to actually *talk* to one another instead of watch TV.'' She mugged a face at her family, making them smile.

Pete watched the interaction and sensed a respect between them that hadn't been there before. ''I was afraid you'd all hate me,'' he admitted.

The chorus of protests would have soothed him but for the one voice that remained conspicuously silent.

Pete looked at the man who would always be his beloved son, no matter how old they both got. ''I know you had your heart set on taking that fancy ski vacation. You planned it after I lectured you about making time for your family, and then I ruined your trip. Like what you'd done wasn't the right thing, somehow.''

He could see that his words struck home, and he smiled ruefully. ''You did a generous and good thing, Jim. Your family would've had a ball at that resort, and you would've gone back home more relaxed. But, there's something about this mountain…the isolation, the closeness to nature, that puts things in perspective.'' Hell, he sounded like a sentimental idiot.

''Seeing your mountain was always part of my plan, Dad.''

''Making you see how important you are to each other was mine. And I knew that it couldn't happen in a two-day stopover here, so it *sure* wasn't going to happen while you were skiing, or shopping, or sitting in a hot tub. You needed a full week on the mountain without distractions.''

''So your answer was to trap us?''

''That was my answer, yes. My interfering, domineering, well-intentioned answer." He laughed shortly. "I don't know what I'm doing most of the time when it comes to you, son. But I always have good intentions."

Something flickered in Jim's eyes. He looked at Sharon, and she smiled. A second later, he grudgingly joined her.

"Did I say something funny?" Pete asked.

Sharon shook her head. "You said something universal."

Jim's expression grew serious. "It reminded me how important you are to me, Dad. How much I love you. How lucky I am that you love me, and have my best intentions at heart."

Pete couldn't speak. The damn lump was back in his throat, and getting bigger.

"See, Daddy?" Bethany said with a bright smile. "Grandpa Pete's not invisible here, either!"

Undercover Santa
Janice Kay Johnson

Dear Reader,

I'm possibly a little twisted, but I've had this plot in mind for years, just waiting for that question from an editor: "Would you write a Christmas story for an anthology?" At last the call came. Then came the tough part. I had to explain to my editor that, yes, I had a story in mind, but it didn't involve the usual trappings of eggnog and long-lost family and bittersweet celebrations. I did have Santa in my story, but, see, Santa is really an undercover cop. Because, um, someone wants to kill Santa Claus, and this kid and his mom get mixed up in it.

Yeah, that's me. I just had to mix up the gentle legend of St. Nicholas with cops and guns and even a little violence. The funny thing is, I knew I could also make this story sweet, funny and emotional, all those things that Christmas represents to all of us.

Is Christmas in my home this eventful? Heck, no, unless you count the year when Mom (that's me) was taking a bath and our new kitten climbed the tree, which toppled over onto my three-year-old, who screamed and screamed until Mom, naked and wet, raced out of the bathroom, stepped on broken ornaments and bled copiously, but lifted the tree from the screaming child.

Okay, no guns, but definitely violence (I bled quite a lot), humor and almost-heroism. Hmm… Maybe that's where I got my story idea…?

Merry Christmas!

Janice Kay Johnson

CHAPTER ONE

REED MCCALL SHOVED padding into red velvet pants and buttoned up the fur-trimmed velvet coat. The knee-high black leather boots were too damn stiff. The belt buckled right over his now-round stomach. The rental agency knew what it was doing. Grimacing he adjusted the wig and pulled on the hat.

His one non-standard addition was the handgun worn in a holster at his waist, beneath the coat. He experimented with shoving up his coat and grabbing the butt. It was awkward, made worse by the fact that he usually wore his gun in a shoulder harness. Unbuttoning the coat to reach it there would have taken too long.

Reed gave himself a disbelieving stare in the mirror. He could not believe he was doing this.

The fake beard, white and flowing, had stuck nicely. He gave it an experimental tug and felt his skin pull. The bushy white mustache felt as secure. He was just glad the wig, already itching, wasn't glued down.

Wig! He uttered a sharp expletive. Look at him! He was dressing up as Santa Claus! Him. Sergeant Reed McCall, who was pretty damn sure he'd never been a kid himself, and wouldn't know what to say to one if he met it in a dark alley, never mind found himself dangling a snot-nosed, greedy-eyed brat on his knee.

But he'd promised to serve and protect, even if it was Santas-for-hire he was protecting. He was a man who took orders, he reminded himself, however distasteful. And, Reed thought with grim humor, he wasn't the only cop in the city who was at this very minute sticking a long white beard on his face and swearing at the mirror and fate.

Some sicko had sent an anonymous, ungrammatical note to the *Seattle Times* announcing that Santa Claus would die. Here, in this city, before Christmas.

Then everyone will pay attention, the writer promised.

Unfortunately, the Seattle Police Department already was. The experts decided to take the threat seriously. A too-substantial number of Seattle's finest would go undercover.

As Santa Claus.

Reed put on a pair of wire-rimmed glasses, let them slip down his nose, and gave one last glare at himself in the full-length mirror thoughtfully provided by the department store where he was to endure a four-hour shift as Santa Claus. Today, tomorrow and every day until Santa flew off to the north pole to load the sleigh.

Meantime, his cases would grow cold on his desk.

A perky young woman in a red wool suit popped her head into the room. "Oh, you're ready! Wonderful! Why, you look perfect! The children are so excited.''

He forced a smile. A few head honchos at the department store knew about the substitution, but not the rank and file. Nobody wanted the sicko to postpone plans because he heard the cops were ready.

Her smile faded at the sight of his, which apparently was less than successful. He bared a few teeth, and she beamed with relief.

''Why, the line goes all the way around the store!'' she burbled, as she escorted him out. ''This is one of our biggest days of the year.''

Catching sight of the lineup, thick with anxious mothers and wide-eyed children, Reed felt his stomach clench with tension.

God help me, he thought.

Nonetheless, he lifted his hand in a benevolent wave and mounted the steps to his throne. As the photographer bent to make adjustments to his camera, Reed scanned the people waiting and the immediate area with a cop's practiced wariness.

One man stuck out near the head of the line until he hoisted a toddler onto his shoulders. Poor sucker had gotten stuck bringing junior, Reed decided with scant sympathy. Shoppers were clumped at nearby counters and sales tables, all but arm wrestling for the best buys. To one side of him were girls' clothes, which to his jaundiced eye looked one hell of a lot like miniature versions of the same things worn by the teenagers he arrested in a normal day's work. To the other side were fancy dresses. Racks of floor-length gowns, shimmering with glitter and sequins, reared like rows of tall SUVs and vans in a jammed parking lot. Good cover. Someone could be on top of him before he knew it. Couldn't the idiots who arranged this have put Santa Claus in a more open location, where he had a chance of defending himself? Reed wondered irritably.

At a signal from the photographer, one of his elves let a weary-looking woman approach with two children. One was a toddler who hung back behind mom, the other a bold kid who was missing his two front teeth.

"Ho, ho, ho." Reed sounded as falsely hearty as a middle-aged man swearing to his wife that he never looked at other women.

Giving up on the sound effects, Reed patted his knee.

The boy clambered up. His sister let out a wail that would have cleared a lane down I-5.

"Now, honey," Mom soothed, hoisting her. "Santa Claus will bring you presents if you tell him what you want. See? Jonathan *likes* Santa."

Jonathan squirmed. "I've got all kinds of stuff I want," he announced. "There's this really cool chemical warfare set, where you make slime and gases that smell so gross! I want that, and a skateboard, and…"

He rattled on while Mom coaxed. Finally losing patience, she held out her sobbing, kicking daughter. Reed took her effortlessly in his big hands—hell, it was a lot like subduing a struggling suspect—and planted her on his knee.

She screamed bloody murder while Jonathan and Reed flashed grins for the photographer.

"Thank you *so* much!" Mom said, taking back her daughter, whose screams were starting to sound hoarse. The boy stopped one step down and turned back.

"Oh, and I want Doom Castle and all the warriors, 'specially the bad guys! You won't forget, will you?"

Mom chuckled and grabbed his hand. "Santa never forgets anything, does he?"

"Never," Reed promised, trying to keep the grim note out of his voice. "Merry Christmas!"

The next kid pissed on his lap. In the midst of scared whimpers and a brave smile for the photographer, she gave up the battle and peed. Warm dampness soaked his thigh. Reed couldn't even blame her. This kid had to have been in line for hours to do something she didn't want to do, all so her parents could have a photo.

When she shot him a scared glance, he managed a smile, gave her an awkward but comforting pat and said in a low voice, "It's okay. You've been waiting a long time. I'll bring you that American Girl doll." At his piercing look, her mother gave a tiny nod and smile.

His elves mopped his lap, then summoned the next kid, who had green snot bubbling out of his nose. Reed shuddered, waited while this mother blew her brat's nose, and lifted his gaze to the line of eager parents and unhappy children vanishing out of sight around the shoe department.

Three hours and fifty minutes to go, and that was just today. He already had piss in his boot, he'd probably catch the plague from one of these carriers, and his hearing would never be the same. How could he survive two weeks of this?

He half hoped the writer of that note would show up and put him out of his misery.

"THERE." MEGHAN PLACED the star atop the glittering Christmas tree in their front window. Stepping back, she marveled, "Isn't it beautiful?"

Her five-year-old son slipped his hand into hers. "The beautifulest ever," he agreed. "I bet with that star, Santa can find it. Huh?"

Her heart sank. Here they went again with that Santa Claus nonsense. She didn't believe in lying to children, and hated the cultural necessity of sneaking around in the middle of the night so that Ted could awaken on Christmas morning to gifts from Santa, who had improbably squeezed his fat bulk down their narrow chimney. Meghan had always downplayed the story and tried to avoid outright lies, including taking Ted to visit a fake Santa.

But guess what? *This year,* thanks to the eager chatter of his best buddy, Colin, Ted was determined to sit on Santa's lap and personally deliver his list.

Now she smiled down at her small, determined son.

"Our tree is shining like a beacon in the window. Maybe we should put on coats and go outside to see how pretty it looks. What do you think?"

He looked up at her, a frown furrowing his brow. "Couldn't we go see Santa Claus? We could look at the tree on our way."

"Tonight?" she asked in dismay.

"Colin says pretty soon Santa will be too busy to see kids. That's what his mom told him. She said they had to go today or it would be too late."

She should have kept Ted home from school this week, Meghan thought grumpily, to save him from exposure to the commercial version of the holiday.

With a sigh, she knelt in front of the kindergartener. "You know Christmas isn't really about Santa Claus and getting presents. We've talked about it."

He nodded and in his deep, old-man voice said, "I know. But Colin's mom said Santa Claus is about miracles, just like Jesus." He looked worried. "Is that bad to say?"

"Of course it isn't bad to say!" She hugged him. "You can say anything to me." She might regret that promise about the time he turned fifteen or sixteen, Meghan thought ruefully.

"Oh. Well, isn't Santa supposed to bring stuff you really, really wish for?" He gazed expectantly at her.

Meghan turned that one over in her mind. Agreeing wasn't *exactly* a lie, was it? That was the myth. "Supposed" didn't mean it was true.

"Yes," she said cautiously.

"I have something I really, *really* want. It's something I know you won't buy for me. But I thought maybe, if I asked Santa..."

Oh, no. She didn't want him to believe in Santa wholeheartedly, but she didn't want him to be crushed, either. What could he possibly want so badly?

"Can you tell me what it is?" Meghan asked.

He shook his head. "Colin says, if I ask Santa, maybe I'll get it. He says Santa can give you anything you want."

Colin was *not* Meghan's favorite little boy, right about now.

"That's not really true," she said. "For example, if you wanted a horse, Santa would know that you don't have any place to keep one and it would be cruel to the horse to bring it to you. Things you ask for from Santa have to be practical."

Specifically, practical for *her* to buy.

"It's not a horse."

"Then?"

"Please?" Ted asked. His gruff voice squeaked, like a teenage boy's when it was changing.

Meghan sighed. "Okay. I give up."

"Now? We can go now?"

She couldn't think of anything she less wanted to do on a chilly evening. The tree shimmered, coals glowed low in the fireplace and she'd been thinking a cup of cocoa would taste sublime.

But it was Saturday night. They had plans tomorrow and wouldn't be able to stand in line at the mall. This might be the last weekend for Ted to see Santa. Since he had no school tomorrow, if he missed his regular bedtime it wouldn't matter.

"All right," she conceded.

"Yeah!" He flung his arms around her neck and squeezed, hard.

"Get your boots on, and let's hurry. It's already seven."

Snow flurries had left the streets slushy and slippery. She drove carefully, easing up to stops. Northgate Mall was farther than downtown, Meghan calculated. Parking was chancier there, but surely on a Saturday evening, she could find a spot. The hills had been sanded, thank goodness, and by the time she crossed the freeway on Pine, roads were wet but bare.

Miraculously—she made a face at her own choice of word—a parking spot opened right in front of the big double doors to one of her favorite department stores. Not, as a single parent, that she could afford to buy here often, but browsing was fun.

She glanced at her watch. "Oh, no! It's after eight already. I hope Santa hasn't packed it in for the night."

"You mean…" her son's voice quavered, "it might already be too late?"

"Let's go see."

Warmth met them inside, along with piped-in Christmas music and a delicious fragrance that made her think of cinnamon-topped apple pie. A display of winter boots turned her head for a wistful moment before Meghan, conscious of her battered, worn-down-at-the-heel boots she'd had since college, hustled Ted past.

"Oh!" the first clerk they saw exclaimed. "You'd better hurry." She gave directions to Women's Special Occasion Dresses, beyond which Santa was holding court.

Meghan was almost embarrassed by the sense of urgency that had her racing through the store. For Pete's sake, would it really be so bad if Santa *had* hung it up for the night? But, seeing the expression on Ted's grave face, she knew it would be. For some reason, this meant a great deal to him. The least she could do was give him this chance.

Women's Sportswear, Children's Clothes, and finally... Meghan drew in a breath that came near to being a sob of relief. There he was, an imposing Santa with snowy beard and velvet red suit, a child on his lap.

"Oh, you just made it!" A green-garbed elf smiled and took their names.

Meghan paid. Two five-by-seven-inch photos would be mailed to her. Because she and Ted were late, the line in front of them consisted of only two other parents with sleepy-eyed children. Ted and she watched as the others took their turns on Santa's lap and the photographer called, "Merry Christmas!" just before he snapped the pictures.

Nobody else appeared behind them. When Meghan

looked closely, she saw that the elves and photographer all looked exhausted. Not until she got close could she read Santa's face.

How very *un*-Santa-like he was, she thought in vague surprise as Ted clambered onto his lap. His expression was nearer to grim than merry, and when he glanced at her she saw that his eyes were a chilly gray behind the small, wire-rimmed glasses. Above the flowing beard, his face was hard and angular.

Well, perhaps he was younger than most of the jolly souls who played Santa, she decided forgivingly; with the economy as tough as it was, he might well be a laid-off aerospace engineer picking up much-needed income. And he, too, was undoubtedly weary.

She transferred her gaze to Ted, who sat with his customarily straight back, his shoulders squared, and studied Santa's face feature by feature.

"Ho ho ho," Santa declared perfunctorily. "What do *you* want for Christmas, young man?"

"Can you really get me anything?" Ted asked.

Santa looked startled by the preternaturally deep voice coming from the slight figure on his knee. "Well… Perhaps not *anything,* but I try."

Ted pressed his lips together and nodded. His nervous gaze flicked to his mother before returning to Santa's face. "What I want for Christmas is…" he drew a deep breath "…a new father."

Meghan sagged. She would have tried to buy him almost anything. But this… Even aside from the compressed time frame, a husband was not in the cards for her. No way, no how.

She had a fleeting second to be aware of someone approaching behind her. An elf, no doubt, to hustle this last customer away so Santa and company could go home. She opened her mouth to say, "Ted, you know I can't..." when something hard and cold jammed against the back of her head.

"Be good, and I won't kill you," growled a man's voice right by her ear.

CHAPTER TWO

A GUN TO HER HEAD. Someone was holding a gun to her head. In her shock, everything was suddenly weirdly clear and yet slow.

Meghan gave a strangled gasp and tried to cry, *Save him, please save him.* Somehow, nothing came out but his name. "Ted!"

Santa Claus half rose and swung her son away as if to drop him off the far side of the dais. With his other hand, he groped under his coat.

"The kid, too!" the man behind her snarled. "Bring that kid here, or I'll kill the mom." The barrel pressed painfully against her scalp. "Get your hands up! Now!"

Santa froze, his gaze flat and oddly lethal above the wire-rims.

The man shoved her forward. "Take your kid's hand. Don't try anything."

She sobbed as she reached out for Ted, who stared past her with wide eyes. She took his hand and lifted him down to her side.

"Over here," the gunman ordered Santa. "Raise your coat."

In this bizarre, slow-mo world, Meghan was still

startled to see the dark, cold metal of a handgun nestled in the waistband of Santa Claus's red pants. On Santa's knee, Ted had been nestled right up to a gun. She wanted to feel mad about that discovery instead of scared.

As the man behind her divested Santa of his weapon, she whispered, "Please. Let us go. We don't have anything to do with this."

"You have everything to do with it." He tossed the gun down and sideways, so that it skidded under the red cloth skirt of the dais. "Santa, keep your hands up. You first." He apparently jerked his head to indicate direction. "That way."

Meghan was vaguely aware of the green-garbed elves gaping as their strange procession headed between racks of prom dresses. Frantic thoughts flitted through her brain. She could shove Ted away, scream, "Run!"

Would the kidnapper really shoot her in cold blood? What did he *want?* Why oh why hadn't she been firm?

"Ted, Santa Claus is no more real than your father's promises to visit. No, we aren't going. We're going to stand outside on a snowy night and admire our tree and then sip hot cocoa before bedtime." That's what she should have said. Then they'd be safe at home, all this something she'd read about in the morning newspaper, a freakish event happening to someone else.

Except he'd said, *You have everything to do with it.*

What did he *mean?*

A last rack of pastel-colored dresses meant for mothers of the bride parted with a frothy swish. An inconspicuous door painted the same white as the wall faced them.

"Open it."

The doorknob turned under Santa's hand. Inside was a short vinyl-floored hallway with a couple of doors opening off it. At the far end was an Exit door, which Meghan saw with dismay was barred by part of a steel clothes rack. Their kidnapper had been here already, preparing.

"In there." The barrel of the gun left her head briefly as he waved his hand.

There was a stockroom, it appeared. Santa entered ahead of her and turned as the kidnapper shoved her in. Falling over Ted, she stumbled into the soft bulk beneath red velvet, her nose burrowing into the strip of white fur down the lapel. Hard hands lifted her upright.

Meghan snatched Ted off the floor and faced the threat.

Gray hair pulled into a short ponytail, he was a big man gone to seed, his belly hanging over his sagging jeans, his chin covered with white stubble. The gun in his hand pointed directly at her.

"Stay here," he ordered. "First head that pokes through the door gets blown off." With that he withdrew and closed the door with the decisive "snick" of steel.

Santa Claus let out a blistering string of obscenities

that had her covering Ted's ears with her hands. Then he yanked off his hat and wig and flung them to the floor. A moment later the glasses joined them with a crunch.

Meghan watched openmouthed as this...man stripped off the red jacket and unbuckled padding beneath to reveal a broad-shouldered, lean physique in a gray T-shirt. He was ripping off the beard, wincing at each yank and swearing afresh, as he stalked behind the first of what seemed to be rows of tall metal shelving units stacked with cardboard boxes.

"Mommy?" Ted quavered.

She squeezed his shoulders and waited until their fellow hostage reappeared. He'd shed the beard, but bits of something gluelike stuck to his chin like tiny wads of toilet paper festooning an adolescent shaver. Given the temper she saw in his icy gray eyes, the sight wasn't the smallest bit amusing.

"Hold these shelves," he ordered brusquely.

Meghan squeezed Ted again and obeyed, bracing the groaning, wavering metal uprights as he scaled the shelving unit like a ladder. When she tilted her head back, she saw him trying to push up ceiling tiles. A single, vicious expletive announced his lack of success.

With a thud, he returned to the ground.

Meghan crossed her arms. "Who are you?"

His frowning gaze looked surprised to find she existed, never mind that she was present. "Sergeant Reed McCall, Seattle Police Department."

Her eyes narrowed. "You expected this."

"There was a threat," he said curtly.

"A threat." Now she was getting steamed. "There was a threat against children sitting on Santa's lap, and no warning was issued."

"How could we suspend visits to Santa? Even assuming we had in Seattle, what about Bellevue? Everett, Tacoma? Where to draw the line? What if he just waited until next year? We took what we thought were reasonable precautions..."

"You mean, you carrying a gun." Meghan glared at him. "Fat lot of good that did!"

"It would have if store personnel hadn't set us up right next to those tall racks of dresses, where the son-of-a..." With a glance at her son, Sgt. McCall swallowed the last word. "Where the SOB could sneak up on us."

"You could have insisted they move it."

"Not without people asking questions. Then he might have been warned."

"And my son and I would be safely on our way home right now instead of locked in a storeroom guarded by a crazy man with a gun!" Her voice rose until it trembled at the end.

"Uh..." The policeman looked wary. "Why don't we sit down and talk about this?"

"You're not Santa." Her son stared accusingly at the powerful man in red velvet pants that sagged low on his hips, revealing blue jeans beneath. "I won't get my wish."

Tears sprang into Meghan's eyes. "Oh, Ted..."

The big police officer surprised her by kneeling.

"We're, uh, his bodyguards. He's listening. Santa hears even if you don't sit on his lap." He cleared his throat. "Or so I'm told."

Meghan didn't know whether to be grateful or irritated by the lie, but Ted's face cleared and he gave a nod.

"Oh, okay."

McCall looked up at her, his expression softer than she'd seen. "There are no chairs. I'm sorry."

"We can sit on the floor." She glanced toward the door and lowered her voice. "Do you think he's really right out there?"

"I'm not real eager to stick my head out to see, but...yeah. Why would he stuff us in here and just leave? Besides, where's he going to go? Somebody would have called 911 and a patrol unit would have been here within a couple of minutes. He's trapped."

They were trapped. Meghan sniffed and nodded. Ted's hand crept into hers.

"Over here looks best, away from the door." McCall glanced down at Ted. "Let me see if I can find a blanket or something."

She settled herself and Ted in the corner away from the door on the hard, vinyl-covered floor. Leaning against the wall, she let Ted curl against her.

"That man wouldn't *really* shoot you, would he?" Ted asked.

"I don't think so, but he was scary, wasn't he?" She smoothed his short, stiff hair. "We'll be fine."

"We're lucky Santa has bodyguards, huh?" His

voice had taken on a slower cadence, evidence that he was tiring. It was well past his bedtime.

A ripping sound preceded the return of Reed McCall, who carried an armful of quilts she saw were hand-stitched.

"Best I could do."

The hard, cold floor under her rump and Ted's wriggle against her side squelched any qualms. "They look wonderful. Thank you."

He nodded and dumped them in a heap beside her. Meghan took one to sit on and another to spread over Ted. "Teddy, why don't you try to sleep while we wait?" she murmured. "Put your head on my lap."

The five-year-old squirmed into position, snuggled into the quilt and lay quiet.

The policeman lowered himself to sit with his back to the wall kitty-corner from her, facing the door. When he stretched out his long legs, his booted feet bumped hers. "Sorry." His mouth twisted. "I'm sorry you got involved."

"Me, too." She lifted her gaze from Ted's face to meet those gray eyes. "I shouldn't have yelled at you. None of this is your fault."

The lines beside his mouth deepened. "It was my job to prevent it. I didn't."

"I don't see how you could have," she admitted. Meghan drew a deep breath. "Did the threat say what he *wants?*"

"Attention." His brows knit. "'Now everyone will pay attention' were, as I recall, his exact words."

Why did she have the feeling there had been more

words that he remembered quite well? Ones he wasn't going to share with her?

She looked down at her son, who was listening rather than drifting into sleep as she'd hoped. Her arm tightened protectively on him. "There aren't any other doors or windows?"

McCall shook his head. "We just have to wait."

"Shouldn't they have given you a cell phone?"

"What could I tell them that they don't already know?" he answered logically. "The guy snatched Santa and a mom and kid. He's holed up with us in a storeroom. I don't know a damn—er, darn—thing more than that."

She appreciated his belated effort not to swear in front of Ted. "I suppose that's true."

They sat in silence for several minutes. Her thoughts jumped as if hyperactive. Why had she ever surrendered to Ted's pleas, despite her convictions? What was that awful man *doing* out in the hall? Why couldn't they hear? Was anybody trying to negotiate with him yet? What if the store clerks hadn't seen where he'd taken them? He wouldn't hurt a child, would he?

Somewhere in there was an uneasy awareness of the large man brooding a few feet away. The oversize red velvet trousers and knee-high black boots were incongruous with the faded T-shirt, the powerful muscles in his upper arms and his brown hair, rumpled from being beneath the wig. She wondered if he'd felt silly dressing up to play Santa Claus, then shuddered at her memory of why he had.

"Why us?" Meghan asked herself as much as him. Perhaps as much to distract herself *from* him as because she expected any response.

His voice was gruff. "Because you were at the end of the line, I assume. Why today and not yesterday or last weekend or the weekend before? Who knows?"

"He said this has everything to do with us." She kept begging him for answers, as if he had any.

"Maybe he needs a mother and child to get that attention. Holding a cop hostage won't light up the press the way this will."

Ted stirred. "Do we have to stay the night?"

Meghan tried to smile. "Yes, I'm afraid so, honey. Are you comfortable?"

He'd slid down so that his head bobbed against her thigh, where he had pillowed it. "I wish we had cocoa."

"I do, too." She had a fleeting, grateful thought that she'd unplugged the Christmas lights. She had considered leaving them on so that they would be glowing in the front window when they got back from visiting Santa.

As if the possibility of a house fire was her greatest worry.

The policeman nodded at her son. "How old is he?"

"I'm five," Ted answered with dignity. "I go to kindergarten."

Reed McCall eyed Ted as dubiously as if a cat had just spoken to him. Children apparently weren't hu-

man and capable of conversing. "Yeah?" He had the
same falsely hearty tone he'd used to say, Ho ho ho.
"Kindergarten, huh."

"I take it you don't have children," Meghan said
dryly.

"That obvious?"

She nodded. "You weren't a very good Santa."

Ted half sat. "*I* thought you were a good Santa.
Your beard looked real and everything."

"Thanks, kid." McCall smiled, lifting one corner
of his mouth.

Meghan's heart skipped a beat. For an instant, that
forbidding face looked…gentle. Perhaps he wasn't
good with children only because he hadn't had a
chance, not because he was the type of grump who
would turn out his porch light on Halloween and bel-
low at eight-year-olds who cut the corner on his lawn.

McCall rubbed one hand self-consciously over his
chin. "I never thought I'd say this, but…I wish I had
some cold cream."

A giggle rose to stick in her throat. "Oh dear."
She clapped her hand over her mouth.

He tried to scowl, but she could tell he didn't mean
it. "You think that's funny, huh?"

"I'm sorry!" Her giggle came out like a hiccup.
"I don't know why, but…it is funny!"

This rueful smile wasn't so much kindly as sexy.
"You should have seen me buying the damned stuff
at the pharmacy. I was as self-conscious as a fourteen-
year-old boy buying…" He shot another look at Ted
before meeting her gaze again. "Uh…you know."

The subject of condoms did nothing to reduce her ridiculous awareness of him.

She didn't ogle men she didn't know, so why was she sneaking peeks at him out of the corner of her eye? Why did she notice every time his booted feet bumped hers? Tingle when his gaze moved idly over her?

Because she and Ted *needed* him, Meghan told herself firmly. He was suddenly all to her because he had to be; they had no one else.

Chilled by the reminder, Meghan suppressed a shudder. "I wish he'd do…whatever it is he intends to do. Waiting is the worst."

They heard the doorknob turning at the same instant. Despite his seemingly relaxed posture, Reed McCall got to his feet as if he'd been a tiger crouched in hunt. He took up a position halfway to the door, putting himself between her and Ted and the kidnapper about to step into the storeroom.

As terror seemed to turn her blood to ice, Meghan had the awful feeling that she was going to get exactly what she'd wished for.

CHAPTER THREE

THE DOOR SWUNG OPEN HARD enough to have knocked Reed back, if he'd been lurking behind it. The kidnapper's head appeared around it.

"Are you hungry?" he asked. "I'm going to make 'em send in food. I can get you some, if you want."

Reed blinked and turned his head to see the woman gape. The little boy sat up.

"*I'm* hungry."

"Shush," his mother whispered, her wide frightened eyes staring at the scum.

"Pizza, maybe. What kind of pizza do you like?"

If the bastard hadn't been holding a gun in his hand, he could have been behind the counter at Domino's or Pizza Hut. His gaze was inquiring, even amiable. As if he *cared* whether they wanted mushrooms or not on their pizza.

"It's okay, kid," the big man said. "Whaddaya want? Plain cheese? I'll get plain cheese for you."

Reed's stomach rumbled. Damn it, he was starved. "Everything for me," he said.

"Ma'am?"

In a small voice, the boy's pretty mother said, "I'm not hungry. Thank you."

"I'll just get you a drink, then," he said kindly. Eyes as cold as the north pole met Reed's. "Don't try to come through that door."

He withdrew again.

The moment the door snicked shut, the woman burst out, "You'll eat his food?"

"I'm hungry," Reed defended himself. "Damn it, I haven't had anything since breakfast. I've had a hard day. I had a kid pee on me, a little girl stab me in the eye, a punk too old to believe in…" He remembered the boy. "He, uh, punched me in the stomach to see if it was real. I've been sneezed on, grabbed, and had to listen to lists so greedy, the brats should be Enron executives." He let himself go plaintive. "I can't think on an empty stomach."

She let out an indignant whuff of air. Apparently he wasn't measuring up to her idea of a hero. "What if he poisons you?"

The idea had occurred to him. After all, the original note had said the writer would kill Santa Claus. That was him, right? But why resort to poison when putting a bullet in Reed's brain would be a hell of a lot easier? Made for a more dramatic death, too. Nah, he felt safe eating the pizza. Assuming the negotiator outside didn't decide to starve them out. Reed really, really hoped his colleague wouldn't do that.

Reed hesitated and then went back to the corner where the mother and kid were ensconced. They were distracting in ways that made him uncomfortable.

The kid…well, he didn't like kids. But this one didn't seem bad, as they went. He'd been polite on

Santa's lap, and he'd wanted something of substance, not a heap of toys that wouldn't make it through airport security these days. He wasn't sobbing or drumming his heels or whining. He was almost kind of cute, so damn solemn, his shoulders so square, as if he was trying hard to be a man. Then there was that deep, gruff voice that sounded like it was resonating in a chest one hell of a lot bigger than his scrawny one.

Yeah, Reed figured he'd gotten lucky as far as the kid went.

The mom, too, in one way. She was taking this decently, not crying or whining or despairing any more than her boy was. She'd gotten a little steamed, but he couldn't blame her. Maybe the city *should* have issued a public warning.

He just wished she was…oh, hell, *bony.* Or downright fat, instead of the tiniest bit plump, by modern standards, which made her perfect, by his. Or she could have been a perky cheerleader type, if she had to be pretty—he never had been drawn to the bubbly, petite blondes. She could have makeup plastered on— that would have been a turnoff.

She could be anything but what she was: a gentle, sweet-faced woman with a cozy, shapely body, wide gray-green eyes, a cap of red-brown hair so thick and glossy his fingers tingled to plunge into it, and that translucent skin redheads sometimes had, in her case dusted with a few freckles. With her tenderness toward her son, she was so far outside Reed's experience with women, he didn't know what to make of her or say to her.

He should be planning, and instead he found his gaze drifting to her full breasts beneath a sweater that probably draped more tellingly than she knew. Or the soft curve of her mouth would snag him, or the lilt of her voice.

Damn it, he was horny! Horny and baffled, because she wasn't his type and this sure as hell wasn't the time or place.

Letting his back slide down the wall until he was sitting on the floor, he frowned at the door and deliberately didn't look at her.

Maybe he was being punished from above. Taunted with what he was assigned to preserve and protect but could never have.

Or maybe instead, Reed was being given the most powerful of reasons to protect this woman and this child.

He was being given a reason to die, if it came to that.

"What's your name?" he asked abruptly.

"Meghan Kane." Her voice was soft and musical. "And this is Ted."

Okay. He was sorry he'd asked. *Meghan.* He liked her name, thought it suited her.

He was even sorrier about the next words that came out of his mouth.

"Your husband going to be getting worried?" The kid wanted a new daddy, but that didn't mean she wasn't dating or even living with someone the boy didn't like.

She bit her lip. "I'm divorced."

Divorced? What kind of idiot let a woman like this get away?

"Anybody waiting for you?"

When she shook her head, the heavy silk of her hair swung, reflecting the light in shimmering strands of gold and auburn and chestnut.

Reed's fingers curled into fists against his thighs.

"What about you?" she asked tentatively. "Do you have a wife?"

"No." He sounded curt, then felt like a jackass. "Cops and marriage don't go together."

"You mean, your job makes marriage harder." She put the slightest emphasis on the last word. Those wide, grave eyes studied him. "Surely not impossible."

She was right, of course; his partner had a sweetheart of a wife, two school-age kids, and a happy homelife so far as Reed could see. Nonetheless, a divorce or two or three was the norm for cops.

"I'm not happily-ever-after material," he heard himself say. As if they were on a date and he was issuing his standard warning.

Voice tinged with bitterness, she bowed her head and gently rubbed her son's back. The kid's eyes had drifted closed. "Apparently I'm not, either."

"That's ridiculous. You look like Mrs. Cleaver."

"What?"

"Not her, literally." He felt like an idiot, stumbling

to explain a remark he shouldn't have made. "I mean, you look like the perfect wife and mother. How could you not be marriage material?"

"Thank you." Tiny lines creased her brow. "I think. I do have a career, you know."

"Yeah? What do you do?" They had to fill the time somehow, didn't they? It wasn't as if he really cared. He was just idly curious, that was all.

"I book and plan conventions and special events for a downtown hotel. I'm good at it."

"I believe you." She could talk *him* into booking with her. Reed wondered if she attended any of the fancy shindigs she planned. He imagined her in a sleek evening gown, green to bring out the color in her eyes. She would be curvy and unbelievably sexy…

Clearly *not* reading his mind, she asked tartly, "Do you? I gathered that you think I look like a housewife."

Ah jeez. He had to open his mouth in the first place.

"I didn't mean that. Just that you look like…" *I'd like my wife to, if I had one.* The thought was a shock. He sure wasn't going to share it. Reed harrumphed. "Like the opposite of the women I see in singles bars. That's all."

"Oh." Meghan was quiet, her head bent. A minute or two must have passed before she asked, "Why do you think you're not marriage material, aside from your job?"

He'd never told anybody this, but, hell, why not?

Reed rubbed his hands on his velvet pants. "My childhood sucked." His voice was harsh. "My parents stayed married, but I don't know why. Mom let my father beat me and her both." Uncomfortable with having revealed even that much, he shrugged as if indifferent. "I figure the generations echo each other. I'd rather not, thank you."

Her head shot up, her eyes brilliant with emotion. "You actually think you'd beat your wife or child, the way your father did?"

Again he moved uneasily. "I like to think I wouldn't, but I don't have any model for a normal family life to look back on, either. I don't know how you discipline a kid. How you express anger at someone you love." *Love.* What was he talking about? The word wasn't even in his vocabulary. He muttered an expletive, then gave a guilty look at the boy and was grateful to see that he was sound asleep. "I don't know why I'm telling you this."

"Because we have to talk about something." Her face was soft with compassion. "Or because we both know we might not survive this."

"The Seahawks. Why don't we talk about them?" he asked desperately.

"I don't watch football." Her nose wrinkled daintily. "I actually don't watch any sports, except the Olympics every four years. Well, and Ted's soccer and T-ball."

He wasn't that big a fan, either. He'd worked to put himself through college and hadn't been able to play ball. These days, he'd hang out with the guys, have a couple of beers and watch a game now and again, but his interest was limited. He was probably lucky she hadn't taken him up on his suggestion and discovered how little he knew about the players or the season so far.

He nodded at her. "What about you? Why are you divorced?"

"I'm a walking cliché." She looked away. "I dropped out of college to put my husband through dental school. The next thing I know, I'm pregnant and he's sleeping with his technician. I was apparently... inadequate."

With heat, Reed said, "You mean, he was a jerk and a fool."

Her cheeks turned pink. "Why...thank you. But I was sick to my stomach for months, and then maybe preoccupied..."

Reed's gaze held hers. "You were sick to your stomach because you were carrying *his* child. He should have been holding the damn bowl, not screwing around. You're better off without him."

"So I tell myself." She heaved a sigh. "But I don't always believe it. I don't always believe Ted is better off without his father."

"Doesn't he see his father?"

"Once in a while." As if she couldn't help herself, she gently stroked her son's hair. "When Gregory doesn't cancel."

"You know, I'm developing a real dislike for this guy."

Her smile held mischief that belied the sadness in

her eyes. "I'm starting to think you're really a softie. Hey, maybe you'd like to coach Ted's T-ball team."

Reed shuddered. "You've hit me at a weak moment. Anybody will tell you, I don't like kids. If I go to hell, I'll probably spend eternity playing Santa Claus, with an endless succession of sobbing or greedy kids on my knee and me having to be jovial."

She laughed aloud. "How did you get picked for this assignment then?"

"Every Santa in the city is a cop. The brass wasn't picky."

"Oh." At the reminder of their predicament and the reason for it, the life and color left her face.

Reed cursed himself for not continuing to distract her. "We'll be okay. The fact that he wants to feed us is a good sign."

"Do you really think so?" Her eyes begged him for the truth. Or, hell, for a lie.

"Yeah. I think so."

Very, very softly, she said, "I'm scared."

Reed made a sound in his throat and scooted closer to her. Close enough to take her hand. "I'll do my damnedest to keep you and your boy safe."

Her hand was smooth and fine-boned. It quivered, then turned to squeeze his in return. "I know you will," she said simply. "I have faith in you."

A band closed around his chest, constricting his air and making his heart lurch. How many people had ever had faith in him? Depended on him, sure—his fellow cops assumed he'd pull his weight. His friends assumed he'd show up when he said he would. But had anybody in his life ever believed in him completely?

He didn't like the answer. Tried to convince himself that she didn't, either. She was buttering him up because she needed him to keep her and the kid safe. That was all.

He started to release her hand, but her fingers bit into his and her gaze became intense. "If you have to choose, please take care of Ted. I'd rather die than have anything happen to him."

Reed hesitated, then gave a reluctant nod.

"Promise me."

"I promise." His voice was low, rough, raw with unspoken emotion.

Apparently satisfied, Meghan nodded and, to his regret, released his hand.

As if on cue, the door burst open.

CHAPTER FOUR

THE SMELL OF PIZZA WAFTED into the storage room with the kidnapper. He edged two boxes in along the floor with a booted foot. From one hand dangled a bag of canned drinks. In the other was the gun.

He nodded at Reed McCall. "You. Come and get the pizza."

Meghan sat close enough to the police officer to see the flicker of anger in his eyes, but after an instant he gave a sharp nod and rose easily to his feet. The kidnapper's gaze never wavered as Reed fetched the pizza and carried the two boxes back to the corner.

The kidnapper propped open the door with his rubber-tipped foot, so that they could all see a slice of the hallway and the door at the end, leading back out into the store. It seemed to be braced with pieces of bent metal, too.

"In case they try anything," he explained, then came to them and held out the bag of drinks to Meghan.

She took it and peered inside. Several types of soda were available, as well as bottled water. "Um...thank you," she said awkwardly.

He waited until Reed resumed his seat, then lowered himself a few feet away, on the other side of Meghan. "Let's eat!" he said jovially.

She hesitated, then decided to wake Ted. Who knew when they'd have a chance to eat again? But when she gently shook his shoulder, he only burrowed more tightly against her, his body heavy with sleep.

Meghan looked up. "He doesn't seem to want to wake up." She bit her lip, not wanting to offend their captor. "He doesn't mind it cold, if some is left."

The big man shrugged. "No skin off my nose." Gun aimed at Meghan, he reached forward with his free hand and flipped open the top box. "Ah. Everything on this one. Plain cheese on the other. Help yourself."

Despite herself, Meghan felt her stomach cramp hopefully. Dinner had been soup and green beans, hours before. "Thank you," she said politely. "Um...do you have a name?" Her cheeks flushed. "Of course you do! I mean, is there something we can call you?"

A slice of pizza held in one beefy hand, he appeared to consider. "Nick," he said at last. "Call me Nick." The idea seemed to please him, because he laughed. "St. Nick. That's me!"

"There is a certain irony," Reed said, tone dry.

"Yeah, yeah. I like irony." The grizzled face sobered. "That's the idea, you know. Who will pay attention if I don't?"

"Pay attention to what?" Meghan asked timidly. Didn't they always say you should get your captor to talk, let him see you as an individual, lead him to develop sympathy for you? Or—she frowned—did it work the other way around, with the Stockholm Syndrome, where the hostages were the ones who came to identify with their kidnapper?

His eyes met hers. In them, she saw pain she could imagine only in her fear for Ted.

"Do you really want to know?"

She nodded. "If you don't mind telling us."

Reed popped the top on a cola and guzzled, as if not interested. But Meghan could feel his attention, his senses giving off radioactive waves like a military dish searching the heavens.

Nick set down the pizza. Sad lines sank deep in his face, as if once contorted in grief, it couldn't regain the jovial look it had once had.

"My wife died two weeks ago. Emily. Emmie, I called her. She had cancer. Started in her breast, then spread." Fury twisted his mouth, while bitterness ate at every word. "I had changed jobs, and I thought we were covered with insurance, but turns out the bastards figured out a way to deny our claim. We sold our house, begged for money, but by the time she had the lump out of her breast it was too late. I'd have done anything—*anything!*—to save her, but I couldn't. Nobody cared but me. She was a kind, loving woman, Emmie was." He fell silent for a moment before finishing starkly, "I missed a lot of work to nurse her. Got fired three weeks ago. They were sorry, they said. But they had to have somebody reliable. Nobody I worked with even came to her funeral."

Despite the gun, which never wavered during his story, Meghan felt tears burn her eyes. "I'm sorry," she said simply. "Nobody should die because they don't have the money to pay for health care. It's…it's obscene."

He regarded her with approval. "Obscene." He seemed to savor the word. "That's what it was, all right."

"Did you try…" Meghan stopped herself. What possible good would it do now that his wife was dead and buried to suggest alternatives for finding health care coverage? His Emmie's life was over, as was his for all practical purposes. Whether she, Ted and Sergeant Reed McCall escaped from this with their lives or not, Nick would go to jail.

Unless what he wanted was to die, she thought with a squeeze of fear. He might intend to join his Emmie, once he'd made his point. If he feared nothing, how could he be stopped?

"So," Reed said, after wiping his mouth with the back of his hand, "to avenge the medical establishment's fatal neglect of your wife, you kidnapped a nice woman, her little boy and a Santa-for-hire."

"I just want some attention." Nick's faded eyes begged for understanding from Meghan. "Nobody would have listened if I hadn't done something spectacular. Nobody did listen."

"Which isn't our fault," the police officer pointed out.

"You're a cop. You signed on for this." The grizzled, old man looked regretfully at Meghan. "As for you and your boy... I'm sorry. I had to choose some-one. You see why, don't you?"

She shook her head. "No. I don't work for an in-surance company or a hospital or...or for whoever employed you. I book conventions for a hotel!"

Chilling her, he said in a flat voice, "Nobody would listen. I had to make them."

"Why didn't you just go to the newspapers? Col-umnists would have written with outrage about your wife's death! Then you might have gotten sympathy. Now you'll be the villain, not the victim."

"I tried," he said stubbornly. "Nobody even called me back."

"What if the police refuse?" Reed asked. "Or the newspapers and TV stations? Then what?"

He reached for a piece of pizza. "Things are going good out there. They won't refuse."

"But if they do?"

"Let's not talk about that." He took a big bite and chewed with apparent enjoyment that was a stunning contrast to his grief of a few minutes ago. "Tell me about you," he said around the bite, nodding at Meghan. "Why did you come so late tonight?"

Because the fates were against her.

"Because I've been refusing to bring Ted." She explained her stand against the commercial side to Christmas and her distaste with the necessity of lying about Santa Claus. "Only he wore me down," she admitted with a sigh. "We had plans tomorrow, with my sister and her children, so tonight was the last chance we might have for him to visit Santa. He was so determined.'' Remembering what her small son had wanted so badly, Meghan lapsed into silence.

''He going to get a new daddy for Christmas?'' Their captor appeared to find the idea humorous.

''Do you mean, if we're still alive to celebrate Christmas?'' she asked tartly.

He gave her the sad look of a dog who had been chastised. ''Everybody behaves, you'll be alive. I'm not a bad guy.''

We want sympathy, she reminded herself, *not to antagonize him.*

Even so, she sounded strained. ''No. He won't get a new daddy for Christmas. I'm not interested in remarrying, even if I had a good prospect offering me a ring.''

''Why not?'' Unexpectedly, it was the cop who asked. He seemed momentarily to have forgotten the gun being held on them.

''Because I trusted a man once.'' She swallowed. ''I don't think I can again.''

He scowled at her. ''You see a kid being a brat, you decide they all are?''

''Of course not!''

''Then how in hell can you brand all men with your ex's lousy character?''

Her mouth opened and shut. Did it again. She must look like a fish out of water, she thought in despair. Finally she found words. ''I've seen the same thing happen with too many other marriages. Men…men stray.''

Nick listened, his interested gaze darting between their faces.

Reed shook his head in disgust. "You know, I had the sense to realize the minute I saw you that you're not much like most of the women I know. I don't figure all women are like the hookers we book every night. But you, you've got all men lumped together as if, drug dealer, airline pilot or priest, we're made of the same material. Lady, haven't you ever met a man you *knew* was different?"

You. The single, simple answer sang in her heart and knotted in her belly. *He* was different. Reed McCall had never married because he was afraid that, with his heritage, he couldn't keep his promise to cherish and protect. He cared about those promises, honored them. If he ever held a woman's hand and promised to forsake all others, Meghan thought with awe and a hurtful cramping in her chest, he would keep the promise.

He was that kind of man.

"My father had an affair," she said dully. "I found out after he died, when I went through his papers. It was just…just before I discovered Gregory was cheating on me."

He swore, his eyes darkening. "I'm sorry."

"No. You're right. I know—I think—not all men are like that. My brother-in-law…"

"But you can't be sure, can you?" he asked with quiet understanding. "Because if your father did and your husband did, maybe your brother-in-law is cheating on your sister, too."

Meghan bit her lip until she tasted blood and nodded.

"I never cheated on my Emmie. Never would have." Their captor wiped a tear away. "She was the only woman for me."

She saw that, in an odd way, this whole horrible scheme was his final way of expressing his love for his wife. He needed somehow to make the world see that she had been too good to have been treated so shabbily. He must feel that this was the last gift he could give her: an outraged public that would insist nobody else die because insurance companies and hospitals turned their backs.

"Why's the boy want a dad so much?" Nick asked.

"I never knew he did," Meghan admitted. "Of course it hurts when Gregory makes an excuse or just forgets to come." She looked down through misty eyes at her son's face, relaxed and so very young in sleep. "Ted has friends whose dads are really involved with their sports teams or whatever—one of them has taken Ted fishing a couple of weekends along with his boy. I guess…I guess Ted has just decided that the next time they ask at T-ball if someone's father can take over batting practice that week, he should have one to volunteer."

"But he has you." Once again, it was Reed who spoke.

"I'm not a man."

Those clear eyes touched on her, lowered, then returned to her face. "I did notice." His voice was like gravel.

Warmth pooled in her belly despite everything. "You regret not having a better male role model," she said, forgetting the third presence. "Ted needs that, too."

Sharply, Reed said, "I regret that *neither* of my parents was strong, loving or honorable."

"But…it's your father you're afraid you'll take after. Not your mother."

He looked away, flinched. "I'm a man," he said harshly.

Trying to dismiss her sexual awareness, to keep her tone neutral, she retorted, "I noticed."

"Touché!" their kidnapper cried with delight. "She's got you there."

Meghan turned her head. "Did you and your Emmie never have children?"

His face sobered; the lines deepened. "To our deep regret, no."

"Did you think of adopting, or…?"

"Our lives seemed busy enough. We didn't discuss it until too late. We went to one agency, but they turned us down. We were too old. They would have let us have a teenager, but a child that age would never have been *ours*." New grief shadowed his eyes. "You see how selfish we were?" He stopped himself. "No. How selfish *I* was. I think Emmie wanted to adopt all along. She would have taken a teenager, even then. No, it was me. I suffered from that curse, male pride. I wanted to pass on my genes. If not that, something of myself. I didn't think of the child at all, what *I* could have given. And so in the end I lost." He sat silent, brooding, his gaze on Meghan but unseeing.

Only the gun, held in a steady hand, suggested that he was not so caught up in the past as to forget the present.

Watching him, Meghan asked, "What would Emmie think of what you're doing now?"

His face flushed. "She'd want me to be heard."

"At any cost?" Meghan asked softly.

As he continued to stare at her, the hair on Meghan's arms rose. How dumb could she be? She'd baited him, and now he was angry. She *felt* his reaction, just as she knew that, on her other side, Reed tensed.

But Nick only heaved himself to his feet abruptly. "Finish the pizza if you want." In his retreat, he kicked at the doorstop, sending it into the hall. The door whispered shut in his wake, leaving thick silence behind.

CHAPTER FIVE

"I MADE HIM MAD," Meghan whispered fearfully.

Relaxing back against the wall now that their captor was gone, Reed shook his head. "Doesn't matter."

Her wide eyes turned to him. "How can you say that? He has the gun."

"He's had a plan all along." Reed shrugged. "He'll do what he intends to do."

She shivered. "Why doesn't that comfort me?"

Feeling tactless as hell, Reed swore. "I'm sorry. I have a big mouth! Listen. I really don't think he plans to hurt you or your boy." He hesitated, unsure how much he should tell her, then decided what the hey. "His original note threatened Santa specifically. Maybe he wrote it in hopes cops would go undercover as Santa Claus. Could be he has a grudge against police he hasn't mentioned yet. I think if he's mad at anyone here, it's me."

"Gee, why doesn't that make me feel better, either?"

He grinned at her. "I don't know. It should. As he says, I'm paid to take risks."

Her forehead crinkled. "Why do you? I mean, why did you become a police officer?"

Uncomfortable with self-analysis, Reed moved uneasily. "It just always interested me. Once I took a few criminology classes, I was hooked."

Those clear eyes saw right through him. "What did your father do?"

"You've got me there," he said lightly. "He was a cop. A lousy one, from talk I heard. We lived in Idaho. Small town. He could throw his weight around all he wanted, so long as the good ol' boys were behind him. It was a power trip for him."

Another power trip. Provoking fear in his wife and son had apparently mattered, too.

She laid a hand on his forearm, then took it back so quickly he wondered if she'd felt the heat that singed him. Pink touching her cheeks, Meghan said, "As much as you seem to have hated him, I would have thought you'd do almost anything else but be a cop."

His mouth crooked. "That's what I told myself. I left home and never looked back. Started working my way through college. I was thinking of becoming a lawyer. He did hate lawyers." Reed smiled reminiscently. "I had this fantasy of meeting him in court. Just blowing him away, getting him to admit he'd violated the law. Public humiliation for him was on my mind a lot that first year or so." He moved his shoulders. "Anyway, I took the first criminology class with that in mind. Finally realized one day that cops didn't have to be like my father. That maybe I could even make up for his abuses, in some cosmic sense, by being a good cop." Another wry smile.

"You've got to remember, I was all of twenty-one, twenty-two when I decided that."

"Does he know you're a police officer?"

"Probably. I talk to my mother once in a while."

Every time he heard her wispy, lifeless voice on the phone, he wished he hadn't called, but he had enough memories of her from his childhood, bandaging his knee, hiding escapades from his father, hugging him with maternal fervor, to make him feel obligated. One day she might decide she'd had enough, and he wanted to be sure she knew she could turn to him.

Meghan nodded and looked down at her sleeping son. Reed's gaze followed hers and he studied the boy's face, rawboned for a kid that age. Did he get teased at school for his voice and his odd air of maturity? If so, he had a refuge at home. Reed could see that, if only in the way Meghan's hand curled tenderly around his thin shoulder.

"You must be getting stiff," he said abruptly. "You haven't moved in a long time."

"I'm all right," she protested. "I don't want to wake Ted."

He didn't want the boy awake, either. What if he talked nonstop, or got scared, or had to pee?

"If you want to get up and move around, we can shift him over here," he offered.

His pulse tripped over her quick, sweet smile. "Thank you. But really, I'm fine. For now, anyway."

"Why don't you try to lie down, sleep yourself?"

Her face pinched. "I don't think I could."

"It may be hours before anything happens."

Her eyes dilated. "What…" She swallowed. "Um, what do you think *will* happen?"

Reed cursed himself for raising her fears again. "There's a negotiator out there talking to him right now. If all goes well, they'll strike a deal and we'll walk out of here."

"And…and if all *doesn't* go well?"

"A SWAT team may try to break us out of here." Or he would make his move, but Reed didn't tell her he was only waiting for the old man to get tired, become careless.

Her whole body shifted, as if to cradle her son. "That's when people die, isn't it?"

"Yeah." He made his voice soft. "There's always a risk. But they're good at their job. It's one old guy, getting soft in the belly. He won't be hard to bring down."

Head bowed, she murmured, "That makes me sad, too. Which is silly, isn't it? When he's threatening us. But I feel sorry for him, too. For him and his Emmie."

Although Reed had taken everything the bastard said with a grain of salt, he couldn't help feeling some pity, too. How the hell had a country as prosperous as the U.S. of A. come to a point where a kind old woman was allowed to die just because she didn't have enough money to pay for the doctors' golf memberships? How had the claims adjuster felt when he or she sent the denial? Had anybody anywhere fought for Emmie? Or was the indifference so huge, nobody along the way had suffered even a twinge of conscience or disbelief or outrage?

"Two wrongs don't make a right." The old saw didn't seem to be answer enough, and yet Reed believed it with all his being. Most of the scum he arrested day in and day out had become what they were because of wretched childhoods—mothers addicted to crack, fathers who walked out, abuse, neglect and poverty. Yeah, they deserved pity, too, but he cuffed them anyway. They were a danger to decent people.

The thing he reminded himself constantly was that a wretched childhood didn't mean you had to become scum and prey on other people. Plenty of abused and neglected children became doctors, carpenters, social workers and even cops. You made choices. St. Nick had made one tonight: to terrify a pretty, kind mother and her little boy. Reed wouldn't be too quick to forgive that.

He was pretty damn sure Emmie wouldn't be, either. He just wished Nick would remember as much.

"No," Meghan said musingly. "I know I shouldn't feel any sympathy at all for him, but I do." She frowned. "The only thing is… Have you noticed how quickly his mood changes? Sometimes he seems genuinely sad, and the next second he's eating pizza or giving you a cold look. Just like that." She snapped her fingers.

"Yeah. I noticed." That was one of the reasons Reed had been so careful thus far. In his experience, genuine crazies were the most likely to have that kind of hair-trigger mood as well as the sort of split per-

sonality that let them cry for you even as they were
slitting your throat. Oh, yeah. He'd noticed.

"Is he telling the truth, do you think? About what
he wants?"

He drew his knees up and braced his elbows on
them. "Your guess is as good as mine."

She nodded and fell silent.

Reed said nothing and watched as she brooded,
then began to nod off. When her head started to fall
forward, then jerked up again, he shifted on the hard
floor so that he was right beside her, the boy's skinny
body between their thighs.

"Lean on me," he murmured, wrapping an arm
around her shoulder.

She started to relax against him, then struggled upright. "No! I can't go to sleep! I need to...to..."

"To watch out for Ted." He made his voice a
soothing rumble. "I know. Why don't you let me do
it for a while?" Inhaling a faint flowery fragrance—
lavender, he thought—that drifted from her hair, Reed
closed his eyes against a surge of emotion that bit
like a knife into his belly. Not lust, although—God
help him—he was feeling that. Tenderness, maybe. A
need to protect.

Gritting his teeth against the pain of this unfamiliar
emotion, he tried to distance himself. Serve and protect. That was his duty, wasn't it?

Only, this was too personal. He would do anything—*anything*—to save this woman from grief or
hurt or disappointment. He wanted to spend the rest
of his life imagining her face lighting when her kid

hit a home run in T-ball or brought home an A on a paper or some day gave a commencement address.

He should want to imagine her face lighting with joy and promise and hope as she walked down the aisle in church toward the man she was going to marry.

Trouble was, when he did, it was from a bizarre perspective: *he* was the man waiting for her.

Yeah. Sure, Reed thought sourly. That was going to happen. Maybe on the day when a citizen could forget her purse at a bus stop and come back two hours later to find it waiting just where she'd left it.

"I *am* tired." Meghan laid her cheek against his chest and made a soft, contented sound. "If I can just…close my eyes…for a few…" The slurred words faded into a slow, deep breath, then another.

Feeling her body relax into sleep against his, Reed let himself bend his head until his mouth touched her hair. Silky, wayward strands tickled his chin. The scent was stronger now. Definitely lavender. His mother had grown a large, leggy gray plant in a terra-cotta pot she put in the garage every winter. In the hot Idaho summer, the elusive fragrance would drift from the deep purple spires at unexpected moments. Eyes closed, he saw his parents' front walk, lined with marigolds, the lawn turning brown in patches despite his father's determined use of the sprinkler, the glider on the front porch where he had huddled with the light out on nights when he was afraid to go in. And the lavender, in its big heavy pot at the foot of the steps. He felt his boyhood anguish, and something sweeter if painful in its own way: the knowledge that this was the woman he would love, if the ability was in him.

She slept against him with the boneless trust and exhaustion of a child. His own body began to ache, but he didn't move a muscle. He studied the individual hairs that made up her glorious shade of chestnut brown: the strands of sun-touched gold, deep brown, rich auburn, all shiny and sleek and springy. He breathed in careful time with her, trying not to be conscious of the swell of her breast against his side. And he studied her hand, clutching his shirt, the skin smooth and pale, the oval of her fingernails unpainted and kept short. Pretty but matter-of-fact, practical.

That was her, he thought. Why the hell he found that very quality so much sexier than he did any sultry blonde or brunette with ample cleavage and a painted, pouty mouth and long, vixenish red fingernails, he couldn't have said.

She wakened on her own, before her boy stirred or their kidnapper returned. Without a watch or clock, he guessed she'd slept for an hour and a half.

First she mumbled something, then burrowed her face against him. His heart may have thudded in surprise and pleasure beneath her ear, because she went still, then slowly raised her head.

His heart took another bump or two at the sight of her heavy-lidded, drowsy eyes, the crease in one of her round cheeks, the softness of her mouth. He felt a violent wrench, imagining what it would be like to see her awaken every morning after having fallen asleep in his arms.

"Did I miss anything?" she whispered.

He shook his head and kept his voice low, too. "Not a thing."

She stiffened as if about to sit up, but he kept his arm snug and she relaxed back against him. "How long?"

"Did you sleep? I don't know. An hour or two."

"You must be stiff."

He made a murmuring sound, neither agreement nor disagreement. He didn't want her to move.

"You make a good pillow."

"You make a good comforter," he said huskily.

Her laugh was a gentle vibration against his ribs. "Thank you."

She seemed contented for a time to sit with her head on his chest, her one arm cramped between them and her hand still gripping his shirt, as if holding on for dear life. Time began to haze.

"I wish…"

When she didn't go on, he almost imagined he'd heard the words when she'd only sighed.

But he looked down until his mouth brushed her hair again. "You wish?"

"We were somewhere else. Snuggling at a movie, maybe." Her head shot up so fast she almost whacked him in the nose. "Oh, dear. I didn't mean…um…"

"I wish we were, too," he interrupted. Yeah. He saw them sitting in a dark, half-deserted theater, nobody nearby, his arm around her, the movie on the screen above losing focus as his awareness of her became paramount. "I think…" Reed cleared his throat. "I think I'd kiss you about now, if we were snuggling at a movie."

She drew back enough that she could look at him with something in her eyes that caught halfway between longing and doubt, as if she didn't believe he could be interested in her. "You would?"

"Oh, yeah." His voice scratched his throat. "Like this."

He slid his fingers around her nape, beneath the thick satin of her hair. She trembled, but didn't pull back. Her eyes were huge and dilated. Reed stole a glance at her kid to make sure he was still blind and deaf to the world, before he bent his head and touched his mouth to hers.

CHAPTER SIX

SANTA CLAUS WASN'T THE only fantasy Meghan had never believed in. Prince Charming was another, along with the romantic notion that the magical touch of one man's lips could awaken a woman, could send fireworks exploding into the velvety sky, could make her heart stop from sheer astonishment, etc., etc.

In one startled instant, she became a believer.

No fireworks, but for all the world her heart seemed to skid, thump and then stop, before taking up a dizzying pace.

Reed's mouth, which only rarely relaxed into a grin, was gentle and even sweet on hers, but it also awakened nerve endings she hadn't known she possessed. A shudder wracked her as she made a soft, helpless sound and felt pure yearning pour through her body. He nibbled her lower lip, she wanted more. Her teeth grazed his, his ragged breath wasn't enough.

Meghan forgot where they were or why, forgot Ted asleep against her thigh, forgot she had never met this man eight hours ago. All she knew was his mouth, the heavy beat of his heart, the scrape of his unshaven jaw against her cheek, the strength of his hand engulfing her nape and the back of her head. Her lips parted.

This time he groaned, a sound she heard and felt vibrate through his body. His tongue stroked hers, and she simply...melted. This hard-faced stranger was making her feel things she hadn't known she could.

He noticed Ted was waking up before she did. His mouth lifted from hers, and he muttered, "Damn," before kissing the soft skin by her ear, then nipping her earlobe.

"What?" she said in confusion.

Gray eyes darkened by unmistakable passion, he grimaced. "We woke him. I'm sorry."

Woke him? For an unmaternal moment, she hadn't the slightest idea what—*who*—he was talking about. Then she felt Ted stir against her, and guilt descended in an avalanche. She'd forgotten her own son! She'd been...been *making out* with a man, while Ted slept on her lap! What kind of mother was she?

She pulled away from Reed quickly enough to give herself whiplash. "Teddy," she whispered, hoping he was too sleepy and bewildered to notice his mother's blush.

"Mommy?" He blinked. "Mommy, where are we?"

She helped him sit up, noticing that Reed had unobtrusively edged away, so that he sat beside her but not close enough to make Ted wonder. She was very careful not to so much as glance his way. She didn't dare see his expression, didn't want to know what he was thinking.

"Remember coming to see Santa? We're still in the storage room."

Puzzlement creased Ted's face, then cleared. "Oh. The scary man." He sneaked a look around. "Is he gone?"

"For now."

Ted nodded, then squirmed. "Mommy?"

"Yes?" she encouraged.

"I have to go to the bathroom." He said it with enormous dignity. "I don't know where it is."

Oh, no. Now she *had* to look at Reed.

He shook his head, his eyes still dark and smouldering, his mouth tight. "I'll go find something." He rose to his feet without any of the creaking and groaning she was afraid her body would demand when she stood up, and disappeared behind the first tall shelving unit.

Ted spotted the pizza box. "I'm hungry," he said instantly. "Except...I need the bathroom first." He scrambled to his feet. "Really, really bad."

She had to go, too, now that the subject had come up. Oh, why had she drank that bottle of water? She should have *known* it would make her have to go. She was an adult, for Pete's sake, with a theoretical ability to foresee consequences.

Like taking her son to see a department store Santa Claus and getting kidnapped?

Okay. Maybe not that.

"Reed?" she called.

"Coming." His voice sounded far away. When he reappeared, he was ripping open a box. "Uh...how's this?" he asked, holding up a beautiful porcelain...soup tureen?

"Oh, no," she breathed.

His glance held irritation. "I'm afraid it's the best I can do on short notice."

"But…it must be horribly expensive." Would the store bill her afterward? First the quilts, now this lovely object that nobody who didn't entertain elegantly would ever even use—which meant it must cost the world.

"Mommy?" Ted was beginning to sound frantic.

"I…" It was about the right size. And…and shape, she decided, the demands of her own bladder encouraging her to analyze the enormous tureen Reed held up like an America's Cup. Why, it was big enough that she could even set it on the floor and… "All right," she said hastily.

"Come on, Ted." Reed smiled at her son, even though it looked as if it pained him. "Let's go set up a bathroom."

"Okay," her son said obligingly. "If we can do it fast."

"You're first in line."

Grateful for the lack of audience, Meghan unkinked her back and scrambled ungracefully to her feet. Her knees cracked and her butt hurt, quilts or no. When man and boy returned, she said with dignity to match her son's, "I think I'll, um, use the facilities, too."

Reed bent and handed her a paper napkin that had come with the pizza.

She accepted it and beat a retreat.

When she came back, she found Reed sitting cross-legged on the floor again and her son kneeling in front of him, apparently examining Reed's police badge.

"Wow! It looks like the ones on TV," he said excitedly.

Reed's gaze found her over Ted's head. "Your mom lets you watch cop shows?"

"No, but I have this friend, and her mom is always watching stuff like that." He held up one hand like a gun. "Bang, bang, bang!"

Meghan's eyes narrowed. "Which friend?"

He turned so fast he fell over. "Nobody! Ow! I mean…"

"Rachel." Meghan guessed. "It's Rachel's mom."

"You play with a girl?" Reed exclaimed.

Meghan turned a dangerous look on him.

"I mean, there's nothing wrong with playing with girls. It's just…I thought…"

"She has this really great PlayStation," Ted said, his expression reproachful. "Mom won't let me have one. So I never get to practice. That's why Rachel is lots better than me at all the games."

"Rachel also plays on his soccer team and is so vicious, the referee has to penalize her constantly," Meghan told Reed. "She's about a head taller than Ted."

"She's really strong," he said with admiration. "Lots of boys are scared of her."

Reed's grin was genuine this time. "Sounds like a good friend to have."

"Yeah!" her son agreed. "I wish I could show Rachel your badge." He reluctantly held it out.

"Evan...he's this other friend of mine, *his* dad is a ferryboat captain, and *he* came and talked to our class." Ted gazed hopefully at Reed.

Meghan made an abortive step forward.

Looking at her rather than Ted, Reed said, "Do you think your class would be interested if I came to talk to them?"

The five-year-old bounced, even from behind his exuberance plain. "Yeah!"

"I'll tell you what. Once I'm back at work, I'll ask my captain if I can take time to do that. Okay?"

"Okay!" Eyes sparkling, Ted turned. "Did you hear, Mom? Sergeant Reed—he said I could call him that—he's gonna come talk to my class!"

"He said he'd *try,*" she corrected. "There are lots of criminals, you know. He may be too busy."

Darn it, he should be looking grateful instead of irked at her effort to bail him out, she thought in exasperation. He had no idea how persistent Ted could be, once he'd taken a vague, "Maybe," and turned it into, "I promise."

"But he won't have to be Santa anymore. 'Cause Christmas is, um, real soon." The five-year-old's face scrunched in worry. "What if we're still here when it's Christmas?"

"Christmas Day isn't until Wednesday," she reminded him, voice steady. "We'll be home by then."

Home, or... No! She wouldn't even think about any other possibility.

"Besides," she said wryly, "isn't Santa supposed to be able to find you anywhere?"

"I guess so." Ted's voice was even gruffer than usual. "Yeah. Sure."

He was scared, she realized, but determined not to show it. Her heart swelled with a sudden rush of love that brought tears to her eyes. Meghan blinked so he wouldn't see them.

Reed, however, did. Gaze riveted on her face, he tensed as though to stand up, then deliberately relaxed. "That's the story," he said.

Ted turned to him. "You must know for real, if you're Santa's bodyguard."

"Never met the big guy." Reed spread his hands at Ted's obvious disappointment. "He's got a lot of people working for him."

"And elves!" Ted reminded him eagerly. "Elves, too."

"Haven't met them, either. Sorry," he added apologetically. "I'm just, uh, a temp. That means I was borrowed for this assignment from the police department. First time. Santa probably doesn't need bodyguards very often."

"Oh." Ted nodded as if satisfied.

Well, thank heaven for small favors. At least Reed had managed to avoid any truly outrageous lies.

"I wish you could have been our bodyguard, too." Ted sounded wistful. "So the scary man wouldn't a got us."

"Yeah, kid." His mouth twisted. "I wish I'd done a better job, too. So it was just me and him, and you and your mom were safe at home."

"But we're good company, right?" Ted scooted

closer to Reed and laid a small, reassuring hand on his knee. "That's what Mom always says. That we're good company for each other. So we can be for you, too. Huh?"

The big, tough police officer had the strangest expression on his face as he gazed down at her son's hand, then his face. "Uh…" He cleared his throat. "Yeah. You're good company."

"'Cept I slept a lot." Ted's voice brightened. "But now I'm not."

"Right."

Meghan moved forward. "Do you want some pizza now, Ted? It's cold, but you don't care, do you?"

"No! Can I have a pop, too?"

"Why not?" She sat down again, a safe distance from Reed, and rummaged in the plastic grocery bag for something Ted would like.

While he happily munched on a slice of cold cheese pizza, Meghan said, "I wonder what time it is. I wish there was a window."

"It's got to be the middle of the night." Reed's mouth hardened. "And if there was a window, I'd break it."

"That was a silly thing to say, wasn't it?"

"No. I knew what you meant."

Aware she was babbling, she still couldn't seem to stop herself. "It's just that I've lost any sense of how much time has passed. It could be midnight, or eight in the morning. If I hadn't slept," she added fretfully, "I might not have lost track. Or maybe I would have anyway. Is time supposed to go really fast in a situation like this, or really slow?''

He looked thoughtful. ''I've actually never been kidnapped before. I guess it could go either way. If you were alone, I imagine time might crawl. But with us talking… Who knows?''

And kissing. They'd done that to pass the time, too. Meghan would have trouble believing she *had* kissed him, except every time she looked at him, it came back with a rush when his eyes met hers. She knew the scrape of the dark bristles on his chin, the feel of his lips, the shiver of his muscles when her hand splayed on his chest. And instead of being ashamed, she wished very, very much that someday he would kiss her again.

Which was about as likely as Santa Claus producing a new daddy for Ted by Wednesday morning at dawn when he rocketed out of his bedroom with his voice cracking as he yelled, ''Mommy! Mommy! Wake up! It's Christmas!''

Reed's voice deepened. ''What do you wish?''

Her eyes widened in alarm. She hadn't thought out loud. Had she? ''Wish?''

''You said, 'I wish,' earlier but you didn't finish.''

''Oh.'' She sagged in relief. ''I wish it was Christmas Eve, and we were sipping hot chocolate in front of the tree.''

''And Sergeant Reed was there, too, right?'' her son prompted.

She smiled to cover her fear that Reed knew quite well what she'd been wishing for. ''Right. I wish Sergeant Reed had stopped by to see our tree, and we'd offered him a cup of cocoa.''

''Maybe I will stop by.'' His voice sounded husky, just the way it had when he said, *I think I'd kiss you about now, if we were snuggling at a movie.*

The heat in her cheeks betrayed her, but she managed to say steadily, ''That would be nice. Please do.''

''Why is the scary man keeping us here?'' Ted asked.

Meghan did her best to explain without frightening him further.

''He wants to be on TV?'' he asked, amazed. ''That's what he wants?''

''Uh...pretty much. So he can tell people what happened to his wife.''

Ted sat with a very straight back, but his voice shook. ''Do you think they're letting him be on TV right now? So we can go home? 'Cause I don't really want pizza. I want a waffle. With jam.''

She knew exactly what he was saying: he wanted home. The familiar. She did, too, so badly her throat closed at the image of the two of them eating breakfast together, Ted's heels bouncing off the legs of the chair, the tea kettle whistling because the water for her tea was boiling, the neighbor boy starting his car outside with the roar that told everyone for a block around that he hadn't yet fixed the muffler. It might be rainy and blustery outside, but their kitchen was bright and sunny and cozy. If only they *were* there, she thought, with a deep ache.

Meghan held out her arms to him, and when he tumbled into them she whispered, "Me, too, teddy bear. Me, too."

Blurred by her first real tears of the night, she saw Reed watching her hold her son with an expression that she imagined for a moment was longing.

Or perhaps it was, but he longed for his *own* home, his girlfriend, or…or just friends or his dog or whoever or whatever he loved most.

It had to be her exhaustion and her fear, not just the kiss, that made her begin a wish that went absurdly beyond fantasizing that Reed McCall would kiss her again.

I wish… Meghan formulated the words as clearly as if she were asking a genie for a boon to be granted. *I wish that he could somehow fall in love with me. And with Ted. So that he'd want to be part of our mornings, and to be a father to Ted. And a lover and husband for me.* And finally, *I wish he was looking at us like that because he wanted to hold us, and not because he was thinking about somebody else.*

The pain under her breastbone told her that her yearnings were just as foolish as Ted's. Sniffing, she laid her cheek against her small son's head and closed her eyes so she couldn't see the lean, dark, sexy man who had set her to dreaming.

After all, she thought very sadly, there was no Santa Claus. So how could Ted's wish come true? And hers never would, because she didn't believe.

CHAPTER SEVEN

HE HAD TO BE GETTING TIRED. That was the only explanation for him getting so softheaded. Yeah, as kids went, this strange little gruff-voiced, spiky-haired boy was fine. Kinda sweet, even. It was nice that he had actually worried about Reed being lonely if he'd been held captive alone.

But we're good company, right? So we can be for you, too.

Reed wasn't used to having anyone worry about him. The kid should be crying and telling him what a lousy cop he was for letting them get kidnapped, instead of comforting him.

Still, he didn't get misty-eyed over kindergarteners. He sure as hell didn't wish desperately that he'd be with the kid and his mother the next time they sat at their breakfast table eating waffles.

What was he imagining? That he'd have spent the night? If a woman like Meghan Kane had an affair at all, she didn't casually produce her lover at the break-fast table so her five-year-old son could get to know him, too.

No, for her an affair would be furtive, guilt-ridden, and as separate as she could possibly make it from her real life.

He wouldn't put her through that even if she could be persuaded, Reed thought gloomily, watching out of the corner of his eye as she held her son and murmured soft words of reassurance to him, her hair shimmering as she dipped her head. She was too nice for that.

Too nice for *him.*

So why had she kissed him at all? He hated to think it was some kind of payment for services to be rendered. A way of saying, *Please, please, save my son and me!* He'd rather believe she had at least been attracted to him, swayed by the moment.

She wasn't interested, or so she said, in remarrying. Reed wondered what kind of man it would take to change her mind. Probably not somebody who wore a white lab coat, given her ex's profession.

Did she go for the banker type? Charcoal-gray suits, well-cut hair and razor-sharp minds? Or maybe artists, with wild curly hair, paint-stained hands and flights of imagination? Or, given the fact that both her father and her husband had committed adultery, maybe all she wanted was a steady, reliable, faithful guy who held a nine-to-five job and came straight home for dinner and whose idea of a wild time was taking his family to Disneyland.

Reed had a bad feeling that the last time he'd worn his suit he had taken it to the dry cleaners and then not remembered to bail it out. It had probably been given to the Salvation Army by now. His flights of imagination tended to involve the next moves of crack

Play **LUCKY HEARTS** for this.

exciting FREE gift!
This surprise mystery gi
could be yours free

when you play **LUCKY HEARTS**

...then continue your lucky streak
with a sweetheart of a deal!

1. Play Lucky Hearts as instructed on the opposite page.
2. Send back this card and you'll receive 2 brand-new Harlequin Superromance® book These books have a cover price of $5.25 each in the U.S., and $6.25 each in Canad but they are yours to keep absolutely free.
3. There's no catch! You're under no obligation to buy anything. We charge nothing— ZERO—for your first shipment. And you don't have to make any minimum number of purchases—not even one!
4. The fact is thousands of readers enjoy receiving their books by mail from the Harleq Reader Service®. They enjoy the convenience of home delivery...they like getting the best new novels at discount prices, BEFORE they're available in stores...and they love their *Heart to Heart* subscriber newsletter featuring author news, horoscopes, recipes, book reviews and much more!
5. We hope that after receiving your free books you'll want to remain a subscriber. But choice is yours—to continue or cancel, any time at all! So why not take us up on o invitation, with no risk of any kind. You'll be glad you did!

Visit us online at
www.eHarlequin.c

Exciting Harlequin® romance books— FREE!
Plus an exciting mystery gift—FREE!
No cost! No obligation to buy!

YES!

I have scratched off the silver card. Please send me the 2 FREE books and gift for which I qualify.
I understand I am under no obligation to purchase any books, as explained on the back and on the opposite page.

With a coin, scratch off the silver card and check below to see what we have for you.

LUCKY HEARTS GAME

336 HDL DRPE   135 HDL DRPV

FIRST NAME

LAST NAME

ADDRESS

APT.#

CITY

STATE/PROV.

ZIP/POSTAL CODE

Twenty-one gets you 2 free books, and a free mystery gift!

Twenty gets you 2 free books!

Nineteen gets you 1 free book!

Try Again!

(H-SR-11/02)

The Harlequin Reader Service®—Here's how it works:

Accepting your 2 free books and gift places you under no obligation to buy anything. You may keep the books and gift and return the shipping statement marked "cancel." If you do not cancel, about a month later we'll send you 6 additional books and bill you just $4.47 each in the U.S., or $4.99 each in Canada, plus 25¢ shipping & handling delivery per book and appli taxes if any.* That's the complete price and — compared to cover prices of $5.25 each in the U.S. and $6.25 each in Cana it's quite a bargain! You may cancel at any time, but if you choose to continue, every month we'll send you 6 more books, you may either purchase at the discount price or return to us and cancel your subscription.

*Terms and prices subject to change without notice. Sales tax applicable in N.Y. Canadian residents will be charged applic provincial taxes and GST.

dealers or con men. He didn't work nine to five, and he'd never been to Disneyland.

All of which let him off.

He scowled. Had he been wanting in?

A quick nap. He'd be himself again, if he could just catch some shut-eye.

The boy, of course, decided he wanted to talk.

"You never shoot people, do you?" he asked, eyes wide and troubled.

In Reed's experience, most boys hoped he had. They wanted to hear every gory detail.

"I've been a cop—a police officer—for thirteen years," he told the kid. "I've had to shoot men twice. We all hope we'll never have to do that, but sometimes it happens."

Ted seemed to shrink. "Did they die?"

Reed tried not to notice how the boy's mom was reacting to the brutal reality of his job.

"One did. The other didn't."

"What did they *do?* To make them shoot you, I mean? Were they really, really bad?"

"Yeah." He pushed away the fleeting, dark memories. "One had just shot at me. The other had shot my partner. Both times, I had to take some time off the job to think about what I'd done and be sure I hadn't hurt somebody just because I was mad."

"Oh." The boy digested that. "Do policemen get mad a lot?"

"We try not to. We try to stay calm, even when people are screaming at us or we're scared or upset.

Our job is to calm other people down, help them not be scared, catch bad guys.''

Looking pensive, the kid said, "I wish *I* could call you when *I'm* scared."

There he went again—a knife straight to the heart. Reed fought the image of himself sitting on the side of the boy's bed, soothing his fears until he sighed, nestled a hand into Reed's and slept again. Only then would Reed quietly stand, ease out of the room and go back to his lover? wife? waiting in their wide bed, the pillow of her breasts soft, her hair scented with lavender.

He tried to hold on to his cynicism. This kid was good. Hell, maybe he'd make a politician someday. He knew how to go right for the jugular.

Reluctantly, Reed looked up and met Meghan's eyes. She smiled at him with gentle approval and a touch of shyness. Reed swallowed. Damn it, she was as ruthlessly effective as her son!

"Just think how much you'll have to tell all your buddies when you go back to school," Reed said to the boy. "Your Christmas vacation has probably been more exciting than theirs."

Mom's smile dimmed.

"Yeah. I guess so." Ted was silent for a moment. "My dad, too. I can tell my dad. I'll bet he'll think I was really brave."

"I bet he will."

His mother hugged him. "You *are* brave." Her voice said, *The hell with what your father thinks.*

"Maybe he's really worried," Ted continued, sitting up straighter. "Maybe he's out there right now, and the policemen are having to grab him to keep him from coming right in here to rescue us!"

This pang in his chest made Reed want to punch the kid's daddy. A man who didn't bother to show up to take his son for the weekend, who couldn't make time to talk to the kid's kindergarten class, sure as hell wasn't out there fighting to risk life and limb to sweep his son from harm's way.

Reed wondered if the bastard had any idea what a great boy he had. Did he even know him? Did he guess that Ted made up stories in which Dad figured largely?

Hell, did he care?

Reed had told the truth. He didn't get angry often. But all of a sudden, he was blazing, steaming mad.

His eyes met Meghan's, and she saw his fury and raised her brows slightly as if in surprise.

"Yeah." Reed had to clear his throat. "Yeah, kid. Maybe he is."

Meghan smiled gratefully over her son's head.

"Aren't you getting sleepy again?" she asked the boy.

He yawned. "No. I want to be home in bed. In my *own* bed."

"Tomorrow night." Her voice was as soft as a lullaby.

Drowsy, he asked, "Promise?"

"For sure," she said firmly, lying for all she was worth. "Now, why don't you lie down again? Put your head on me. I make a good pillow, don't I?"

Immediately her gaze flew to Reed's, as she remembered telling him he made a good one, too. Heat stained her cheeks, the color deepening when he couldn't help taking a slow, hungry look at her lower lip, caught between her teeth.

Damn, he wanted to kiss her again.

Maybe if the kid fell asleep...

Even the thought made Reed feel like a scumbag. He was a cop on duty. Their lives were on the line here. And him? All he could think about was necking with his fellow hostage—despite the fact that her five-year-old kid was all too present.

Get over it, he told himself irritably, his brows drawing together. He wasn't a randy sixteen-year-old, even if he'd acted like one.

Abruptly shoving himself to his feet, he growled, "I'm going to go listen at the door. Maybe I'll get lucky and overhear our kidnapper being interviewed for KOMO-TV."

He actually pressed his ear to the cold metal door. Silence. Then he heard something. A footstep? And a guttural noise like a shout. His adrenaline rose and he flexed his fingers. Was something going down?

If so, it was over. He heard only more silence. Experimentally, he slowly turned the doorknob. No resistance. But when he tried to ease the door toward him, just a fraction of an inch, it wouldn't budge. The bastard had wedged it with something. Frustrated, Reed let the knob roll back. For lack of anything else to do, he returned to their corner.

The boy seemed to be falling asleep again. Meghan

was watching Reed with wide, anxious eyes. "Did you hear anything?" she whispered.

He shook his head.

Her shoulders slumped. "Oh."

Suddenly restless, angry, unwilling anymore to do nothing but sit and wait for their fate, he rocked on the balls of his feet and rotated his shoulders to loosen up.

"If we just knew what was happening..." Her voice was thin, hopeless.

"He may be napping out there like a baby." The idea infuriated Reed.

"Would he dare?"

"If he's got all the doors blocked."

"I hate this!" She looked surprised at her own vehemence, then let out a puff of air. "I'm sorry. Of course I do. You hate it, too. That was another silly thing to say."

"Damn it, quit apologizing!" He dropped to a crouch in front of her and gripped her chin, lifting her face. "Who made you think everything you say is ridiculous? Your idiot of an ex?"

Her eyes were clear and bottomless as she stared up at him in astonishment. "No... I mean..."

"It was, wasn't it?"

Another excuse to punch the bastard, if he got a chance. Too bad he was an upstanding officer of the law who would never do such a thing.

A man could dream, couldn't he?

"Has anyone ever told you how nice you are?" she asked unexpectedly, her face softening.

"Nice?" Reed let her go as if her velvety skin had burned the pads of his fingers.

"Is that bad?"

"Big tough cops aren't 'nice.'" He could just imagine the crowd in the locker room holding their sides and howling at the idea of Reed McCall being "nice."

"Well, they should be!" she said strongly, then stiffened at a scraping sound. "Did you hear...?"

"Yeah," he breathed, and swiveled toward the door just as it swung open.

St. Nick again, flannel shirt hanging open to show that big belly pushing against a white undershirt, his expression jovial. The cold hollow of the gun barrel ruined the mood.

"Still awake?"

Reed grunted.

"Boy's asleep, I see." St. Nick shook his head in apparent disappointment. "Didn't get any pizza."

"Actually," Meghan said timidly, "he did wake up and have some."

"Ah!" He beamed. "Good, good."

"Has anybody interviewed you yet?" she asked.

A cloud darkened his face. "They haven't decided if they're going to 'allow' it yet. Anyway, it's the middle of the night, they say. Can't get journalists out of bed. We'll wait until morning." His finger stroked the trigger, Reed saw with narrowed eyes. "They think I'll get careless. Morning? Sure. I can wait."

"What...what time is it?"

"Four o'clock," he said, sounding cheerful. "Dawn

on the way. So." Gaze bright, he looked from one to the other of them. "You folks holding out okay?"

"The woman and the boy are scared." Reed stood. "Let 'em go home. You still have me."

"But that wouldn't do! Not at all. You're only part of the point." The idea seemed to amuse him. "Part of the whole."

A fruitcake. That's what he was, Reed realized anew. Unfortunately, a fruitcake with a plan, the worst kind.

What worried Reed was that the plan might be one hell of a lot more involved than St. Nick had revealed to them.

And he seriously doubted that the plan involved letting them stroll out so they could peacefully return to their separate lives.

At least, not him.

Santa Claus will die, the note had said. *Then everyone will pay attention.*

So far, Santa Claus hadn't died.

CHAPTER EIGHT

TED STIRRED AND LIFTED his head.

Meghan stiffened. She didn't want him to interact with a kidnapper. So far his worst trauma had been the snatching, the scary march through the store, the sight of "Santa" transformed into an angry cop. But it had all happened fast, and the time since had been no more than uncomfortable and inconvenient for him. She wanted to keep it that way.

But, too young to understand the unspoken pressure of her hand on his shoulder, he struggled to sit up.

"Well, if it isn't young Ted." Their captor's eyes twinkled. "Bet you're wishing for your own bed, aren't you?" Waving the gun at Reed, the heavy, white-stubbled man snapped, "Sit. You make me nervous, standing there waiting to pounce."

Reed backed slowly away into his corner, sinking to a sitting position with his knees drawn up and his arms resting on them. Meghan could feel how very *un*relaxed he was, despite appearances. To her, he looked like one of the big cats, a panther perhaps, stretched languidly on the ground watching potential prey, only the twitch of a tail and unblinking eyes betraying intense interest.

"I *do* want my bed," her son blurted. "Sir. Please."

Nick's cold gaze left Reed and warmed to a genial blue. "You'll get it. Think of this as a camp-out. Are you in Cub Scouts yet?" At Ted's head shake, he continued, "Or maybe your dad takes you camping sometimes?"

Another head shake.

"Tsk, tsk."

Meghan hadn't known anyone actually said that. Fascinated by this vestige of Victorian language, she felt again a peculiar, unsettling inner conflict about this man. He was crazy! He had to be, to threaten to kill them so some TV station or journalist would interview him and give him a chance to rant and rave. But then he had these moments when he would have looked like everyone's grandfather, if only he shaved and cut his hair. Plump, kindly, courtly, in the old-fashioned sense.

Maybe she was the crazy one!

"You live in the glorious Northwest, and you've never been camping?" Nick continued. "Son, tell me you've been up to Mount Rainier? In the early summer, when the avalanche lilies are blooming, or later, when you can pick huckleberries by the handful and gorge on them?"

Ted shook his head uncertainly, while Meghan felt a pang of guilt. She *should* have taken Ted up to Rainier, the magnificent volcano that on clear days hovered like a guardian angel over Seattle. But it was a long drive, and they were always busy, and she'd thought he was too young...

"You do need a new father," Nick concluded, with a brisk nod. "Smart of you to ask."

"But *he*," Ted jerked his head toward Reed, "isn't really Santa, so my wish might not work."

"Who's to say?" The man holding the gun chuckled benevolently. "Who's to say?"

As much to turn his attention from Ted as anything, Meghan said the first thing that came into her head. "There's pizza left. And pop. If you want anything."

"Why, that's kind of you." He beamed at her. "I just might have a piece of that cheese pizza, if some's left. My stomach is feeling a mite unsettled from all that pepperoni and sausage and onion and garlic and who knows what. Plain cheese just might settle it."

As if he'd patted her on the back, Meghan felt a wave of approval from Reed. He'd *wanted* their kidnapper to sit down and stay.

Of course he had, she realized with a chill. So he could try something. But that's when people died, as even he had admitted.

It was impossible to watch the men on each side of her with equal vigilance, but she tried. If Reed made a move, she'd throw herself over Ted. She didn't like the idea of him having to go through life with the memory of his mother's lifeblood pumping out onto him, but that was better than him not having the chance to go on through life, wasn't it? Of course, she didn't like the idea of dying, for that matter. She wished she'd talked to Reed earlier, when Nick wasn't here, about what he intended. It seemed to her that their chances were best if they just waited. Nick had the gun. Unless he actually fell asleep…

She took a 7-Up from the bag, hoping he wouldn't notice that there was a cola, full of caffeine, left. "Would you like a drink?"

"Yeah, but let me have the other." He smiled at her, as if unsuspecting that she'd had an ulterior motive. "I say, if it doesn't have caffeine, it isn't worth drinking." He chuckled at his own humor.

Darn.

Meghan made the switch and handed over the can of soda.

After flipping the top and taking a deep drink, he said, "Looks like you've made yourself cozy here. Nice quilts."

"I think they're hand-quilted." She stroked the top one, which she thought was a pattern called Irish Chain, in this case with the small squares red against a white background.

As he munched pizza, he made other chatty remarks. Meghan was the only one to respond. Reed sat in what seemed to be sullen silence, but she feared was really an alert state of readiness. Ted listened with wide eyes, not exactly scared but not lulled into friendliness with this stranger, either.

She, on the other hand, probably sounded like an idiot, making polite conversation with a man who might shoot them all at any time. She couldn't seem to help herself. It must be congenital, or maybe a social onus laid on good girls: *you will always be polite*. Semihysterically, Meghan wondered if the social mavens who made up the rules had ever dreamed of a situation like this.

Once she felt Reed shift slightly, the movement so small it probably hadn't been visible, but she was so attuned to him now that she knew when he breathed. She tried very hard to make her glance at him casual. Their eyes met, and his held reassurance and a warmth that had the opposite effect he'd probably intended. It was as if, in the one split second that their gazes clung, he was conveying something. A message. If he'd been a husband or lover, she would have been certain he was silently saying, *I love you.*

One last time. Just in case.

She shivered, stole another peek and saw that his icy gray eyes were unwaveringly fixed on their captor. She'd imagined that look. Of course she had.

Nick, however, contemplated Reed and then her with a bright, interested expression. Shoving the pizza box away with his foot, he said, "Well, I'm going to be sorry I ate that. My Emmie wouldn't let me eat junk food. Fed me too well," he patted his belly complacently, "but only good stuff. Roasts and potatoes and stews and the best macaroni salad you've ever had. Insisted we have a vegetable with dinner every night! She was a fine cook." His gaze turned inward. "She couldn't eat herself those last months. Just faded away, still cooking as long as she could, then picking at her own food, pretending to be eating. But she tried to take care of me." He was silent for a moment. "She always took care of me."

Driven by impulse, Meghan reached out and touched his knee. "I'm sorry," she said quietly.

He looked down at her hand, then into her eyes, his own sad and yet kind. "I know you are. You'll be a loving wife and make some man as lucky as I was."

Wrung by pity, she hardly noticed that, in looking at her, he'd let his gun hand sag so that momentarily the barrel pointed down.

Reed launched himself right over the top of Ted. Meghan had a blurred impression of Nick's startled face and Reed's violent one, of Ted's open mouth. She heard a scream and realized only as she rolled to cover Ted with her body that *she* was the one screaming.

A thud was followed by the sound of struggle: grunts, snarls, profanity and the smacks of flesh hitting flesh. Whimpering, Meghan pushed herself and Ted, inch by inch, away from the battle. The quilt bunched beneath them but slid along the hard vinyl floor.

She didn't get far, because the fight didn't last long.

"Meghan." The voice was insistent. "Meghan, you're safe."

Shuddering for breath, she froze. Beneath her, Ted wriggled.

"Sit up," Reed ordered.

She lifted her head with all the enthusiasm of a turtle peering out of its shell. What a coward she was! Meghan thought with dismay.

Their kidnapper lay facedown on the concrete floor,

Reed straddling him and holding his arms behind his back at a painful angle. The gun, she saw with a wild glance, had skidded across the room and come to a stop against the first metal shelving unit.

Nick labored for breath and his face had a bluish hue.

"Meghan." Reed was being remarkably patient, considering. "Would you *carefully* go out and call in the cops."

She stumbled to her feet and held out her hand. "Ted…"

"Leave Ted here."

Because she would be in some danger when she opened the outer door, Meghan realized. Of course Ted had to stay.

"Mommy, I want to come!" he wailed, scrambling up and launching himself at her.

"I'll be right back," she promised, gently unprying his fingers. "You help Reed if he needs anything."

He watched with big eyes as she left the storage room. In the silent hall, she had to stop for a moment and take slow, deep breaths to gather her courage. It felt as if they'd been in there forever, leaving her frightened of the outside world.

The door to the store proper was barred and jammed with tangled pieces of clothing racks, just as the outside one was.

"Hello?" she called. "Is anyone there?"

Muffled voices answered, but the door was sound-proofed and she couldn't hear what they said.

"I'm coming out!" she yelled, then began unbracing bent pieces of metal. When the last one gave way, Meghan swallowed and inched the door open.

Black-clad SWAT team members engulfed her.

"Ma'am?" one asked. "Did you manage to escape?"

"No. Reed..." Too friendly. "Um, Sergeant Reed McCall—he's in there with us?—um, he overpowered our kidnapper. He'd like you to come help."

They wanted her to stay behind. She refused. Ted was in there, and she was going back.

She pushed past a couple of beefy cops in time to see Reed rise to his feet and shake his head.

"Let's not cuff him right now. You'd better run him by Harborview for a checkup. I don't like his color."

"Will do," one said, heaving Nick to his feet.

Gasping for air, he gave her a smile probably meant to be jaunty, and let himself be led from the room. Watching him go, Meghan realized tears were rolling down her cheeks.

"Mommy?" Ted tugged at her hand. "Is he in big trouble?"

"I...yes."

He sounded as troubled as she felt. "Is he *that* bad a man?"

"I don't know," she admitted.

Reed was conferring with the other cops. His cheek was swelling and scraped, his dark hair spiky as if he'd run fingers through it, and a frown seemed permanently carved on his forehead. He *matched* all those other men, she realized, as bulky in the shoulders as they were, as hard. With a sinking heart, Meghan understood that he was a stranger to her, that the closeness of the night had been an illusion.

A guttural shout from out in the store turned all their heads. More shouts, and Reed and the other cops jostled in the doorway and disappeared out into the store. Ted and she were left alone.

After a hesitant moment, she said, "Let's go see what happened," hoisted her son onto her hip and retraced her steps.

All she could see, through gaps between prom and mother-of-the-bride dresses, was that policemen had spread out through the store. Perplexed, she watched them make a kind of line, like searchers beating the woods for a missing child, and begin a systematic hunt that involved poking through racks of clothing.

Nick had escaped. She couldn't imagine how. He was overweight and slow, and he'd looked like he might be suffering from angina. He must be hiding in the center of one of those racks, shielded by brand-name jeans or leather coats, or hiding behind a display in the china department. But he must know he wouldn't be able to get out of the store! They'd find him eventually. He had just made things worse for himself. Reed, nice enough not to cuff him, would be mad now, and she didn't blame him.

Even if, secretly, she hoped they didn't find Nick.

As if she'd summoned him, Reed himself appeared with another officer.

"The son-of-a..." His gaze met Ted's. "Nick ran for it. You've probably figured that out. We'll get him, of course. In the meantime, I've gotten permission for you to go home. Siegel here will escort you. You'll have to give a statement eventually, but you can go home and sleep first. Take a shower, have lunch, dinner, whatever time it is when you wake up, then call and a patrol unit will pick you up to take you down to the station.''

Feeling weirdly numb, she nodded. ''And...and you?''

She didn't even know what she was asking. Yes, she did. *Will I see you again?* she wanted to beg.

He took a step toward her, stopped himself with a visible effort. Voice harsh, he said, ''I've got to stay. Meghan...I'll call.''

She didn't believe him.

''That would be nice,'' she said politely, social training once again permitting her to be courteous to the bitter end. But she knew he wouldn't call, and her face probably told him as much.

A muscle jerked in his cheek, and he said again, ''Meghan.'' Then he rubbed a hand over his face, wiping away all expression, leaving only his eyes alive, intense. ''Go home,'' he said, and turned away.

Bereft, Meghan squeezed Ted so hard he complained, ''Mom!''

She loosened her grip. ''I'm sorry. Oh, sweetie, I'm so sorry.'' Striving for composure, she turned to the uniform-clad police officer. ''We're ready to go home, please.''

CHAPTER NINE

MEGHAN GUIDED TED'S HAND, holding the cookie cutter. "Okay, push down hard." She helped, pressing firmly, then letting him lift the cookie cutter with a star cutout inside it.

Frowning in concentration, he shook the dough loose on the cookie sheet, to join all the others they'd already cut out: trees, candy canes, bells and fat Santa shapes. For some reason, the first Santa they'd made had given Meghan a pang.

"It's full," her son said eagerly. "Can we bake them now? And decorate them?"

"You bet." She smiled at him. "Do you want to cut some more out while these bake?"

"I'm kind of tired of it," he admitted.

She kissed the top of his head, showering him with flour from her apron. Laughing, she said, "You go play or watch TV while I finish. We'll have to let these cool before we decorate them. It'll be a while."

"Okay." He left the kitchen and she heard the television a minute later.

He'd been watching more than usual since the kidnapping, she thought, but she hadn't done anything about it. She'd been disturbed last night to hear, through his closed bedroom door, the sound of him yelling, "Pow! Take *that,* you bad man! Pow! Pow!" She guessed he had to process the things he'd seen and feared. So far, he hadn't seemed upset enough that she felt he should see a counselor.

Was that a bad decision? she worried, as she automatically cut out more Christmas cookies and spread them on the second sheet. Would she find out when he was sixteen and it was too late that he'd been traumatized for life?

Smiling ruefully, Meghan peeked in the oven, decided the first batch was done and took them out, popping in the second sheet.

Somehow, she felt pretty sure Ted hadn't been *that* scared. She was probably the one who needed counseling. Ted seemed absorbed in his everyday life. She, on the other hand, was waking in the morning with an instant sense of loss. Her Christmas cheer during the day was fake. It almost seemed—water running unheeded in the sink as she gazed unseeing out the window at the quiet afternoon street—as if she was in mourning.

That was it. She was sad, for no reason she could quite put her finger on. She didn't like to think of Nick in a jail cell, assuming they'd found him—and how could they have failed to? And Reed... Well, Reed was the crux of the problem, if she was honest with herself.

She missed him. But how could you miss a man you'd known for less than twelve hours?

With a sigh more heartfelt than she had intended,

Meghan dragged herself back to the present, turned off the running water and dried her hands.

She couldn't miss him. Not really. He'd simply represented a...a *possibility*. That was it. A possibility that wouldn't be realized.

But she should be grateful to him, because he'd made her realize that she should take a risk with her heart again. Ted did need a father, and she needed a husband, best friend and lover.

That man wouldn't be Reed; she'd never see him again. He hadn't even made the effort to be at the station when she went to make her statement. In the two days since, he hadn't called, much less rang her doorbell.

No, he was probably kicking himself for having kissed her. It had been an impulse for him, no more. Even if he'd been interested at all, he'd made clear that he wasn't a marrying man, and he must have realized that she *was* a marrying woman. With a young son, she had to be.

So that was that.

She needed to shake this cloud of grief for what might have been, and be grateful for what was. They were safe, thanks to Reed. Their Christmas was waiting to unfold. She had a job she loved. Also thanks to him, she was willing now to look for possibilities.

What more could she want?

But when the oven timer went off, she didn't even hear it, because she was looking out the window at the slushy street, wishing a car would turn onto it, that a man would be striding along the sidewalk, hunched against the cold, glancing at house numbers, hesitating outside.

Her mind knew he wasn't coming, but her heart continued to believe in the impossible.

REED SCOWLED AT HIS computer screen, then hit the backspace key repeatedly. Where in hell had his mind been? It would take him all day to write this report if he kept making stupid screwups.

"Merry Christmas!" someone called behind him, and a voice across the squad room called back, "To you and yours, too."

They weren't helping, he thought irritably. Why this year did it seem as if every hard-bitten cop in the city had suddenly become imbued with Christmas spirit? Brown from Vice was collecting toys for the shelters. People were still bringing in bags of food for Christmas baskets. A decorated tree twinkled by the window, a wreath hung on the captain's door, and mistletoe—mistletoe!—hung above by the coffeepot.

Everybody was in the mood but him.

Playing Santa had killed his Christmas spirit and uncovered the greed that lay at the heart of the holiday.

Predictably, a small earnest face appeared before his mind's eye. "What I want for Christmas is a new father."

Not every kid who sat on his lap was greedy, he admitted to himself, uncomfortably. Only a few. Plenty of the kids had asked for modest gifts. A few had even said what they wanted most was for people to be nice to each other and not make war or steal cars or shoot anyone. Scared kids had smiled bravely at the camera for their mothers' sakes. Even most of the greedy ones had been eager and hopeful enough to remind him they were just young.

Reed glared at the computer screen. He hadn't typed a single word. He seemed to have this trouble a lot these days. Brooding had become his principal occupation.

Call her. Ask her out to dinner. Or just ask how she and her son are.

In a black mood, he ignored the taunting of his inner voice and stalked to the other end of the room for a cup of coffee. A receptionist who'd been lingering hopefully under the mistletoe caught sight of his face and made herself scarce, to his relief. He didn't want to kiss her.

He wanted to kiss Meghan Kane. Now and forever.

An illusion. It was a goddamn illusion! he snarled at himself. Circumstance heightened emotions. They'd both be disappointed if they got together for a garden-variety date. Nobody fell in love, happily-ever-after, in just a few hours. And he wasn't the happily-ever-after kind anyway. He'd always known that.

Yeah, but wouldn't at least calling her to find out how she and Ted were be the decent thing to do? He didn't want to hurt their feelings. Maybe the closeness had existed only for those pent hours, but it had existed. He couldn't have imagined it.

He couldn't have imagined the way her lips parted and her hand clung and her body melted.

Heart and mind at war, he swallowed bitter coffee and made himself start typing.

A DAY LATER, HE FOUND himself in her neighborhood. Not because he'd intended to stop by her house, but just—oh, hell, admit it—because he was curious. He would drive by, see what her place looked like. See her tree in the front window, the lights she'd undoubtedly strung on the eaves even though he didn't like to think of her teetering on a precarious ladder, convince himself by the homeyness of the scene that she didn't need him.

Her narrow street had cars parked to each side, allowing only one lane of traffic down the middle. Christmas Eve, and people were home. Every house on the block had Christmas lights on as dusk deepened the gray sky. The slush lingered, icy in spots, messy in others. He spotted her house number and a parking spot at the same moment.

Telling himself he'd just sit here for a minute, Reed backed his car into the narrow space between a BMW and some teenager's beater. Then got out. But only because a neighbor's huge camellia bush, dark and wet, blocked his view of her narrow brick house.

Hands shoved in his pockets, the collar of his coat up to keep the cold out, Reed crossed the street and stood just to the side of her house. Sure enough, a tree was in the window. Even from here, he could see that the decorations were motley, some probably handmade. Bright and cheerful but not color coordinated. Homey and child-oriented, popcorn and papier mâché as well as gleaming red and gold and green balls.

Just what he'd expected.

Movement flickered in the window and Reed froze, trying to make himself invisible. It was Ted who appeared. He stood staring out, probably unable to see much beyond the glass with night falling. Reed waited for him to do something kidlike. Damn it, wasn't this Christmas Eve? Shouldn't he be excited? Why was he staring out at the dark street as if he were searching for something, or someone? Why did he look sad and anxious?

Maybe he hoped—even believed with all his heart—that his dad would come by.

Cursing the jerk, Reed found himself doing something really stupid. He was climbing the steps to her front porch, lifting his hand to ring the bell. *This isn't any time to drop in on someone,* he told himself, and pushed the button anyway. For Ted's sake.

Reed heard an explosion of movement inside, as if a pack of dogs were racing for the front door. On reflex he stepped back, just as the door was flung open. No rabid German shepherds. All that appeared in the opening was one small boy, whose face lit when he saw Reed.

"You came!" he cried.

"Ted? Did you answer that?" his mother called sharply. "Who is it?"

Reed looked over her son's head at Meghan, hurrying from somewhere deeper in the house, wearing leggings and a fuzzy purple turtleneck sweater that came to midthigh. Her hair shone and her cheeks were flushed; on one hand she wore a padded mitt as if she'd been taking a hot dish from the oven. He was vaguely aware that something delicious was cooking, the aroma mixed with the Christmasy scents of fir and holly and spice.

He just stood there on her doorstep and waited, the space in his chest where his heart should have beat feeling...not right. Or maybe right. He didn't know. A huge knot had formed inside, unbearably tight.

God help him, he was terrified.

When she saw him, Meghan stopped. Completely still for a moment, she searched his face. At last her tongue touched her lips and she took a deep breath, crossing the last few steps to the door.

"You're here just in time for dinner," she said simply, and held out her hand.

The knot loosened, just a strand or two eased by relief. "You're sure?" he asked, not letting himself step across the doorjamb.

Her smile was sweet. "I'm sure."

"Yeah!" Ted grabbed his hand and tugged. "We've been waiting and waiting."

Letting himself be pulled forward, Reed looked at her again, brows lifted.

Meghan half laughed. "He kept saying you'd come. He was absolutely positive."

"He wasn't waiting for, uh, his own...?"

She shook her head. "Nope. For you."

The knot loosened further. He could breathe again. He lifted Ted, slung him over his shoulder, and closed the distance that separated him from Meghan. Her head lifted naturally, as if she too had been waiting, when he bent to touch his mouth to hers.

The merest brush of lips, and his heart beat again. This kiss was a promise and a hope, gift enough for him this Christmas Eve.

Stepping back, she laughed at him. "You're losing my son."

With a grin, Reed swung the boy back to his feet, lightly cuffed him on the back, and said, "So, you missed me, huh?"

"Yeah!" Ted said again, in that gruff voice, vulnerability on his upturned face. "Did you miss me and Mom?"

Reed smiled at the boy, then at his mother. "You could say that."

"How come you took so long to get here?"

"Sergeant McCall is always busy being a police officer," Meghan reminded her son, letting Reed off the hook. She hesitated. "Did you catch Nick?"

Reed shook his head. "I don't know how he did it, but he vanished into thin air. We can't even figure out who he was or when or where his wife died. If I didn't know better, I'd say we made him up."

"I'm...almost relieved," Meghan admitted. "I felt sorry for him, even though I was scared."

Ted tugged at Reed's hand again. "That man with the gun? *I* think he looked like Santa Claus. Lots more like Santa Claus than you do. I think he was trying to give me my wish.''

Meghan opened her mouth as if to say something, then closed it. Reed sure as hell couldn't think of a rebuttal. Their eyes met and held, communicating plenty they couldn't say in front of a five-year-old.

Their kidnapper was a lunatic. Of course he wasn't Santa Claus.

But it did seem as if crazy St. Nick had given them all their wishes.

Even the ones they'd been too dense to make. That *he'd* been too dense to make, Reed admitted to himself.

All he knew was, he'd never been luckier than when a little boy had sat on his lap and said, ''What I want for Christmas is a new father,'' or when a lunatic chose to throw three lonely people together for one miraculous night.

Epiphany
Margot Early

Dear Reader,

One of the gifts of a positive love relationship is that it broadens the world of each person involved, causing each to become bigger, better and stronger. Chris Good Rider's and Carmen Dinesen's horizons begin to stretch from the time they meet. Like many people, Carmen never felt accepted by her parents and believed she had to adopt a false persona to meet their approval. Chris encourages her to be herself.

Epiphany means "appearance." This Christmas, love appears to Chris and Carmen and Carmen's little sister, Bizzy. Love brings no one security, but it brings both Chris and Carmen courage and wisdom, the courage to live each day fully, to look farther and reach higher, and the wisdom to enjoy every moment of happiness to its fullest, without the cloud of fear.

My Christmas gift to you is *Epiphany*—and every wish for peace, joy and love for you and yours.

Sincerely,

Margot Early

CHAPTER ONE

Thanksgiving Friday

BIZZY DINESEN LIVED in a silent world, and her name
sign was the sign for B rocked smoothly over the
mouth. She was twelve years old. She saw more than
other children her age—and less, because her eyes
were so often on people, reading speech or signs. Her
language was visual; all her senses were exceptionally
strong, except the one she lacked.

And she wanted a horse of her own.

She wanted to adopt a mustang from the Bureau of
Land Management's Adopt a Wild Horse Program.

For Christmas.

Every time Carmen saw her sister's eyes—the clear
turquoise of the stone of that name—tearful over this
impossible issue, she felt helpless. They lived in Santa
Cruz, in a rented apartment, and Carmen could not
afford to keep any horse, let alone a wild horse for
her little sister to gentle. She ran the treadmill of
someone trying to get by.

So, as pitiful substitute for Bizzy's having a horse
of her own, here they were *again* in a private equestrian ring near the university, with front row seats for

Montana Blackfeet Chris Good Rider's demonstration
of Plains Indian Horsemanship and Wild Horse Awareness Handling.

Beside them, two women discussed one of Chris's
bestselling books, *Wild Horse Sense*. Carmen didn't
bother to listen. She had paged through Bizzy's au-
tographed Chris Good Rider books, mostly to enjoy
the pictures with her sister. Her only interest in horses
was for Bizzy's sake. The friendship she and Bizzy
had developed with Chris over the past two years was
for the same reason.

Bizzy never cared that she couldn't hear Chris,
couldn't watch him and watch Carmen interpret at the
same time. It had become moot because even though
recording equipment wasn't allowed at the mustang
presentation, Carmen had received the usual okay
from Chris. By now, he always made an exception
for his young Deaf friend and her older sister, so that
Carmen could sign his words to Bizzy later.

It had also become a tradition for Bizzy to ride his
horse in the ring after the presentation, while Chris
and Carmen had long, deep conversations; afterward
all three would shoot baskets behind the barn and eat
dinner at their favorite Thai restaurant. And although
Chris Good Rider was a long way from fluent in
American Sign Language, he'd learned many of the
master signs. Bizzy had given him a name sign,
pinching a lock of hair near the back of her head, for
the feathers he wore in his hair at demonstrations.

So Carmen didn't mind him. As hearing people

went, as hearing *men* went, he was…nice. And interesting.

From the time she was small, Carmen had known two worlds and two languages. Her first language had not been the language of sound but the language of eyes and of faces and of emotion—and of signs. Spoken language had eventually followed. She was a *CODA,* a hearing child of Deaf adults.

Capital "D" Deaf. Lowercase "D" deaf could mean someone whose hearing was nonfunctional for ordinary life, someone who maybe didn't sign—well, it could mean a lot of things. Just as VERY-HARD-OF-HEARING could mean someone with a hearing impairment who struggled to live on the same terms as hearing people—instead of becoming culturally Deaf and choosing to live among the Deaf and communicate mostly in sign.

Carmen anticipated no pleasure from the presentation today—although Chris was, of course, a pleasure. Attending Chris's workshops with Bizzy always reminded Carmen of what she couldn't do for her sister. Carmen was an interpreter and taught at the Santa Cruz School for the Deaf, where her parents had taught until their deaths and where Bizzy went to school—but there was still tuition to pay. Riding lessons and Chris's presentations were the closest she could come to making horse dreams come true. Time with Chris was always bliss for Bizzy.

And it was *for* Bizzy.

That was obviously his only interest. Giving time to a good cause.

A year and a half had passed since Carmen had realized how she felt about Chris—and that her feelings were pointless. Her first instinct had been to avoid him. For a few reasons.

But that would have been selfish. Here was this wild horse expert, and he'd gone out of his way to befriend Bizzy. What was more, he kept learning more signs and thought signing was fun.

Beside her, Bizzy sat on the edge of her seat as Chris entered the ring with his mustang, Looks Up. His hair was long and loose—straight, black Indian hair. Carmen supposed his looks didn't hurt the popularity of his books or his training methods. One of Carmen's Deaf friends, who'd come to a presentation with them once, had thought he looked like the Native American actor Michael Greyeyes.

He looks as good, anyhow, Carmen reflected.

He wore his usual publicity clothes, which he insisted were his favorite and most comfortable clothes—a knee-length dark-brown deerskin shirt and deerskin leggings and moccasins. Porcupine quills, bells and beads. He'd painted Looks Up, his red bay splashed-white pinto, and feathers dangled against the mustang's mane and tail.

Wired to a microphone, Chris greeted everyone with a Blackfeet phrase, and added, "I said, 'Hello, all my relatives.' Because we are all related. I'm Chris, and this is my relative Looks Up." The pinto.

Carmen had heard this introduction so many times she could have given it herself. She checked to see that the tape recorder was going.

"Looks Up was wild when we met, and he'll always be wild. I'm domesticated. But this horse and I are related, and what we do is look and listen to each other's language." He picked Bizzy out of the crowd with his eyes and smiled right at her.

Bizzy beamed at Chris, her eyes glistening.

Carmen gritted her teeth and smiled. She should have stopped this friendship long ago. Then maybe Bizzy wouldn't want a *mustang* of her own.

Okay, she wasn't thinking about his friendship with Bizzy. Chris was…interesting.

Yes.

For a hearing guy.

Her own hearing was perfect, but that was irrelevant.

"See, Looks Up and I know each other's language, and I've shown him this microphone. He hears my voice coming through it, and he has no reason to fear it. You don't want to give a horse a reason to fear anything. Think about it. Do you like to be afraid?"

Fear, Carmen believed, was good when it aided survival. In surfing, for instance. But when she'd realized she was falling in love with a really hot Indian who was someone else's boyfriend, she'd also become afraid.

And that wasn't a life-and-death situation.

Loving Chris was intoxicating…distressing…bleak. Yet it was a lesson. She was in love with someone who was indifferent to her, and she was not dying from it. Instead, she was—well, *resigned* to the situation.

''Mustangs can make good saddle horses, and you won't find a healthier horse. In the wild, they breed for survival. Out there, if you're not healthy, you die. Today, Looks Up and I will show you how wild horses can be gentled. When you leave here, you can speak with a representative from the BLM and learn more about adopting mustangs.''

Carmen was sure she knew everything there was to know about adopting a wild horse—except how to get the means to do it.

She wondered, idly, if there was an organ she could sell. What about a kidney? Was it legal to sell your own body parts?

When Chris turned away to face another part of the audience, Bizzy tapped Carmen's shoulder.

Carmen began interpreting, focusing on Bizzy, finding the right pictures to reach the essence conveyed in a familiar voice talking vigilant gentleness, a oneness with another that became mastery.

But then Bizzy touched Carmen's hand. She wanted to watch Chris again.

Carmen returned to the organ-donor idea. What about hair? She didn't have *lots*—it ended a few inches past her shoulders, and it was straight but *thick*. Everyone thought it was a great color, like a mouse who'd spent a lot of time in the sun and salt water.

Okay, forget that idea. What about…

No. Forget moving to Big Sky Country. Here in Santa Cruz, Bizzy had a good school for the Deaf, and a Deaf community. It was a community to which Carmen would never belong but one in which she was embraced as a welcome guest. It was a world she understood. Someday, Bizzy would probably marry a Deaf man. Bizzy's friends were Deaf; she had no friends who weren't.

Carmen made a point of having only friends who were Deaf or could surf—not on the Internet—or both. In high school she'd virtually lived on a surfboard and at the beach.

Chris Good Rider couldn't even swim.

Carmen liked surfers because they never seemed to judge her. None had ever told her she idolized the Deaf, and none ever seemed to think it curious that her fingers sometimes moved even when she was talking, like Bizzy's did when she spoke. Like a Deaf person's would. Carmen didn't *mean* to do it. She'd been raised almost as though she were Deaf.

Almost.

Just enough to make her wish, too often, that she was.

The Deaf should be held in a certain awe. To her, they seemed to have a precious power. It wasn't silence. It wasn't sign language. It was something Carmen had spent two decades of her life coveting. It was solidarity in a human experience—in the experience of seldom or never being able to hear and understand the speech of other humans. A world that hearing people, including herself, could not fully understand. As a child, she'd imagined that someday she would be Deaf and had cried when she learned she never would be. That her parents would never truly understand her—nor she them and their DEAF-

WORLD. That she would always be different from what they wanted because she would never be like them.

It had been a dismal revelation. All its repercussions still made her angry and sad. Her parents had died in a single year when she was nineteen. Ever since, her life had been centered on raising her sister, the Deaf child they'd really wanted.

She knew it was foolish and she'd talked to counselors about it, but Carmen still occasionally felt there was something wrong with her because she could hear, that she would be a more valuable person if she could not.

That Bizzy was her parents' favorite had never stopped Carmen from loving her furiously. Which was why now, eight years after their deaths, she was trying to make up for Bizzy's not getting a horse for Christmas.

An evergreen studded with lights had decorated the entrance to the equestrian center. Wreaths and red bows spotted the riding ring.

To Carmen, Christmas was a time for granting Bizzy's wishes. It seemed ages since she'd wanted—or dreamed of having—anything for herself. Except to keep what she had. That, she wanted very much.

The presentation lasted an hour and a half.

At the end, fans swarmed down for autographs, and Chris said into the microphone, ''Looks Up and I are glad to sign your programs if you'll give us just a few minutes.''

Carmen touched Bizzy's shoulder. They would have lots of time with Chris later, when they went out to the Thai restaurant.

But Bizzy still gazed straight ahead, tight white-blond curls sprayed over the hood of her sweatshirt.

Chris had come over to the railing, and Bizzy jumped up to hug him. He smiled as he held her, and Carmen reflected again, from the safe comfort of distant and absolutely unrequited love, that he was handsome. Strong cheekbones, eyes that were almost black, curiously like her own in color, and a perfect bow mouth. She knew the look of his mouth well. All his features. Her business was watching faces. Hands…hands she simply saw—but faces she watched, because signs only became language when facial expressions were attached.

After a moment, Chris held Bizzy away from himself. "Want to stay and ride Looks Up?"

The usual question. Dependable as the sun's rising.

What if someday he *didn't* offer?

The question clearly hadn't occurred to Bizzy. She spoke in the low, slow precise way she'd learned at the Santa Cruz School for the Deaf. "Thank you." She turned to grin at her sister.

Brat, Carmen thought happily.

Chris hugged Bizzy once more, meeting Carmen's gaze over the curly blond head.

It wasn't a usual Chris look.

No, she'd imagined it.

Naturally, she, like Bizzy, had given Chris many of the long hugs goodbye that were usual among the

Deaf and always seemed uncomfortable with hearing people.

Except this hearing man.

He said, "Hello, Carmen."

Perfectly normal.

Her voice croaked when she answered.

That was probably normal, too, and her fragile mind would again develop selective amnesia about the incident.

He released Bizzy, gave the twelve-year-old an extra hug, and turned to the line of autograph-seekers.

Bizzy gazed after him, then looked at Carmen. Her eyebrows, the tilt of her head, the pace and movement of her hands, spoke to her sister. Pointing to Chris. *NICE.*

Yes.

WHILE WORKERS CLEANED the empty rows, Bizzy rode Looks Up, the red-and-white pinto, around the ring.

Carmen leaned against the edge of the ring, her nostrils full of the smell of horses. Beside her, Chris smelled like some kind of smoke, maybe sage. Up close, his shirt was exquisite, the sleeves decorated with porcupine quills, the chest beaded in black and white. It was a kind of relief—and also a venture into another world, the hearing world—to stop watching for signs, to read Chris's clothing, to study something so external.

She said, "Bizzy wants her own horse. For Christmas."

He made a movement with his mouth that she recognized and had never been able to read. A look that told her he wanted to conceal his thoughts and feelings. It reminded her that he was Hearing. He did not wear his emotions.

It made her accentuate hers, or at least her frustration that Bizzy wanted a BLM mustang. Not the other kinds of frustration. "Let's see. A small enclosure and a gentling pen... Feed. Vet bills..." She let her face show helplessness. Annoyance—at him.

But he was watching Bizzy and strode across the ring to correct something.

She sighed.

Any way she looked at it, unrequited love had nothing to recommend it.

He returned to Carmen. "Ever thought of leaving Santa Cruz?"

"Definitely not. My work is here, and I faint if I can't smell the ocean. Why? Are you going to suggest I move to Nevada or Wyoming and educate the very hard of hearing?" She grimaced. "Yes, I've thought of leaving Santa Cruz. It's a bad idea." By now, he ought to know why, but the guy could hear and couldn't surf. What did she expect?

She repeated things she'd already told him, speaking about the DEAF-WORLD. Explaining. Describing a people self-isolated and unified by a common trait.

Cautious, she studied his profile while he watched Bizzy. He made a motion with his hands, and Bizzy understood. She nudged the Pinto to a lope.

In a minute, he would tell Carmen he'd grown up poor but had always had horses. Then he would say he guessed that wasn't really true, which it absolutely wasn't. His father was a rancher who now leased out his acres for other men's cattle and raised horses for fun.

But his mother lived on the reservation.

He said, "You have a boyfriend?"

"Are you changing the subject?"

"Actually not."

She had poise. In spades, truly. She surfed goofy-foot in triple overhead. Her eyes snapped at him. "I faint when I can't smell the ocean," she repeated.

"You'll get over it."

Oh, man.

Yes.

Yes, she would. But this wasn't the typical course of their conversations. "What do you mean?"

"What would you say to marrying a guy who'd make it possible for your sister to have a horse? A wild horse? And you'd never have to work again."

Carmen choked. Coughed.

The horse snuffled as Bizzy slowed him to a trot.

"I know," Chris validated her dismay. "It's a shock. But at least he's rich."

Undoubtedly. Books, presentations all over the country, a public television documentary…

"A lot of women marry older men."

Older? Carmen grew uneasy.

"And he was just—" a shrug "—seventeen when I was born."

She blinked. Slowly.

He was chewing on his lip. "What do you think?"

I think I'm going to die. Not only did he not want her for himself. He wanted to hand her over to his father?

He smiled suddenly.

"What?" She could hardly speak.

"You passed. I wanted to see— Never mind. Want to marry me?"

Now she was really going to throw up. "Don't do that to people!"

He laughed. "I know you'll say yes. You love my long hair. Admit it."

"Shut up!"

"It's nice to hear you yell. Sometimes I forget you have a voice. Worse, *you* forget."

Aloofness and cynicism were her shields against the world to which she'd been assigned by birth. Only with friends did they disappear. She remembered, then, that he was a friend and that friends were good. She threw her arms around his neck and held on, because sometimes he hugged as long as a Deaf person. Because sometimes he was unutterably, wonderfully *real*. Even as she hugged him, she said, "I know you don't love me, and it doesn't matter. I'll love you just as much anyhow."

His arms were holding her too lightly, as though some energy had drained from them since the last time they'd embraced, months before.

She stilled, sensing the difference.

They separated, though he still held her arms. "It

isn't for love, Carmen. Not that I don't think we can love each other. My father has given me a year to marry. If I do, he'll give me the ranch. If I don't, he's handing it over to an oil company for exploration and drilling.''

Perspiration beaded her face. The love-hate way Chris usually spoke about his father now made sense. Mr. Good Rider, Sr. was not above strange and archaic forms of parental pressure. ''Well. No pun intended. That's a whole year.'' Really, it wasn't so bad. She would still love him, he still wouldn't love her, and she would get to be with him always. It would be great.

''The year started in December.''

Looks Up's hooves struck the soft ground.

''Last December,'' he added. ''Christmas Day.''

Carmen squeezed her eyebrows together and tilted her head forward as she said, ''You didn't ask what's-her-name.'' Carmen remembered the name—*Renée*—perfectly but chose not to use it. ''Why?'' She became aware that her fingers, at her sides, were moving as she spoke, signing, and she remembered that hearing people found it strange.

The first time she'd seen Chris notice, he'd just smiled at her, as though he understood her better than she knew.

Maybe better than she understood herself.

Now, he didn't seem to see.

''We broke up a year ago.''

''You said she didn't mind our having dinner together.''

"Mmm. So. Yes?"

Carmen hugged herself, protecting herself. He could have offered this to many other women. Beautiful women. Rich and famous women.

He was asking her.

It would make possible something she wanted. Truly wanted. In a very real way.

A horse for Bizzy.

But it was insane! For all that she'd thrown her arms around his neck...

The veil dropped, and the picture cleared.

When she'd embraced him, she'd still believed he might love her.

He did say we can love each other.

"No."

He sighed and shut his eyes. "We only have to make it last two years."

She did groan then.

"And you *do* love me. Don't you?"

Did he care? For a moment, she wondered if maybe he did.

But he glanced at a lock of his own hair and said, "You run your fingers through it when we hug."

"I'm affectionate!"

"No. You're crazy. You wish you were deaf. I don't know anyone else who's even thought for a second they'd like to be deaf."

Her expression transformed to irony. "You must love the sound of your own voice, saying things like, 'Please marry me. If you do, my father will give me his ranch.'"

He paled slightly, although he stood straight and warrior-like as ever. Crazy Horse must have looked like this man, she thought. But acted lots better.

"At least you didn't lie," she murmured, almost to herself.

He was quiet so long that she turned to watch Bizzy. She wanted to weep. She hadn't brought *this* on herself. Unrequited love, yes, she'd invented the concept, but not this.

She felt...devalued. And wasn't sure why. "Chris, you can't marry someone you don't love and expect to fall in love with her. That's a joke."

"I didn't say I don't love you."

She waited for him to say he did.

"Bizzy wants a horse. What do *you* want for Christmas?" he asked.

She smiled. "Your heart. I will cut it from your chest and eat it."

He looked interested. And a little dangerous.

Carmen slid along the railing of the ring and away from him.

Bizzy was watching them expectantly, and Chris gave her some nonverbal direction that seemed individual to the two of them. She nudged Looks Up, and the mustang broke into a trot.

Chris put back his head and gazed up at the rafters high above, as though they held the answer to some burning question. Looking at her again, he said, "Okay. I like you. I like you a lot. I think you know that."

Friend, not-friend, Bizzy's friend... He wasn't stu-

pid, and her ambivalence no longer played. Carmen
watched a piece of straw half-buried in the loose
earth, half-expecting it to move. "I know you have a
girlfriend. Or did. That's what I know." And thinking
that Chris didn't like her, Carmen, had been better
than thinking he did and was spoken for and yet continued to take her and Bizzy out to dinner. Because
if she admitted the truth, she'd have to admit he
wasn't marriage material and tell him to get lost. But
none of it was true. He'd broken up with his girlfriend
a year before. What had happened? *Was it because
he likes me?* "You acted like a *friend*. And
now…this."

He started to smile again. "I'll still be your friend.
Even though you want more."

She ignored that. "Why did you break up?"

"Infidelity. Hers." Cold now.

Bizzy rode past again.

"Carmen, I don't *want* to marry anyone. I don't
think I can do it. Marriage is a failing proposition.
For me, anyhow."

"I'm so flattered you thought to include me in your
personal disaster."

"It's not funny."

"Am I laughing? I've never been so insulted in my
life." She thought of her parents. Their rejection
didn't count; it had been too grave, too hopeless and
too sad. No, this was the Great Insult. "You want to
marry me for two years so your father will give you
his ranch. Next you're going to tell me we have to
have a child to fulfill some other dictate of his."

"Fortunately not."

She walked into the ring and stood waiting for Bizzy to come around again.

"Carmen."

"I'm taking my sister and going home. Thank you very much for the good food and all the time we've spent with you up until today."

"I'd *like* to have a child with you."

"I'm sorry."

Bizzy slowed Looks Up.

Chris glanced up at her on his horse and said, "Your sister and I are getting married. Do you think it's a good idea?"

"IT'S BEAUTIFUL," he said over pad Thai, "and stretches between the reservation and the Sweet Grass Hills. They're sacred. The name is translated wrong. The Piegan—" it sounded like "pagan" "—means Sweet Pine Mountains. But it doesn't matter. My father's ranch reaches them, touches them. We, the Piegan, the Blackfeet, have vision quests there. It also touches the Badger-Two Medicine Mountains area, the last stronghold for the practice of our religion."

Bizzy was squinting, speech-reading. *Good,* thought Carmen. Too much finger-spelling. *I can't marry him. He can't sign.*

Sure, he was learning. But fluency took years.

In his truck on the way to the restaurant, she'd told him she wasn't going to marry him. It was, she thought angrily, the first time she'd ever spoken in front of Bizzy and deliberately hidden the fact, turning her head to look out the window as she uttered the words. Another reason not to join Chris in his stupid, near-sighted scheme.

"I will make the ranch a place for Blackfeet families," he said now. "So people commit not to drink and then they learn about their fear. They learn from being with horses, because horses are prey animals. People are predators. If they learn to be with horses, they can learn to be with each other."

Carmen felt the single toll of a bell inside her. This mattered to him for reasons he'd never told her. Saying no suddenly seemed complicated.

And selfish.

Bizzy said with perfect diction, looking at each of them and both of them, "When are we moving to Montana?"

"I CAN'T BELIEVE YOU SAID THAT to her!" She shoved open the sliding door to the balcony of her apartment. She could hear the ocean. Bizzy had gone to bed. "How can I tell her I'm actually *not* going to marry you and we're not moving to Montana?"

"I'm a desperate man."

"You're too conceited to ever be desperate."

He was good at not looking hurt. She wondered if he'd had practice, like she had.

"I have a life here, you know," she said, as though he'd suggested she didn't. "I have work. I have relationships with people." Her tongue tangled over that one.

"With Deaf people," he said. "Do you ever sing?"

"What?"

He sang softly, *"Good King Wenceslas looked out/ on the feast of Stephen..."*

She frowned.

"Or dance?" he asked.

"Sometimes."

"Play musical instruments?"

She sighed, silently, the way she'd learned to sigh.

"Carmen, you can hear. Bizzy can't, but you can. And Bizzy can do a whole lot of things—including have relationships with people who aren't deaf."

"You don't understand."

"What I don't get—" He sat on her couch and seemed surprised it was so comfortable.

"Don't even think about it. You're not sleeping here."

"—is why you won't ride my horse."

"You know why."

He gave one nod and seemed to detach from her.

In fact, he was thinking about her. Carmen's mother had died on a horse. They'd been on a trail ride, together; her mother was inexperienced, while Carmen had taken lessons and helped at the university stables since she was small. Carmen and her father had decided not to tell Bizzy how her mom had died.

"Look, Chris, when people become—more than friends—they change. I don't want you to change. But you'll want me to change, and I don't want to."

"I might want you to sing me some love songs.

Shall I sing to you?'' He started singing—in the language of the Blackfeet.

Like the ocean. A sound she wouldn't have known if she'd been born Deaf.

''There's no ocean in Montana,'' she broke in. ''I've always lived by the ocean.''

''I'll let you ride one of my horses.''

''Thank you for small favors! You said Bizzy could have one.''

His eyes showed he'd discovered something about her.

She felt the guilt; she did want to ride.

He probably understood all of that, too. He knew her pretty well.

''Come sit down with me. We can make out. Maybe you'll like it.''

''Leave. Now.''

He stood. ''I'll be back in the morning.''

There was no lingering embrace. Neither of them smiled.

When he'd left, she sat out on the balcony with a beach towel over her jeans and her bare feet and listened to the waves and imagined she was surfing— and never living by the ocean again.

THE NEXT MORNING, he came to the beach with her and Bizzy. While Carmen surfed, Chris sat in the sand with her sister. Even in jeans and a hooded sweatshirt, he felt out of place. He and Carmen lived in different worlds. The only reason he'd asked her to marry him was that he'd found he didn't want to ask anyone else. Couldn't imagine *wanting* to ask anyone else.

When she fell in the low waves and came walking through the water in her wetsuit, tugging her board like a bad dog behind her, he got up and walked through the sand and into the wet sand and the foam, until the water stuck his jeans to his legs. He told her he'd asked her to marry him because he didn't want anyone else and didn't think he ever would.

''The words are, 'I love you.' In sign language, this is how you do it. Try it.'' She splashed past him.

He said, ''Thank you.''

THE NEXT AFTERNOON, after Bizzy was through at school and Carmen at work, they all went to the courthouse. There were no rings, just paper, vows and a kiss that didn't last a moment more than the occasion demanded.

He took the bigger belongings she and Bizzy wanted to move and left for Montana with Looks Up.

He did not kiss Carmen again.

When he'd gone, Bizzy looked and signed, YOU MARRY CHRIS, WHY? ME. MUSTANG. THANK YOU.

Carmen shook her head and said with signs that she and Chris were in love.

She couldn't face why she hadn't used speech.

Only that she'd had a lot of practice lying in her parents' language.

CHAPTER TWO

December

MOUNTAINS, HILLS, trees, rivers and snow. So much snow, glittering, reflecting a million blinding suns. Carmen leaned around Bizzy, her own straight walnut-colored hair blending with her sister's foamy white curls, and stared through the aircraft window until finally a city—almost a city, anyhow—came into view and then the airstrip.

The plane touched ground.

The air over the tarmac was colder than she'd imagined air got.

Chris was inside the terminal, in a faded denim sheepskin-lined jacket, Levi's and basketball shoes—*not* Sorel boots like those she'd bought for her and Bizzy, at his suggestion. In fact, he looked no more prosperous than any other Indian in the terminal.

He looked cold.

He also looked gorgeous.

And he was her husband.

No. Not really.

Nor was she his wife. But she was the only woman

he'd been able to imagine marrying at the time they got married.

It was probably a better start than a lot of couples had.

Bizzy walked up to him and hugged him.

Carmen tapped her on the shoulder. "Do you need to use the bathroom before we drive to the ranch?"

Bizzy blinked at her, started to open her lips and sign NO, then stopped. She looked for the rest-room signs, and Carmen pointed them out.

When her sister had gone, Carmen found she couldn't ask the question that was on her mind. The answer was obvious. Or would have been if he'd even kissed her goodbye. "Where do we get our bags?"

Suddenly he was hugging her. "I'm glad you're here." Squeezing her tighter with strong arms.

Her eyes grew moist.

He liked her.

"I'm glad I'm here."

They were still holding each other when Bizzy came out of the bathroom, and when she tapped Carmen's shoulder they both pulled her into their embrace as though she was the only and most important thing in their lives.

THE LANDSCAPE WAS WIDE and clean, the roadside edged in barbed wire, everything snow-covered, plains folding into expansive rolling hills, trees, distant mountains.

"Those hills ahead—they're the westernmost range of the Sweet Grass Hills."

"Are you in a hurry?"

"It's a big state. People drive fast."

What people there were. I-15 north of Shelby was nothing like any freeway she'd ever been on. Just land and every once in a while a ranch house or a place that sold animal feed or extremely large farm equipment.

The space and the enormous sky were terrifying and peaceful all at once.

She and Bizzy sat beside Chris in the front seat of his dual-cab pickup. He glanced past Bizzy at Carmen, then smiled.

"What?" Carmen asked, simultaneously signing the word for Bizzy.

"You haven't fainted."

Bizzy fell into rapid sign. FAINT YOU, WHY?

"The ocean." Her breath felt shallow. The air was too thin and dry.

Bizzy took her hand and held it, but Carmen pulled her fingers loose and hugged her sister. Soon, briefly, a male hand held the back of her head, fingering hair against her scalp and neck. Only after a moment, when his hand drew back to the steering wheel, did she turn to Bizzy and sign something else she couldn't speak. That everything that mattered to her was right there in the truck.

THE GREAT LOG RANCH HOUSE seemed more like a mansion than a home. A green Humvee sat in front of one bay of a three-car garage. Snow draped the roof and the lodgepole fences.

"How the other half lives?" Chris murmured. Two heelers, one blue, one red, barked steam at the newcomers. Chris spoke sharply in Blackfeet and then introduced them, signing their names for Bizzy, using the hand-sign for each word. How could he stand not wearing gloves? "Blue. And Red."

Signing and speaking at the same time—even two words—was hard for beginners. He'd practiced.

Carmen's reply, whole sentences in simultaneous sign and speech, in gloves suitable for Mount Everest, was much more difficult. "Are they your dogs?" Her lips were numb.

"No. I haven't had a dog since I was sixteen."

Which was six years after his parents divorced. Carmen remembered that—and how aloof he became when he spoke of it. Like now. The dog story would be bad. "Was this ranch in your dad's family?" *And can we go inside?*

"Old property. New house. The other one's over that way." He nodded. "It's falling down."

Wondering if her nose was going to turn black and fall off, she measured the exterior of the massive log house. "I'm not doing the windows. That'll be your job."

He laughed. "Okay." A basketball hoop hung above the door of the center garage bay. All snow and ice had been swept from beneath it. With the toe of his shoe, Chris kicked a basketball from behind a planter and into his hands. He dribbled once and sank a basket.

Bizzy rebounded with *her* Mount Everest gloves and passed to Carmen.

He was always too tall for them, and he was good, but they were quick. Bizzy, who played with no sound cues but the vibrations in the ground, from the ball or another player's signaling foot taps, had eyes that were everywhere at once. Carmen knew she felt the ball like a heartbeat. Like a drum.

She concentrated on the ball, on sinking baskets, on this spontaneous half-court game, and soon warmth crept through her limbs and even to her fingers and toes. What she'd wanted to ask him in the airport occurred to her again. Were they going to sleep together? That night? Gazing up at a huge window pane reflecting sky and clouds, she missed the ball.

He caught it. "Dreamer."

No, *he* was. With his place for Blackfeet families to stay and heal—with horses. From alcoholism. "Is there an alcoholic in your family?" she asked.

"Three."

Bizzy watched the exchange with interest while Carmen counted family members. His mom who lived on the reservation, his dad who lived here, and Chris.

He shot a basket, and this time nobody rebounded. "Horses can heal individuals—they saved me—and my dad. And individuals can heal families. Also we can save more horses with adoption. Some people think there are too many. So the BLM destroys them. Sometimes. There's a holding pen near here and a reserve near Crow Agency."

He'd told her there were Deaf people on the reservation; he knew one girl who had no language.

"Do you think you might—" Carmen stopped. "I need to go to the college and to Bizzy's school." Bizzy would start in January. "To see about teaching."

"Yes." He wasn't replying to what she'd said but to what she hadn't. She wanted to start classes for the Deaf population. On the ranch. He looked into her eyes. "We'll be able to organize things in the new year. Everything we want."

Bizzy spoke. "Looks Up. Where is he?"

"Waiting to see you. Let's take your bags in, and then we'll go to the barn and make him a happy horse."

Reading his lips, Bizzy smiled and signed happiness.

Carmen asked, "Is your father home?"

Chris nodded to the Humvee, then glanced up. At one of the balconies stood a tall man, stout-bellied, black hair faintly streaked with gray and worn in one long braid. His cheekbones were broad, his straight nose echoed in his son's. Chris's father came to the lodgepole rail and looked down at them, his smile warm. "*Oki, niksokowa.* I'm Floyd."

"I'm Carmen." She signed, "This is my sister Bizzy. Bizzy is Deaf."

From high above them, the big, heavy warrior man made the signs for *Hello, Carmen,* using a C for Carmen's name sign, and *Hello, Bizzy,* using a B for Bizzy's.

"That's good," Bizzy told him.

"You talk well. Better than me." He winked.

Snow puffed on the hill that separated the house from the highway, and Carmen turned to watch the vehicle approach. It was a red Land Rover.

Floyd said, "I was wondering when she'd be back. Went into town."

Chris picked up Carmen and Bizzy's bags to take them inside. Over his features lay a placid contempt. For his father?

Floyd moved silently away from the balcony rail.

Carmen tried to take her backpack, but Chris got it first. "He's Blackfeet?" she asked. "Your dad?"

He set down the bags. HALF. Right index finger sliding across the midpoint of the left. Prepared for the question.

She raised her eyebrows. MOTHER?

"Blackfeet."

Bizzy showed him the name sign she'd made for the tribe, so they were still standing there when the Land Rover pulled into the driveway and the driver turned off the engine and got out. She was a pretty Native American, probably a little older than Chris. He was thirty-one, three and a half years older than Carmen. The woman wore small, wire-rimmed glasses. Her hair was twisted into a knot that lay against the fur-lined hood of her parka. "Hi. I'm Renée." She shifted her purse and held out her hand. "I'm Floyd's wife. I teach at the college."

Oh.

Oh.

Now, she *was* going to faint.

Ignoring his stepmother and former girlfriend, Chris turned to Bizzy. Tilting his head toward the house, he put his hand against his tilted head, then index and middle finger on each side of his nose, beneath his eyes and away. This was followed by two fingers together high on either side of his head, like a horse's ears. He pointed at Bizzy.

She had understood him, and she grinned. From her room, she could see horses.

Chris hardly noticed Renée's leaving and slipping into the house. The silent communication with Bizzy took all his attention. Sign language felt more economical than English or Blackfeet. He liked talking in pictures. And understanding that way.

He pointed to Bizzy, then made the unique spinning gesture that began as an open hand near the right side of the face, then spun downward.

Bizzy beamed, and Carmen managed to laugh, rubbing her chest at the same time. A finger to her lips and away to say, TRUE. Bizzy *was* beautiful.

And she was happy. For now. So Carmen would be happy, too, for the next few minutes, anyhow, even though Chris had lied to her. When he'd asked her to marry him and she'd asked about what's-her-name, this was the kind of information she should have received.

Chris gathered their bags again. The door was massive. The trees that had made the logs on each side of it had been gnawed by porcupines and scratched by bears. Why had Chris's father built a six-thousand-square-foot house? Often, when she saw a big new house, she wondered if the owner didn't know who he was and had tried to express himself with what was material—a pretty sad thing.

Floyd Good Rider should know who he was. He was the son of a rancher and had lived his whole life on this ranch.

Spitting distance from the reservation.

Maybe that gave him reason to wonder who he was.

Like me, Carmen thought, *hearing in a Deaf family.*

They left their shoes just inside the door. The entryway was vast, the ceilings great vaults rimmed by upper walkways with lodgepole railings. As her face began to tingle with restored blood flow, Carmen thought of the land outside, rolling hills with mountain views, 360-degree beauty. How many acres came with the house? . *Hundreds of thousands.* One didn't ask. Chris had told her that much back in Santa Cruz when she'd said she wouldn't know how to fit in if she moved to Montana. *Don't ask how many cows or acres. Besides that, follow the Golden Rule.*

Carmen paused beside a photograph of a man in a Blackfeet war bonnet.

"Steals-Horses-Many. My father's mother's father's father." He grinned at Bizzy, who was working out his speech and showing amusement at his signing father-mother-father-father. "The Good Riders will use his name again when the right child is born."

He said it without emotion, and Carmen wondered

why *he* hadn't been the right child. "So, is Good Rider your real name?"

"Ha, ha." Gently he grabbed her head as though to rub his knuckles on her scalp, an answer to her teasing. The touch became a caress instead, one both of them instantly broke. He nudged her toward the stairs.

As promised, Bizzy's room looked out on a paddock. At the window, Bizzy gestured and made an L sign. Looks Up.

Chris pointed out another horse to her, a strawberry roan mustang mare with red patches edging each side of her white face. Her legs, mane and tail were the same red, her coat faintly speckled like pale cinnamon ice cream. Chris very slowly finger-spelled the name. M-A-N-Y C-O-U-P-S. He touched spread fingers and palms to his chest, then drew them away in fists.

Brave.

A reasonable name sign, Carmen thought, for to count coup was to touch the enemy in battle, an act of courage.

"I want you to ride her," he told Bizzy.

Bizzy clasped her arms about herself. A moment later, she indicated another paddock, with two horses A black mustang stood alert at the far end, but Bizzy pointed at a black-and-white appaloosa gelding, nearly leopard-spotted, closer to her room. "What's his name?"

Again, Chris arduously spelled. C-R-E-E M-E-D-I-C-I-N-E. The bow of his mouth curving into something that even Carmen could only call completely charming, he pointed at her, made the shape of a bottle with his hands, pantomimed drinking from it, crossed his fists on his chest and pointed at himself.

A slight flush had appeared on his cheeks. He spelled to Bizzy, L-O-V-E P-O-T-I-O-N.

Grinning, she rubbed her chest, for laughter.

Chris motioned toward the appaloosa, shot his thumb as though launching a shooting star.

Fast.

And gave Carmen a rogue's look.

He showed Bizzy the ornate pine chest of drawers and the door to the vast walk-in closet. "Unpack. Relax. Then we'll ride. Okay?"

Smile.

He and Carmen walked alone down the hall to another room at the corner of the house. Doors opened onto balconies facing in two directions. Big bright windows.

"Different times of the year, you can watch the sun rise and set from this room."

Carmen heard the door click shut behind him.

This means, she thought, *he's going to do something.*

There was one bed, king-size. The headboard, canopy and all parts of the frame were made from twisted limbs and poles of pine, scarred by animals of the wild, who'd left their mark before the tree was cut. It was the most beautiful bed she'd ever seen.

She turned away to examine a daybed by a window facing southeast. It was large enough to sleep on and set in a dormer. Old-fashioned curtains trimmed in lace could be pulled down for privacy, both from the windows and the rest of the room.

She turned, and he was behind her.

"When I asked you about Renée, was it impossible to tell me, 'She married my father and lives at the ranch'?"

He hesitated. Contemplated her for a long time.

Before he'd suggested she marry him, he'd "tested" her reaction to the idea of marrying his father. Now she understood why. His girlfriend's decision to marry his father must have made many things look very different.

"Chris, why do *you* live here?"

"The horses."

It wasn't even a good lie. Carmen backed away.

"I'm adopted," he said. "I don't tell people. All right?"

He seemed certain she understood what he meant. Carmen didn't have a clue, although her life's work was clarifying the confusing and unclear. Making sure people, including her, were clear in expressing their thoughts and in interpreting what language others chose. "It is all right, and I'm glad you told me. I want to know everything about you. What does this have to do with your dad marrying your girlfriend?"

He kissed her. Not immediately but after a moment of looking as though there were no words for what he wanted to say. She'd seen her students look like that. Her hands found his shoulders, then touched his neck, under his hair. They kissed each other's mouths, jaws. Her throat, his hair.

She knew his want, and it was her.

As hers was him.

He said, "Want to live in a tipi? We have a few out toward the hills. Actually, I've been sleeping in one when I'm home."

Then living in the house with his father and Renée was a sacrifice—made for her and Bizzy. That made sense.

"Live in a tipi with Bizzy?"

"A couple of them are close together. She could have her own. I bet she'd like the idea."

"Okay." Too late, she remembered the cold outside. What if Bizzy froze to death? What if she did? "Will we be warm enough?"

"We won't die."

"Oh, good. Just like the guys on the *Endurance*."

"What's that? A TV show?" He was playing with her.

Carmen pushed aside the curtains and sat on the edge of the day-bed. "I'm going to sleep right here. Alone."

He came near and crouched before her. Close. Big.

Carmen couldn't keep her eyes from him. His nose was straight, neither big nor small. Beautiful and perfect. She let herself feel that he was an emotional mess for living with his father at all, let alone in these circumstances, that *he* should question his identity and that she'd made a terrible mistake.

He said, "I'm sorry. I should have told you about Renée."

She forgave him. He had some personal reason for being at this ranch, perhaps for clinging to his father.

With the thought, the reason became obvious.

He *looked* like his father.

She exhaled slowly.

Everyone must see exactly what she had. Including Chris.

Subterfuge wasn't a big part of her nature. "He's your natural father, isn't he?"

"No. We look alike, but it's coincidence."

Did he really believe that? No, Carmen decided with a glance at his face. He did not. "Does your dad have brothers or sisters?"

"Both." His smile became less patient.

She leaned forward and grabbed him around the neck.

"Watch that if you plan to sleep alone."

"I don't. Not anymore." He had ceased to be her unattainable and trouble-free friend Chris. She still saw the highly successful man but also the rejected son.

As she had been and was, in many ways, a rejected daughter.

He was going to be hers, and no one—not Renée or anyone, even Carmen herself—was going to interfere. She was going to make him hers.

She kissed him on the mouth.

Pulling her up with him, he stood.

Slowing her.

She rubbed his foot with hers. Wool sock on wool sock. It felt good. He felt good. If he wanted to live in a tipi, they would. If— "Bizzy likes her new room."

"She might like a tipi better. Come on. We'll ask her what she thinks."

HE MOTIONED to Bizzy to stay outside the paddock but let Carmen come in. Carmen hugged herself, backing against the rails, as he whistled to the horse they'd seen from upstairs. The black horse.

She watched the mustang come, long black mane flying in the sun, hooves kicking up snow. When his forelock flew back she saw a white star, the only spot of color in the nightness of him.

Chris held a halter and bridle, murmured to the horse as it neared, muscles rippling, breath turning to steam.

No saddle in sight.

She knew he did not intend to ride this horse.

But she would. The split reins were in her hands. She'd taken them from him without asking because she knew that this animal had come to her, had come to help her. To make many things all right.

She had not ridden since the day her mother died.

Carmen spoke to the horse, and his ears pricked, turning to the sound.

"He's three. I've had him since he was a yearling, but I just had him cut—" he let out a small breath "—recently. He still kind of thinks he's entitled to a harem. I can't blame him. I mean, look at him."

Carmen had eyes for nothing else. The black horse was wild and strong. She wanted to ride this beautiful creature with a mane longer than Chris's hair and a tail that dragged on the ground.

The gelding let her touch him. But his ears began to drop back, and she fell away. He watched her with one eye, then slowly relaxed.

Chris spoke to him in Blackfeet, then English. "Epiphany, this is my wife, Won't Listen."

Carmen glared at him and put her left hand on the horse's hump above his shoulder and her right hand in the middle of his back. He wasn't tall. Not much more than thirteen hands. And she was athletic. But when she glanced behind her, Chris sighed and clasped his hands into a step for her. He could mount an unsaddled horse from the ground.

Carmen accepted his hands.

Epiphany began to walk as Chris's boost and her surfing arms, paddling arms, basketball arms, took her onto the mustang. Her jeans slid against the horse's warm back, the only thing warm in the freezing day.

She imagined Chris spelling the gelding's name to Bizzy. Then he could try and explain what it meant. Besides the Wise Men's coming.

Epiphany chose a nervous trot, and she slowed him carefully. Before adoption, wild horses were virtually always gelded by the BLM—for easier handling and population control. Ephiphany obviously hadn't been. Why had Chris waited so long to have him cut? People bred wild mares; still she was pretty sure that owning a wild stallion was against BLM rules.

Where was Chris anyhow? She didn't feel comfortable enough on Epiphany to look. Was he asking Bizzy about living in a tipi?

He could probably talk Bizzy into jumping off a cliff.

The wind sucked out of her as she hit the snowy ground.

For a moment, she thought she was going to die as her mother had.

He pulled up beside her on Cree Medicine, his "love potion" appaloosa, and slid to the ground.

Two eagles soared overhead.

Chris followed her gaze. "I always wondered why humans couldn't get along like that. Mate for life. Build a nest. Feed and protect the babies. Teach them to fly."

Her head ringing, though it had never touched the ground, Carmen made herself stand.

"You all right?"

"How do I call him?" She raked the sleeve of her sheepskin-lined denim jacket across her eyes.

"You work that out between you. He's yours."

She blinked. Stared. "Really?"

"Wedding present."

Carmen gazed across the corral, where Epiphany had retreated, and pretended her body didn't hurt. Nor her heart.

She'd never called her mother "Mom" or even "Mother." Her mother was a letter K rocked gently across her chin, like Bizzy's B and Carmen's C.

Katherine Dinesen had been as blond as Bizzy. She was only forty-three when she died.

Chris mounted Cree Medicine again, from the ground, trotted across the ring and caught the black horse's reins.

A moment later, he handed them to Carmen. ''Cry if you want. He won't mind, and I'll come back and hug you.''

He rode away and left her to mount the black horse from the ground.

But she let her tears run—they were tears of pleasure at the fun she and her mother had been having for the hour before the accident happened, at the acceptance she had felt. At the incredible pleasure she felt now, because a wonderful, intelligent, fascinating man had given her a wild horse. A black stallion-nomore. The horse turned his head to stare at her. Carmen forgot he was wild and put her face in his mane, rubbing the hair against her skin.

He seemed to forget, too.

And to know he was hers.

''WHAT DO YOU THINK?'' Chris asked. He'd pulled up on Cree's reins beside the two tipis where he liked to write when he was working on a book and where he'd slept during last year on those nights he'd spent at his father's ranch.

Carmen eyed Bizzy.

Her sister rode with a borrowed saddle. Chris planned to give her one of her own for Christmas.

The sun rested low in the sky, painting light on the metal roof of a building to the southwest.

Bizzy shivered a little. Hesitantly, she dismounted

from the mare and stroked the horse's nose, then held the reins as she walked to the door of one tipi. Chris jumped down, dropped Cree's reins in the snow, and followed.

They were modern tipis. Carmen couldn't tell what they were made of, but the furthest one had horses painted on the outside.

He and Bizzy came out of the other tipi, and Carmen asked her sister, "Do you think you'll be cold?"

Bizzy signed that she was cold now. But she could have a fire inside.

Great. Smoke inhalation.

Chris said, "Let's go have dinner and get what we need from the house."

FLOYD'S HOUSEKEEPER and cook, Annie, let Carmen chop vegetables and Bizzy make a sauce. "I thought that boy would never marry. Since he was ten years old and his mother left, he's been hopeless."

Why had she left? Because Chris had started to look like his father and it had revealed infidelity on Floyd's part? But Chris had said his father was very young when he was born.

Carmen didn't believe for a second that their resemblance was coincidental. And she doubted Chris believed it, either.

Annie studied Carmen again as Chris came into the kitchen. "I told her I'd given up on you."

"I had to find someone after you broke my heart."

Annie was old enough to be his mother. She shook

her head. "You are no good. These poor girls. You'll make everyone miserable." Her eyes smiled softly.

Bizzy was making the sign for amusement, and Carmen told Annie, "I married him so we could ride horses."

"That's good," said Annie. "Don't expect much more."

Chris sat on a countertop and plucked raw vegetables from the cutting board.

Renée came in.

He and Annie tensed.

Renée took one look at the assembly and seemed ready to leave, but Bizzy said, "Are you hungry?"

Renée said, "You talk really well! I didn't know you could talk at all."

Bizzy smiled and hugged Renée.

Chris looked at the knees of his jeans.

Annie adjusted a setting on the stove.

Carmen dropped the vegetables into a colander with better lettuce than she'd expected to see in so cold a place, tossed them and put them in a salad bowl. "I need to go upstairs." She wondered for just a moment what seductiveness required. She had the kind of boyish, no-hip body a lot of guys liked, and she was a good athlete. That had to be enough. But how did she get Chris out of the kitchen? Oh, hell. "Come with me, husband. You need to learn some signs."

Annie's lips twitched.

Chris eased off the counter, stealing another carrot stick and ruffling Bizzy's hair on the way out.

"THE BARN," he said. "We'll go up in the loft."

The cold stung her face. "Do you always take your girlfriends there?"

"Just my wife."

At least he was quick.

Up in the loft, he wrapped them both in cotton and wool blankets.

She listened to the horses below, out of sight. "What's this Cree Medicine love potion you were talking about with Bizzy?"

"The Blackfeet used to believe strongly in love potions. If a man wanted a woman, he'd bring her lots of horses. If she liked him, she took them into her herd. If she didn't, she ignored them, and in that case, he went to get Cree Medicine. It's foolproof, by the way. No antidote. A hundred percent effective. But, of course, you accepted my horse."

"Sure, but we're still negotiating. I think you should give me more than one."

He rose out of the darkness. Grabbed her and dragged her down with him.

She clutched his body, his hair.

"How many horses do you want, my wife?" He rubbed his face against hers. "Or maybe you just want to hear me say…" His voice had dropped. He said it softly as he touched her. She needed good ears to hear. His words and her own.

CHAPTER THREE

THIRTY FEET SEPARATED the tipi were Bizzy slept from the one Carmen shared with Chris. He'd given Bizzy a stainless steel pot and big steel spoon to bang if she needed them. Blue and Red would keep her company and, Carmen hoped, warm through the night.

After dinner with Floyd and Renée, they'd saddled the horses and packed sleeping bags and everything they needed for the night. The tipis stood on a patch of ground Chris called Bear Hill. Late that night, when Bizzy was tucked in with the dogs, Carmen stared up at the patch of starlit sky where the poles met canvas. This was the first night she would sleep beside her husband. With her head against his arm and chest, she said, "I want to remember this night when we're old."

He blinked in the dark. It was like blinking away a veil to see for the first time the way she must see, that she could look at stars now and believe they might see them together when they were old and look back on this night with fondness. He found her innocence and trust of life wonderful and hugged her, feeling the same absence of guile, of knowledge, whisper through him. If he could ever believe as she did in such continuity, it would be an epiphany. He wanted that awakening, and he wondered if the sun of his own innocence and trust that had set so long ago—if that sun could rise again. He wanted to believe it could, and he too stared up at the stars, memorizing the night.

In the morning, Carmen woke on California time and on pre-work surfing time. But she couldn't hear the ocean. Overhead, the patch of sky was just growing light, and she gazed at Chris and watched him sleep. Putting her face near him, she found his Sun Dance scars where flesh had been torn away, where he'd broken free. Her fingers skimmed above them, imagining touch. Briefly, she knew a satisfied sense— like ownership. *Husband.* Hers. She put her mouth on a scar, then drew back.

Had Renée done the same thing?

How could anyone sleep with a guy *and* his father? Carmen supposed it was like Chris had finally said. *I had to ask, Do I want my father in my life or not? I love my father.*

The love came with a sad and mature resignation Carmen understood perfectly because she had lived it herself.

He woke and saw her. "You have to sing to me," he said, "if you want anything from me."

"I want nothing." She enjoyed her indifference. "What do *you* have that—"

"Okay." He sat up and started to rub his hands over his eyes.

Carmen sang, *"Dashing through the snow..."*

When they came out of the tent, the dogs were chasing every snowball Bizzy threw.

Chris said, "Those are the dumbest heelers I've ever seen. Tell your sister to stop making fun of them."

"You tell her. My horse wants me."

And Bizzy was rolling on the snow, having her own brand of hysterics over dogs who wondered where the snowball had gone. Red lay down beside her and barked.

SHE WAS HIS LOVER NOW. When he would see her again and when they would touch again and when they'd be alone again were never far from his mind. He didn't like this change. He didn't like depending on her because he shouldn't depend on anyone.

Everything, absolutely everything, was temporary. That fact contained all the good and bad of existence. Pleasure was temporary, but so was pain. Happiness and sadness, too.

The next morning, Floyd said he'd made an appointment with his attorney to transfer the ranch's title to Chris.

He and Chris were alone in the kitchen.

His father had never said he was sorry about Renée, or even sorry about the weekend Chris had come home early from a presentation to find the woman he was seeing, the woman he slept with, coming out of his father's room in his father's robe. An apology would have been nice but useless, and he himself wasn't sorry. Sorry she was still around—sorry his father liked her—but not sorry he'd become aware of a deceitfulness that had always been present.

As he'd told Carmen, what could he do? Walk away from his father because his father was being an idiot? He'd tried, when Floyd had said he was going to marry her.

No point.

Renée's betrayal hadn't hurt. Just his dad's.

He'd stopped expecting much from Floyd, so it was just another chapter in the book.

So was the transfer of the ranch.

"Thank you."

"You build this resource center you want to build. I'm going to fix up the old house for me and Renée. I'll keep those acres for my horses. It's enough for us. You have your family here."

Decency could still awe him when it came from Floyd.

"Thank you."

"She's nice."

Chris stilled.

"She can't take her eyes off you."

"It's a good quality." He wished he hadn't said it. He couldn't look at Floyd without feeling...pity? Compassion? Floyd always looked to him now like a man who'd stolen his son's girlfriend. It was sad, and Chris wished it wasn't. Hell, there were only about twelve years between his father and Renée. But even Floyd had to think it was pathetic. Chris didn't think he'd ever look up to him again. The loss of admiration for Floyd hurt worse than the first time he'd heard his father deny the family resemblance everyone else seemed to see. *Oh, all us Indians look alike,* Floyd always joked.

Maybe their resemblance was a coincidence. Even though Carmen, too, had noticed it right away.

But Chris had learned something from her. That there was nothing to lose by saying what was on your mind. "I'm really not your son, am I?"

Floyd smiled. "I've never said you weren't my son. You are."

A truth meant to sound like satisfaction with his adoption. A lie. Same lie, different words.

Chris grabbed the door handle and went out. The thermometer read ten below, and he wore no coat, but it was a long time before he felt the cold.

THEY WERE FIGHTING.

But in a language Carmen didn't know. In the Blackfeet language.

She and Bizzy had met Chris's mother, who'd introduced herself as Ellie, and Bizzy had left the adults and gone outside to brush Many Coups and ride Looks Up. Chris had asked her to. *Will you exercise him for me?*

Carmen saw nothing of Ellie Good Rider in Chris. Except mannerisms. She stood short and straight and unmoving, answering him calmly.

He spoke calmly, too, but his anger, as well as Ellie's, lashed Carmen.

She silently shifted on one of the huge lodgepole

couches in the living room. She sank into its massive cushions as Chris's mother took both his hands in both of hers and coaxed him to sit down. She spoke softly.

He answered with a plea.

Finally Carmen said, "What's going on?"

His mother spun around, smiling. "I want to invite you and Bizzy to meet my friend Martha's granddaughter. She's eleven years old, and she's deaf."

Carmen should have felt a rush of pleasure. She might not have been accepted by her own parents. But she was like them. She should've been thrilled at the prospect of conversing with a Deaf child and felt the importance of helping her feel accepted and acquire what tools she might need in life. Days ago, she would have felt that.

Now she was irritated. Resentful.

Pulled back into something she'd escaped.

She made herself answer. "Does she sign?"

Ellie shook her head. "She's never learned. There are no teachers on the reservation."

Chris's hand slid into Carmen's, almost as though he knew what she was experiencing.

Maybe he guessed.

She'd had to shed her shackles to realize she had ever been imprisoned. But Chris, she suspected, had seen all along. Chris didn't love her just because she could sign. His love had never depended on her ties to the Deaf, on her behaving almost as though she was Deaf. Perhaps her parents' hadn't either—but it had felt as though it did. She'd always felt she had to make up for not being born like them.

But Chris sang to her, whispered to her in Blackfeet. They communicated in sound and word, as well as other ways.

And he had gotten her on a horse again.

In recent days she'd been transformed. She'd become herself as she'd never been in her whole life, except on her surfboard, almost out of reach of her parents' enveloping DEAF-WORLD.

As he lounged beside her, she relaxed into a familiar freedom that reminded her of surfing. She could choose. How to be, how to spend her moments. She could continue to use her skills to help people *and* explore the new world that had suddenly opened before her. And she could love herself just as she was and wanted to be. Braced by this epiphany, she asked, "Are there many other Deaf kids?"

"Oh, a few." Ellie named five or six and seemed as though she could have gone on. Instead she stopped with a cool glance at her son. "But Chris says you might not want to worry about helping people learn signs. I told him he should take you somewhere nice if he wants a honeymoon."

Carmen let a small smile play on her lips.

Chris flushed. "I just said I was going to take you riding today."

"I didn't hear nothing about horses."

What he'd said didn't matter to Carmen. He'd protected her autonomy, not assuming anything about what she would want to do. She liked that. She told Ellie, "I do want to help."

"Then, where's that sister of yours?" Ellie glanced toward the back door, toward the stables. "I'll find her, and we'll go see Martha and Melissa."

Carmen glanced at Chris. "Are you coming with us?"

"Of course. It's our honeymoon."

MELISSA CROW SHOE could not hear. Worse, she couldn't sign, and neither could she speak. She was virtually without language, and the lack reflected throughout her being. Her lank hair was uncombed, her clothing worn indifferently, as though she cared about nothing.

But Carmen and Bizzy together began a miracle as their silent language opened the gate to communication. The pleasure Carmen felt in giving something so important to another reaffirmed her joy in her talents—those she possessed and those she was acquiring. Soon Melissa was using a few signs, and Bizzy was walking her through the yard, pointing out objects and teaching her more. And Melissa, they learned, could play basketball. Bizzy had such a good time with Melissa Crow Shoe that Ellie invited both children to spend the night at her house.

Ellie said Chris had bought her the small ranch house where she lived, a much nicer dwelling than most others on the reservation.

As Chris and Carmen drove away from Ellie's

house some time later, Carmen said, "I like your mother."

"Let's get you some boots."

Riding boots. He'd suggested she bring some, but she'd only had money for one pair of new boots, and she'd chosen the Sorels, knowing she'd rather have warm feet than riding boots.

The boot-buying errand was accomplished at an old western-wear store forty-five minutes from his father's house. Afterward, they headed home to ride.

"That was nice of your mother to ask Bizzy and Melissa to stay," she murmured. "I really like your mom."

"You said that." Chris frowned, eyes on the road and on the sky beyond the windshield.

"I keep thinking you'll say something like, 'Yes, my mom's great.'"

"She is great. She's a Sun Dance sponsor, and she's on the Tribal Council. But even ten years ago I wouldn't have let Bizzy spend the night with her. She was a drunk. With bad taste in men. The last dog I had? One of her boyfriends ran over it."

Oh. She imagined the teenager he would have been. The pain of losing his dog.

She would ask Floyd or Renée or Annie where to get a puppy. *Gosh, I hope those cow dogs don't eat it.*

Maybe a Great Dane puppy.

Her eyes picked out the western range of the Sweet Grass Hills. "I like it here. I wasn't sure I would. But

I feel like I'm becoming someone I was never allowed to be. Thank you.''

His hands rested lightly on top of the steering wheel. ''I think you had it kind of hard, Carmen. But you turned out all right.'' Having Deaf parents and a Deaf little sister must have helped make her who she was, just as knowing nothing about his birth parents had helped shape him.

Nothing?

Yes. Unless Floyd decided to tell him something meaningful, to give him something more than his amended birth certificate.

He wasn't going to search for a truth that was right in front of him, dressed up as a lie.

He said, ''Your parents wanted you, Carmen.''

''To be someone else. They wanted me to be like them. I always wondered why they named me Carmen. It means song, and they never heard one. I'll bet they didn't know what it meant.''

''But what if they did?''

She sat taller in the passenger seat. Snowflakes hit the windshield. More gathered on fence posts. It was what she imagined sometimes. That they'd realized, acknowledged, honored, that she was special but someone they would no more understand than they could a song.

Wishing they'd taken more time to understand was like fishing in a pond with no fish. Or fishing in the ocean for trout.

Here was a well-stocked river. She could help Melissa Crow Shoe and others like her—and she could share in Chris's dream. For a moment she rested her head on his shoulder as he drove.

His hand left the steering wheel and reached up to caress her smooth jaw.

When they got back to the ranch, they rode immediately out to the tipi to make love until their skin tingled and burned from it, until the smoke of pine and sweetgrass and sage drenched their pores, until he knew her as part of himself and believed, just briefly, that she would be with him, in body or spirit, until his heart stopped beating.

Until he believed that someday they would be old together and recollect together the star patterns of their first night.

CHAPTER FOUR

IT WAS RENÉE who drove Carmen to the college and introduced her to an administrator who said she'd see if there was a place in the curriculum for American Sign Language or Deaf Studies.

"Let's have coffee," Renée suggested afterward. "Do you smoke?"

Carmen shook her head.

"Neither do I, anymore, but I'm always hoping someone else will so I'll have an excuse to start again. Isn't that terrible?"

"It's bad for your skin," Carmen told her. Like the sun. Chris had bought her a wool Stetson to keep the sun off and a scarf to help keep her warm while she rode. During the days, while Floyd went out to the old ranch house and talked to carpenters, Carmen worked beside Chris, outfitting different bedrooms for families, writing grant proposals for programs at the center and planning a Christmas Eve party for the battered women's shelter. One day she drove with him to the BLM holding pen and met the retiring ranger.

But this afternoon Bizzy was riding with Melissa on the ranch—Chris was letting Bizzy's friend ride

Looks Up—and Carmen was free to have coffee with
Renée in the student center.

She was the only white person in the room, but she
ignored the fact as easily as she'd ignored being the
only hearing person in a room full of Deaf people.

She and Renée each had a donut with their coffee,
and Renée said, ''You must think it's pretty bad what
I did to Chris. And it was,'' she added. ''But I loved
Floyd. Chris was always—too young for me. I knew
his heart wouldn't be broken, and it wasn't. He didn't
love me, Carmen. You, he loves. Me?'' She shrugged.
''I always knew he liked Looks Up better.''

''He does love his horses.''

Renée laughed. ''You're good. You're good,
woman.''

''Only on a surfboard.''

''That looks like fun. I've always wanted to do
that.'' Renée had lived in California once, earning her
master's degree at UC Berkeley. ''Pretty weird for an
Indian, huh?''

''You drive us to Santa Cruz, I'll teach you to
surf,'' Carmen said. She couldn't dislike Renée. She
had trouble disliking anyone for long.

''You're on.'' Renée leaned forward. ''You know,
I'm crazy about your sister. I'm going to try to ar-
range it so she can take my geometry class here. She's
going to wipe the floor with the kids at her school.''

Carmen thought of all the years she'd spent deliberately not talking with other people who could hear.
The world grew bigger again, and when they left, they
went together to see a litter of Border Collie/Austra-

lian Shepherd crosses, and Carmen paid the owner for a male she and Renée decided was neither the boldest nor the most timid. He had one black-and-gray ear and one that was white and caramel-colored. Renée said, "Do you think Bizzy would like a puppy?"

Carmen's jaw dropped open. "You want to get it for her?"

"Yes!"

The co-conspirators picked out a female that looked like an Aussie and acted like Madonna. "She can handle her," Carmen said. "Bizzy will turn her into a hearing ear dog."

"That sounds like a good thing to have."

"It's more practical than a hearing ear sister." In Renée's car on the way home, Carmen admitted, "I've always had this plan that I'd be there for her in every situation. But that's totally at odds with how to raise a kid. And with Deaf education. As she grows older, she needs to be able to look after herself, and she can. I'm so glad you thought of a dog."

Renée dropped her hand from the steering wheel to briefly squeeze Carmen's fingers. "Thanks. Thank you for being who you are."

Carmen didn't answer. Renée had said Chris loved her. Chris had said so. But Carmen couldn't forget the circumstances that had made Chris propose to her. She tried not to wonder if he would ever have kissed her had those circumstances been absent. They were married, and if his affection was unequal to hers, then the dignified thing was to ignore that fact.

And trust him.

Whether she mattered to him or not, the *promise* mattered, and he would stand by it and be a husband to her and a father to her children.

IF SHE'D ASKED HIM why he was sometimes aloof and edgy and distant, he would've said he didn't know he seemed that way.

The last thing he would've said was that he was waiting for the other shoe to drop, that the feeling of a disaster around the bend had been with him since he was ten years old, and that it always grew worse when life was treating him well.

Life had never treated him so sweetly. A week before Christmas, Chris took Carmen and Bizzy to town to shop for gifts. On the street before they split up, Carmen and Bizzy to shop for him and he to shop for them, Chris told them, "I've never done this with anyone."

"Merry Christmas!" said Bizzy with a big smile. She stood up on tiptoe and kissed his cheek.

They had a long three-person embrace, so long he felt eyes watching him.

And saw, from across the road.

A BLM ranger. One he didn't know. The guy was young, with a mustache and a slouching posture. He nodded to Chris, and Chris smiled. The ranger did not.

Uncomfortably, Chris thought of what had happened several weeks before. Gates left open. Epiphany and Many Coups. A mis-mate. Careless at best.

The BLM should have gelded Epiphany before the

adoption. When that hadn't happened, Chris should have brought it to their attention and remedied the situation immediately. Instead, he'd been caught up by the idea of trying to gentle a wild stallion.

Who'd left the gate open, he or Floyd, was actually moot, although it had been some fight.

They'd laughed afterward.

He wasn't laughing now.

Bothered, Chris watched Carmen and Bizzy head down the sidewalk, then crossed the wide street to where the ranger stood.

"Chris Good Rider. You must be the new wild horse ranger."

"That's right. Hal Martin."

"Nice to meet you. Just saw Stan before he left. He said Montana might start a prison rehabilitation program with the horses, like Colorado." He told the ranger about developments with the new Sweetgrass Hills Family Healing Center at his father's ranch— *his* ranch—and how horses would be used.

The ranger nodded. "Good. Don't like to see them destroyed."

"You ride?"

"Oh, yeah. Took one out of a herd in Nevada when I was sixteen and gentled it. Went off to university, studied journalism—"

"Me, too."

"Never did forget that horse."

Chris liked him, was glad to know him. They talked about individual horses in the group at the holding pen, about a palomino colt Chris wanted to adopt.

He could just tell him. But then Hal Martin would probably have to impose a penalty. The regional supervisor, Clement Haines, could demand that much if he knew. They'd inherited the supervisor when he was promoted out of his last job—after a forest fire debacle that had resulted in the deaths of two firefighters. Haines wasn't known for his leniency. He might revoke Chris's right to adopt wild horses.

Whereas if he said nothing, probably no one would know.

Except Carmen, Bizzy... They already knew Epiphany should have been gelded earlier.

Probably the BLM would rather not know. Everything Chris did was a good thing for the "Adopt a" program. The last thing they'd want was to have to penalize him.

Well, Clem Haines might want to.

Leaving Hal Martin, he wandered toward the feed store, just because that was where he usually went. Bizzy would get a saddle for Christmas. He'd also bought her a drum and Carmen a flute from craftsmen on the reservation. He wanted something else for Carmen, but nothing seemed right.

Except one thing she should probably have.

They should both have.

He scanned the signs on the street, looking for the shop of a Blackfeet jewelry-maker whose son was his best friend when he was seventeen before the son got killed driving drunk. Chris, equally drunk but not driving, had survived the accident. He walked to the shop to tell his friend's father, who had become his own friend and his own sort-of father, that he'd married someone wonderful.

THEY WERE SUPPOSED TO MEET and select gifts for the ranch party for the children's refuge and battered women's shelter. Chris had a list of how many women, how many boys and how many girls, and a suggested list of extra gifts in case others showed. But when he met Carmen and her sister in front of the trading post, he immediately dragged them over to his friend's jewelry store. It was a good place to buy gifts for women anyhow.

"What have you been doing?" Bizzy asked, blinking at his empty hands.

"She thinks she's not getting anything," Chris said.

"I'm getting a horse," Bizzy answered. "Aren't I?"

Laughing, Chris pulled them inside the shop and introduced them to the owner. "You and I," he told Carmen, "are going to buy wedding rings, and while we choose them, Bizzy's going to pick out two kittens."

The blue eyes went wide. Thrilled. "Where?"

The jeweler glanced playfully at the floor behind him. A long-haired tortoiseshell was climbing out of a box. Bizzy hurried over to look in the box. She told the man, "I'm Deaf, but I can understand you if I can see you when you talk."

"Do you know how to talk with those hand signs?"

"Yes," she said. "Want me to teach you some?"

"I would like to learn," he said.

Chris held Carmen's hand, knowing he would come here more often now and bring Bizzy.

But most of all, bring himself. For the friend who'd died and the father who was left.

Carmen wondered if she should tell him about the puppies. Would he think kittens and puppies together were too much? But what he'd told her about his dog dying made it important to her to surprise him. The people selling the dogs were going to hold on to the puppies for her and Renée until Christmas. She would keep it to herself. "Rings are a good idea, aren't they?" she remarked. "I was thinking of getting you a collar and a little heart-shaped tag saying you belong to me and where to return you if you're lost. But, yeah, a ring's nicer."

The jeweler tried signing "kitten," and Bizzy said, "This is CUTE." She showed him. "Chris, can I have three?"

"Kittens? No." He made the NO sign automatically, and he and Carmen both stared as though his hand had acted on its own initiative.

She murmured, "You're good. With your hands."

He chased off the sense of impending doom that had nothing to do with reality and everything to do with his knowledge that all of life was temporary and tragedy did happen.

Right now, he would be happy. Thoroughly happy.

He rubbed his cheek against her hair and howled softly into her ear.

"A collar," she said. "I'll have a beautiful ring, and you'll wear a collar."

They chose hand-cast silver bands. Then Carmen selected necklaces and earrings for the women party guests. In a case beneath a side window, she discovered a hand-carved wooden nativity set. It was for sale, and Carmen looked up at Chris. "I want that." She consulted the jeweler. "Did you make this set?"

"Actually, my daughter made that. A woman woodcarver." He shook his head.

Chris read the price. "Okay."

"Thank you. I'm going to give it to Floyd and Renée for Christmas."

His breath left in one long exhalation. Carmen glanced at him. "She wears that cross with the stones in it all the time. She'll like it. Don't worry."

He sighed again, this time facing the street—and none of them.

"Do you gift-wrap?" she asked the jeweler.

"Sure!"

Against Chris's back she murmured, "The holidays are a good time for—giving. Forgiving."

"Especially for people with nothing to forgive," he answered. A kitten clawed at the sleeve of his jacket, then crawled up onto him. "Bizzy. You like this one? Ah. A girl kitten. And...another girl."

Bizzy had chosen two of the tortoiseshell cats, one long-haired, one short-haired.

"What are you going to name them?"

She squinted at the short-hair he was kissing on the nose. "Christmas?"

He laughed, remembered to make the sign for amusement and found his hands were full of kittens. He handed Christmas back to her. "And the other one?"

"Cute." She grinned at the jeweler and showed him the hand sign again.

All of them made the kitten's name sign together, and then the jeweler opened the case to take out the nativity set and wrap it for Floyd and Renée.

"I DON'T EXPECT you to forgive me," Floyd said.

"People keep using that word today." Chris continued currying the grullo mustang that had come from Utah, one-hundred percent Spanish blood, a descendant of the second wave of horses on the continent. "I forgive you. I forgive Renée. All right?"

"Do you forgive your mother and me?"

"For what?"

"For drinking. For divorcing."

He got out of the stall and secured it. The gelding already felt his anger and snorted uneasily. He walked away, casually rapping the curry comb against a stall.

Drinking, sure. He forgave that. People had forgiven him.

Divorcing? His childhood had ended right then and there. What childhood he'd had. "I forgive you for drinking and for divorcing."

"Just because it didn't work out between your

mother and me doesn't mean your marriage to Carmen won't last."

He must've been talking to someone with a degree in psychology. That would be Renée. "It will last." Chris kept his eyes focused on a bay mare in her stall.

"Son."

Chris swung around.

"I'm glad you found someone. That was my greatest hope in insisting you marry if you wanted the ranch. You've never believed a marriage can last. But I know that's untrue. My parents were married forty-nine years before my father died."

"Your mother and I were alcoholics. Apart, we each became much better people than we'd been together."

Chris had comforted both parents' tears.

It was past.

Something else was not. He stared at his father, holding his eyes by will. "Am I of your blood? Are you my biological father?"

Floyd nodded. He touched his son's arm and turned away, then suddenly looked back. "Let's hear no more about it."

Chris swore at him in two words and instantly regretted it.

Floyd was his father who'd given him life.

And he had said so.

Chris strode after him to say, "I'm sorry. Please forgive me."

His father kept walking and waved his hand as though to say it was nothing.

Chris watched him go, a vigorous man walking slowly, as though his bones felt old.

Why? Why had his father kept it a secret? Why wouldn't he say more?

He will, Chris thought. Because he would continue to ask questions until he could at least begin to understand. Life had taught him that, married or not, having a family or not, he was ultimately alone. No one would ever understand him as well as he could—if he could find the answers. And he would no longer be afraid to ask for them.

He returned to the barn to see Cree Medicine, to rub his face in the horse's mane, to take him out so he could ride as fast as the appaloosa would carry him.

And know he was his father's son.

THEY ALL SLEPT in the house that night.

It was the first night he'd slept under his father's roof in a year.

Carmen went up to bed first. But one of Floyd's horses was lame, and Chris waited to see the vet. When he finally followed Carmen upstairs, she was still awake, lying on their bed in a pair of his sweatpants and nothing else and reading *Great Expectations.* She didn't even look up when he came in.

He said, *"Oki, niksokowa,"* and wondered how he was going to tell someone who didn't look up when he came into the room that his father had admitted he was his father. At the same time he knew he'd be able to tell her because she was someone who could find a book more interesting than him.

He locked the door and took off his clothes. She finally glanced up.

"Ah, my wife. You noticed me."

"Mm."

In bed, he said, "I rode Cree Medicine today, and he told me the Blackfeet teachings again, to keep me out of trouble."

"What are they?"

"To honor *iit-tsi-pah-tah-pii-oop,* the Source of Life. To respect all that is female, because women are the sacred vessels of our being in this world. To respect the sacred always and the traditions and beliefs of all people. To listen. Don't make war over the sacred beliefs of others. Be truthful and respectful in speech. We are related to all things in the universe. To know that it is sacred to give and share my behavior with others." He took a deep breath, looking into her eyes. "And be very slow to anger. Anger is for survival and teaching, not killing or saying hurtful things to other people." He paused. "Teach all children. The earth and all that exists is here to be respected and shared. Obey the teachings of the Source of Life."

He had her attention now. But what words could he use to tell her? There were no words. Only the signs she'd taught him and he'd taught himself. He could never get the grammar right, but he tried.

FATHER, HE SAY, SON-ME. Something like that.

Carmen saw his lips tighten, holding it back, the thing he could not say out loud. "Did he explain why he kept it a secret? Why didn't he just tell you?"

"I don't know, but I plan to keep asking. Obviously he knows who my birth mother is."

Reclining against his chest, Carmen said, "I think we're kind of alike." She wasn't sure how his being adopted and his parents divorcing and his being Indian but growing up on this ranch was like her having Deaf parents, but somehow it was. In what it had done to both of them.

"No," he said. "We're not alike. I'm intelligent and sensitive and good-looking. You're just ticklish."

"You're wrong! No, you're wrong! Stop it! Stop if you want to stay friends...."

A KNOCK ON THE DOOR awoke them before it was light the next morning. Chris threw the covers over Carmen, pulled on the sweats she'd been wearing the night before and opened the door.

Bizzy came in, looked right at Carmen, and began signing, too distraught to speak.

Carmen said, "Epiphany's rolling in his stall, Chris."

"Yes," said Bizzy.

He said, "We'll be right down. Where are the kittens?" He made the right facial expression and signed TWO KITTENS.

"In my room."

"Go check on them."

When Bizzy had gone, Carmen sprang up and began dressing. He was ahead of her, slipping away before she had her shirt on.

Carmen and Chris were in the barn, Chris gently holding Epiphany's head, when Floyd came in, dressed in worn overalls, a jacket like Carmen's shielding him from the bitter Montana cold. Bizzy followed him, carrying a small and worried kitten in each hand, and Blue and Red followed her as though looking for a handout.

''Carmen, tell her the dogs might hurt the kittens,'' Chris said.

Carmen told her expediently, with signs, and Bizzy turned and hurried out of the barn, followed by the heelers.

Floyd handed Carmen a bottle that must once have contained vanilla extract.

''Pour it in his mouth,'' Chris said. ''Mineral oil.''

For colic.

Carmen spoke to her horse, kissed him, opened the bottle and poured the oil into the horse's open mouth.

A truck stopped outside.

Carmen placed her head against the horse's neck, in his long mane. *Epiphany, I'll never miss the ocean again.*

A body pressed against her back, held the horse with her, whispered in Blackfeet.

The vet came in.

He was Blackfeet, about Floyd's age. Chris told him they'd given Epiphany mineral oil. He introduced Carmen and told her, ''Bob Spotted Eagle is our vet.''

"Chris's wife," said Bob. "You're good at catching mustangs, then."

"I mostly want to keep this one."

The vet looked the horse in the eye and made friends as he worked. It seemed like an hour had passed before Bob Spotted Eagle handed her a lead rope. "Walk him, if he'll go with you. Chris, you want me to do an ultrasound on that mare?"

Carmen squinted. "What mare?"

Chris nodded. "Guess so."

Carmen led Epiphany outside. Bizzy had returned and joined her as she walked with the horse, her hand in his long mane. Carmen had taken enough falls from Epiphany's back to learn to watch every twitch of his ears, every movement of his eyes.

Bizzy, deciding Epiphany was out of danger, signed to Carmen that the kittens had seen themselves in the full-length mirrors on Renée's closet doors. It was very funny.

When she went back inside, finding horses temporarily less interesting than kittens, Chris took her place. He was thinking of what the ultrasound had shown him. Many Coups was carrying a foal. Should he tell the BLM?

No. If it was just Hal Martin, he would've considered it. But Clem Haines was bound to hear of it, as well, if Chris told Hal.

Any way he looked at it, it was a mess.

After they'd walked for some time, Chris preoccupied and strangely ashamed to let her know what had happened, Carmen climbed on Epiphany. The horse warmed her half-frozen legs. Watching her, Chris said, "You know the three most important inventions for warfare?"

Carmen thought. "Gunpowder?"

"One."

"The stirrup."

He smiled. "Keep walking. I'll be back."

He was, a minute later. On the grulla. "You ride with me." He lifted her off Epiphany and onto Señor with him. He led her horse, making sure Epiphany looked well and safe and wasn't turning belligerent. Epiphany wanted to lead.

"He just won't let anyone forget he's had Many Coups." It was a half-hearted attempt to confess the truth.

"Oh, *that's* what happened."

"Oh, yes. It did."

He held one arm firm around her waist.

"I'm going to tell you how the Blackfeet got horses." Chris told her about the poor boy who went to the Underwater Spirit from which all things came, and how the boy let the old man take him down in the water and look at nothing. How he was allowed to choose an animal and chose a mallard duck, as he'd been told. And he held the mallard duck by a rope around the neck, but he could not look back, must not look back, and soon he no longer heard the duck but the heavy clop of feet and deep breathing, and finally when he did look, he saw a giant four-legged beast. More horses followed. "When he returned to his village, everyone was frightened, but he knew how to mount the animal, and they called the animal the Elk Dog, and they made the poor boy the chief, and the chief has always had many horses.''

"He chose a *duck?*"

"They taste good."

She twisted around to give him a look just as the sunrise licked them with tendrils of warmth.

He said, "Look at your horse."

She did, and Epiphany's head was up, his ears listening to things humans couldn't hear. He broke into a healthy and happy trot that Chris stopped with a word. "Why don't you ride him before he remembers he'd rather be free."

FOUR DAYS BEFORE CHRISTMAS found Chris immersed in plans for the family healing center, arranging his speaking schedule for the coming year and planning his next book. He hoped to adopt a young horse from the BLM and focus on wild colts. He hadn't ridden for several days, and when Carmen told him that she and Bizzy were going riding, he asked if they would exercise Looks Up and Cree Medicine.

Carmen gladly agreed. She'd ridden Cree Medicine once before, and she loved the appaloosa. She and Bizzy set off on the saddled horses beneath clear skies.

Chris watched from Bizzy's window as they rode away, then took the kittens into his and Carmen's room, where he'd been working on his laptop at a small desk. He couldn't focus. Carmen wouldn't leave him, and he wouldn't do anything to make her want to leave. But somehow, some way, the bird would fall alone from the sky, and everything would change.

It wouldn't be worse than it had been before, right? Wrong.

It wasn't his nature to be afraid. Unconsciously, he separated himself from that which caused him fear—Carmen. She was, he reasoned, someone he'd married because being married was a requirement for saving this ranch. A ridiculous requirement. He and Carmen were friends who happened to sleep together. He liked having someone to sleep with, and she liked thinking he loved her, and he did love her. But not in a life-or-death way.

He picked up the kittens and put them on the dresser so they could look in the mirror and see two more kittens and look at each other in confusion. He was still playing with them when a banshee howl bent the windows and banged the frames. The kittens trembled before he thought to.

Before he remembered the sound of the wind and knew there were some facts that would not accept lies.

Carmen was his wife. Bizzy, his family.

The sky outside had darkened, and the snow flew parallel to the ground. He could not see the highway.

The blizzard had come in fast. Why hadn't he checked the weather before they'd gone?

He thought of these things as he returned the kittens to Bizzy's room and hurried downstairs.

And his epiphany came.

He could not lie about his feelings. To try to feel less would be cowardice. There was nothing left but to live and to love.

And to hope that Carmen and Bizzy had turned around. To hope they were back in the stable already.

And to go find them if they weren't.

Because he did believe. He believed in Carmen and himself, senior citizens looking back on their first night. He believed in that future and wanted it for his and wanted to share with her all the starry nights in between.

CARMEN ENVISIONED correction fluid whiting out a printed error. Around her, snow blew so fast and thick she couldn't see.

Both were called white-out, and if Chris's horse didn't need so much attention she would have signed in front of Bizzy's face to share the comparison.

To make sure her sister stayed alert.

They must be nearing the tipis; if they reached them, they could take the horses inside and stay warm. Carmen had thrown her saddle and blanket on Looks Up, and she and Bizzy both rode Cree Medicine, using the horse's body and each other for warmth. Carmen let the appaloosa lead the way; he would know the way better than she did. She periodically pulled Bizzy's coat collar up higher, trying to shield her sister's nose. But her sister's hands were what kept getting cold. Carmen made her take off her mittens and put both hands under her parka and the layers of clothes, to warm them against bare skin.

Bizzy twisted around and said, "It works."

A moment of comfort.

They were in a Montana blizzard, and all Carmen knew was how not to get hypothermia after surfing and that no one should fall asleep in the snow.

Cree grew restive, and she corrected his head—then wondered if maybe she should let him choose the route. She wasn't even sure if they were still on the ranch. But Cree Medicine might know the way to the tipis.

We could die.

No.

Wasn't going to happen.

They were cold, and Looks Up was just a white-flocked head with the rest of him fading in the horizontal snow, but it wasn't so bad. It was kind of like surfing. She sang "Let It Snow! Let It Snow! Let It Snow!" She sang louder than the wind and thought, *Thank you, Chris. Thank you, Chris. Thank you, Chris.* She was grateful for being able to hear, grateful for not being deaf. She was herself, and she was glad. She would survive this storm.

She could hear.

FROM THE BACK DOOR, he couldn't even see the barn, but the fences would have stopped him if he'd lost his way.

Cree's and Looks Up's stalls were empty.

And the BLM ranger, Hal Martin, and another man in the same uniform stood with their backs to Epiphany's stall, trying to befriend two growling heelers.

The other man was the regional supervisor, Clement Haines.

Chris chased off the dogs in Blackfeet.

Hal said, "Friendly, aren't they?"

Clement Haines said, "Mr. Good Rider? Your vet likes your horses, but I bet you know BLM regulations better than he does. He didn't come to us especially, but we did overhear him mention what had happened here and that he'd cut this three-year-old for you."

The wind howled and pushed and pulled at the barn. Chris said, "My wife and her sister are out riding. Can we talk after I find them?"

The ranger nodded. "In the meantime, we're going to take this horse—" Epiphany "—and that horse—" Many Coups "—back to the holding pen. And I don't think they're going to be yours anymore."

They weren't his.

Epiphany was Carmen's.

And on Christmas Day, Many Coups would have been Bizzy's.

"My wife has the black horse's papers. He's hers."

"Looks like she has some others to choose from. This one's going to belong to the BLM. And you won't be getting any more from us."

Hal leaned back against a post between the stalls, brooding. Eyes on Chris's, he moved his head a millimeter to one side and then back.

The footsteps made almost no sound, but Chris turned.

Floyd ignored the rangers and spoke in Blackfeet,

telling Chris that Renée was putting together food and thermoses of coffee. He would take Rick, his big bay quarter horse. It was a good thing, he said, that Carmen had Cree Medicine. That horse was smart.

Chris answered him in the same language and grabbed tack for Señor.

Hal said, "You have a road we can drive on and look for your wife?"

"You can't drive in this and see." *But thanks.* Thanks for stealing our horses.

"Besides," said Haines, "we have an incident here."

"Think they're on BLM land?" asked Hal.

"Could be." They were a ways from BLM land, but looking for Carmen and Bizzy might make the rangers forget about the horses. Hal Martin might be thinking the same thing. Chris's head was full. Of the women in the storm.

And the thought of a man who wanted to haul two horses in a blizzard.

Chris walked up to him, read his badge and looked into his eyes. "If you take those horses and go off the road you'll spend the rest of your career pushing paper somewhere undesirable. I promise."

Behind him, Hal straightened up and addressed his superior. "I'd like to help with this search. If you can manage these horses by yourself and if Chris will lend me another, I can go along. Another pair of ears and eyes can't hurt."

"Two pairs," said Floyd, leading Rick by them.

Hal's senses and the horse's. The wild horses, especially, would seek each other.

But all Chris could think was that Hal had really meant another pair of hands.

THEY WERE SAFE in the tipi where he'd spent his first night with Carmen. Cree and Looks Up were inside with them, and Carmen and Bizzy were bundled together in zipped-up sleeping bags, signing. Carmen jumped when she saw them. The wind must have hidden their approach.

"You found us," she said. "You look frozen."

Bizzy got up, stumbling out of the sleeping bag, to hug Chris and his snow-covered father. She frowned at the ranger, as though thinking she might be in trouble.

Carmen said, "You all look cold. Pull up a sleeping bag and join us." She told the ranger, "I'm from California. Sorry about this."

"People from Montana get lost in the snow, too. And you don't seem very lost."

Floyd led the horses out, and Chris built a fire. They sat drinking coffee, eating Christmas cookies and listening to the wind.

It died soon, and they got the horses ready to head back to the house. On the way, slowing Señor and Cree to lag behind the others, Chris said, "The BLM took Epiphany and Many Coups. I broke a rule. It's my fault."

Carmen bit her lip. He would find another horse for Bizzy, and Bizzy wouldn't mind so much.

Christmas was a time for giving. Forgiving.

Especially for people with nothing to forgive.

Now she had something to forgive.

She gave Cree Medicine his head and turned to call over her shoulder, "I'll have this one till you get mine back."

CHAPTER FIVE

BIZZY STOOD beside Many Coups's empty stall. She looked up at Chris. "You broke the rules?"

Carmen wondered, *How did she grow up in Santa Cruz with a surfer for a sister without figuring out that people sometimes break the rules?*

But this wasn't "people." This was Chris Good Rider, expert in Plains Indian Horsemanship and Wild Horse Awareness Handling.

Chris said, "I'm sorry."

Eyes filling, Bizzy rushed out of the barn and up to her room.

Carmen glanced at Chris.

He walked away.

THEIR CONVERSATION WAS rapid signing. Bizzy wanted to know how, after all his discussion about the right way to adopt a wild horse, Chris could keep a wild stallion.

Some questions didn't come with good answers.

"I think he probably wanted to see if he could gentle a stallion. But you should ask him."

NO sign. She wasn't going to talk to him ever again, and he could *keep* his horses.

There was a little problem, Carmen told her. Husband. Family member.

How could Carmen be married to him? Bizzy wanted to know. How could *she* stand to talk to him?

Carmen scooped Christmas off the floor and rubbed the tiny kitten's soft belly. "I like him. Yes. Still." *I love him.*

As Carmen tried to get Cute out from under the bed, Bizzy tapped her shoulder. Signed that now Carmen was acting like him, was talking instead of signing, they should never have come here, should never have left Santa Cruz. Nobody cared about her, Bizzy, anymore.

Carmen signed that she was sure Chris would have another horse for Bizzy. And that she'd lost Epiphany. Did Bizzy think *she* wasn't a little mad at Chris? Chris wasn't perfect. But he wasn't bad, either.

Bizzy did a BAD? YES. She grabbed both the kittens and curled into a ball on her bed.

Chris peered in the room.

Bizzy saw him and ignored him with the ultimate shutout of a Deaf person. If she didn't want to know what he had to say, she didn't have to find out.

Carmen told her not to be rude, then got up and walked out.

When she went to look for Chris and her sister ten minutes later, the room was empty. She found them standing by the corral fence under gray skies. Looks Up stood nearby.

Abruptly, Bizzy ran off, then came back and began

signing at Chris with great emotion. From the barn door, Carmen watched her sister call her husband a dolt who thought she, Bizzy, must not have cared about Many Coups at all. Worse, he'd lost Carmen's wedding present when Carmen hadn't ridden a horse since Bizzy was a very little girl. Her diatribe deteriorated from there until Carmen went out to talk with her about not insulting people in languages they couldn't understand.

Bizzy looked at Chris. "Jerk." She finger-spelled it for emphasis and strode off.

CHRIS COULD SEE ONLY one way to get the horses back.

He had a plan.

"Bad idea," said Floyd in the living room that night, after Carmen had followed Bizzy to bed. "You'd be Steals-Many-Horses for one night and in jail for months."

Renée said, "He wants his appaloosa back from his wife. That's the problem."

No. He wanted Epiphany back *for* his wife. And Many Coups for Bizzy.

Most of all, he wanted what his solution would never buy, what nothing would—Bizzy's respect, which he had lost. He wondered if his dad had felt this way after he and Renée were caught.

Hal Martin had said Chris could probably continue his good relationship with the BLM and the Adopt a Wild Horse or Burro program—but those wild horses were going to another holding facility and would be sold to someone else. The ranger's blue eyes had said he was sorry, it was the best he'd been able to do. His mouth had said it wouldn't be smart for Chris to try adopting the same animals twice. Could raise some eyebrows. Of course, Clement Haines wasn't known for his compassion. He'd been sent here after his last region had burned down, taking the lives of two firefighters who'd died only because Haines had refused to let a fueled and ready plane go drop retardant on the forest fire. The story was well-known.

"I like what you do for the horses," Hal had said. "And for people. You should keep doing it. We'll find another good horse for your wife."

Renée bit into an iced and sprinkled cookie and spoke of the firefighters. "Can you imagine a plane just sitting there on the ground and two kids down there trapped, and this guy says, 'The fire's contained, so we'll save the fuel'? What is *wrong* with people?"

Chris shot a look at her, but she'd already gotten up to leave.

It didn't matter that Renée had been the one to say it. He'd been thinking it.

He should be willing to risk everything to get back Carmen's horse. Not just for her, but to strike a small blow against petty evil. To win something very little for the dead.

And for Carmen. The way he'd asked her to marry him—that couldn't be undone. But this was something he could do to help her understand that he loved her for herself.

He could get those horses back.

Even if it cost him…his career.

And it would. To take back what was his. To bring those horses back to Carmen and Bizzy.

Floyd said, "Do what you want. I won't stop you. But ask yourself what Carmen and Bizzy would want. And then look down the generations at the future. Those hotshot kids are dead, Chris. But you're going to save lives right here. You need to work with the BLM. Everything you plan to do with your life depends on their good will. It might be smart to swallow this one. And if you're thinking of letting your wife adopt them back, I wouldn't do that either. If you've done wrong, it's best to accept the consequences." Floyd stood, hunted for his reading glasses and found them.

"The way you have?"

Floyd looked startled—and confused.

"Who is my mother?"

"Your mother is Ellie Good Rider. The woman who gave birth to you is dead. You can do some research and find out her name and everything there is to know about her, and you'll know nothing more than you know right now."

"Why don't you just tell me?"

"She was a good person and a beautiful girl, a fancy dancer and smart in school, everything that almost nobody was when she and I were kids. And after you were born, she started drinking. When you were three, she was walking out on the road and got hit and killed. Your mother and I adopted you."

"Aunt Grace." His mother's older sister. The tribe's first female basketball star, who would've had a scholarship if she'd kept her life together and not gotten pregnant by someone whose name she'd said she couldn't remember. Floyd. Floyd and Aunt Grace had been classmates. "Does Mom know?"

"She figured it out. Not till you were a bit older."

"Is that why she left?"

Floyd pursed his lips. Finally he admitted, "Yes. She loved her sister and she blamed me for Aunt Grace's death."

"She must blame me, too."

"No, son. She's always loved you. I think you may have meant even more to her when she learned whose child you were. Now, let me tell you a story. This is a good one for all of us. It's about the first lightbulb."

"Mm?"

"It doesn't exist. The patent guys were all coming to see it, and Edison gave it to an eight-year-old boy. Said carry it upstairs. The boy dropped it. Thomas Edison had to call everybody and say, 'Don't come today. We need twenty-four hours to make another light bulb.' So they made one, and he called all the engineers, and he gave the new light bulb to the same eight-year-old boy to carry upstairs. He said, 'Don't drop it this time.' And he didn't.

"Think about it." He headed toward the stairs but paused. "And never leave a gate open."

"I never have."

CARMEN WAS IN BED with the lights out. When he opened the door, she said, "The kittens are in here. Don't step on them."

As he shut the door, a kitten latched onto his sock. He picked up Cute and said, "Your new horse sometimes bites."

After a moment, she said, "I'll let you ride him some time. Think you can stay on?"

"I think you're a horse thief."

But he wouldn't be.

He found the other kitten and put them both on the bed.

In bed, he told her about his mother. Then he said, "If I was going to get your horse back, this is how it would look. I would ride to the holding pen on a moonless night, which Christmas Eve will be, and I would take our horses and maybe several more. I would be called Steals-Many-Horses."

Carmen put Cute, the fluffy kitten, on his chest. "You know, I've never ridden Looks Up. I had Breyer horses when I was a kid, and now there's a Looks Up Breyer horse. I'd like to own a famous horse."

Smiling in the dark, relieved and wondering why he felt even better than before the horses had been taken, he said, "He'd own you." He held up Cute, looked at her shadow and her eyes in the dark, then brought her down to kiss her.

"I promised to return them to Bizzy's room before we go to sleep," she said.

Ungrateful brat.

You were her hero.

Light bulbs.

Carmen plucked Christmas from her hair, climbed out of bed and pulled on her sweats. "Give me those cats."

As she set the kittens inside Bizzy's doorway and smiled at the sleeping shape of her sister, Carmen envisioned Chris's horse raid. It would have been almost romantic enough to outweigh the consequences. He, of all people, should not annoy the BLM.

And Looks Up was a wonderful horse. Chris sounded almost as if he might be persuaded to part with him. Carmen liked the idea of his giving her the horse he'd loved more than he'd loved Renée.

WAITING FOR HER in their bed, Chris tried to pinpoint the source of his relief. It had nothing to do with the horses and the BLM—and it wasn't knowing about his mother.

He saw his father's face, heard Floyd's advice again, about the horses and the ranch.

He remembered hearing common sense.

His father had shapeshifted again.

No, Chris's perception of him had.

When Chris had been prepared to act from emotion, Floyd had spoken from wisdom and made him remember how to act.

That was the relief.

He started counting the *life* bulbs he'd dropped.

The car crash, alcoholism, ten or fifteen years of resenting his mother...

Today he'd lost Bizzy's respect—and maybe some of Carmen's. But he'd eventually get it all back. And then do his best not to drop it.

THEY CUT A Christmas tree the next day.

A medicine man came to ask permission from the tree's spirit, while Chris's mother whispered, "You get him to buy an artificial one next year, Carmen. I saw some nice ones at Wal-Mart. This isn't right. Sawing down a big tree like that."

"Should I stop them right now?"

Ellie laughed out loud and the men looked at them, and Melissa Crow Shoe's mother and Renée wandered over to find out what was funny.

Bizzy and Melissa walked off through the snow to look at the frozen river, and Carmen excused herself to follow.

She was with the girls when they all saw a buck and three does stepping carefully through the mantle of the forest floor.

The three of them stood together in stillness, talking in sign.

Carmen felt the best parts of herself weave together in the kind of safety that let her be exactly who she wanted.

Chris found them several minutes later, after the tree was loaded on his truck. Bizzy ignored him and dragged Melissa away toward the rest of the group.

He ignored her, too, and took something from his pocket. "Look." A wallet-size photo of a pretty high-school girl. "This is my birth mom. My Aunt Grace."

"You look like her and your dad."

"Thanks."

He held her shoulder to guide her through the deep snow. "If Looks Up was your horse, he'd still have to be my employee for a while."

"Well, if you pay him enough. And no overtime."

"I didn't say I *would* give him to you."

"Yes, but you want to get another colt and write about young wild horses. You've said so. And if you're doing that, you'll have to take the star of your book around the country with you."

He hugged her to his side. "You and Bizzy are who I'm going to take with me. And now I don't have to put up with those weird Santa Cruz people to see you. You know, a woman there told me she feeds her horse wheatgrass juice every day."

"Oh, she sat behind me a lot. She's also into equine aromatherapy. I'm going to try it. You can take your wife out of California, but you can't take California out of—"

THE STEREO in the living room played a winter holiday CD made by Blackfeet singers. It mixed Christmas carols, traditional Blackfeet singing and original melodies and lyrics.

Women and children sat or played around the huge tree. Bizzy and four or five kids were playing charades, and she was teaching them sign language. Some of the women were recovering from black eyes. One had her arm in a cast.

Chris was the only man present—Floyd and Renée were nominally spending the evening at her mother's house but actually picking up the two puppies—and women who, early in the evening, had watched Chris warily and kept their distance soon sat beside him talking. The healing center's first employee, a counselor named Elaine from South Dakota, talked with the counselors from the battered women's shelter and with the women themselves.

In the middle of the evening, some of the women began singing Christmas carols to their children.

Carmen searched anxiously for Bizzy, not wanting her sister to feel left out.

But Bizzy stood with Melissa Crow Shoe, both studying the hearing and singing people with baffled expressions. They turned to each other and began to sign.

Beside her, Chris watched the girls, too. "The first time I saw you and Bizzy signing, I felt more left out than I've ever been in my life. You two definitely thought you were superior to everybody else at that presentation."

"Thought?"

He laughed and hugged her. "Excuse me. Your superiority made me shy. I thought you were never going to forgive me for not being born deaf."

Carmen didn't even smile. He was too close to the truth.

She listened to the women and children singing and joined in. Bizzy really didn't care. There was no guilt.

With the song vibrating through her, sounding through her, she wondered where her parents were. And if they could hear.

CHRIS WINCED when he saw the sheepdog tumble toward Bizzy. Kittens, a puppy... A horse seemed redundant. Even a horse she'd never seen, one Hal Martin had let him take.

The kind of horse she'd wanted.

A wild horse to gentle herself.

"*Two* dogs?"

The second one was peeing on the hardwood floor.

"That would be yours," said Carmen. "Merry Christmas. Do you like him?"

Chris said, "Nobody pay attention to this dog." His first encounter with his canine friend was to sequester the animal in the mud room so that he wouldn't see anyone cleaning up the floor.

He cleaned up, went back and let out the dog. "Hi." Sat down on the kitchen floor. Spoke in Blackfeet.

Someone tapped his shoulder.

He looked up at Bizzy.

"My dog is going to recognize signs."

"Good." He fondled his puppy's silky ears, one flopped over, and turned so that Bizzy could see his own face if she wanted to look. "Oh, yes, you're cute, little guy."

A tap on his shoulder.

Again, he looked up.

"My dog is cuter. Look at it."

He did, then at her. "I don't think she's cuter than my dog."

When Carmen came in, Bizzy was pointing out all her dog's markings and the intelligent look in her eyes.

Chris said that his dog was a fast learner. He'd only peed on the floor once.

"Come back in the living room," Carmen told them. "Other people got presents, too."

Floyd and Renée opened their nativity set, which Carmen had labeled as being from Chris and her and Bizzy.

Renée got up and kissed her cheek. Chris had turned out the lights on the big tree, leaving only the starlight to shine on what lay below.

Carmen and Bizzy tried the flute and drum. Then Bizzy took her kittens upstairs. Chris finally turned off the lights on the tree, but he didn't lead Carmen up to bed.

Instead, to the mud room, where he pulled on boots and put leashes on both the puppies.

He took her out to the barn with its animal smells and first showed her the paint colt, the young mustang that would be Bizzy's. He dragged his dog out from an unoccupied stall, then led her to the horse she'd called famous.

She petted Looks Up's nose. "You really didn't have to."

"Oh, I know." But he was laughing, and he tapped her shoulder and signed I LOVE YOU.

Finally, Carmen decided, he was getting the hang of ASL's facial expressions.

Her eyes filled with the same emotion, and she lifted her head to tell him in another silent way how much she loved him.

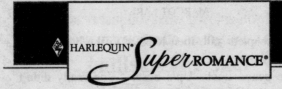

If you enjoyed what you just read,
then we've got an offer you can't resist!

Take 2 bestselling love stories FREE!

Plus get a FREE surprise gift!

Clip this page and mail it to Harlequin Reader Service®

IN U.S.A.	IN CANADA
3010 Walden Ave.	P.O. Box 609
P.O. Box 1867	Fort Erie, Ontario
Buffalo, N.Y. 14240-1867	L2A 5X3

YES! Please send me 2 free Harlequin Superromance® novels and my free surprise gift. After receiving them, if I don't wish to receive anymore, I can return the shipping statement marked cancel. If I don't cancel, I will receive 6 brand-new novels every month, before they're available in stores. In the U.S.A., bill me at the bargain price of $4.47 plus 25¢ shipping and handling per book and applicable sales tax, if any*. In Canada, bill me at the bargain price of $4.99 plus 25¢ shipping and handling per book and applicable taxes**. That's the complete price, and a savings of at least 10% off the cover prices—what a great deal! I understand that accepting the 2 free books and gift places me under no obligation ever to buy any books. I can always return a shipment and cancel at any time. Even if I never buy another book from Harlequin, the 2 free books and gift are mine to keep forever.

135 HDN DNT3
336 HDN DNT4

Name	(PLEASE PRINT)	
Address	Apt.#	
City	State/Prov.	Zip/Postal Code

* Terms and prices subject to change without notice. Sales tax applicable in N.Y.
** Canadian residents will be charged applicable provincial taxes and GST.
All orders subject to approval. Offer limited to one per household and not valid to current Harlequin Superromance® subscribers.
® is a registered trademark of Harlequin Enterprises Limited.

SUP02   ©1998 Harlequin Enterprises Limited

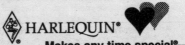

Free book offer!

During the month of November, send us 4 proofs of purchase from any 4 Harlequin Supperromance® books and receive TWO FREE BOOKS by bestselling authors Tara Taylor Quinn and Judith Arnold!

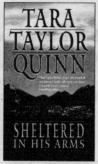

All you have to do is send 4 proofs of purchase to:

<u>In the U.S.:</u>
Harlequin Books
P.O. Box 9057
Buffalo, NY
14269-9057

<u>In Canada:</u>
Harlequin Books
P.O. Box 622
Fort Erie, Ontario
L2A 5X3

_____

ame (PLEASE PRINT)

_____

ddress   Apt. #

_____

ty   State/Prov.   Zip/Postal Code
                                           098 KJO DNDR

receive your 2 FREE books (retail value for the two books is $11.98 U.S./$13.98
\N.), complete the above form. Mail it to us with 4 proofs of purchase (found in all
vember 2002 Harlequin Supperromance® books), one of which can be found in the
ht-hand corner of this page. Requests must be postmarked no later than
ecember 30, 2002. Please enclose $2.00 (checks made payable to Harlequin Books)
 shipping and handling and allow 4-6 weeks
 receipt of order. New York State residents
st add applicable sales tax on shipping and
ndling charge, and Canadian residents
ase add 7% G.S.T. Offer valid in Canada
d the U.S. only, while quantities last.
fer limited to one per household.

2002 Harlequin Enterprises Limited

it us at www.eHarlequin.com

HARLEQUIN *Super*ROMANCE®
2 FREE BOOKS OFFER!
One Proof of Purchase

HSRPOPN03

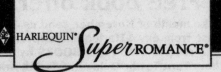

HARLEQUIN *Super*ROMANCE®

It takes a special
kind of person...

**Author Roxanne Rustand
explores the exciting world
of the DEA and its special
agents. Dedicated, courageous
men and women who put their
lives on the line to keep our
towns and cities safe.**

Operation: Mistletoe
coming in November 2002.

**Special Agent Sara Hanrahan's
latest assignment brings her
home for the first time in
years. But old secrets and old
scandals threaten to make
this a miserable Christmas.
Until Sara—with the help of
Deputy Nathan Roswell—
uncovers the surprising truth.
A truth that sets them free to
enjoy the best Christmas ever!**

**First title in Roxanne Rustand's
The Special Agents series
1064—OPERATION: KATIE**

HARLEQUIN®
Makes any time special ®